OUTRAGED

A TOPHER DAVIS THRILLER

BRIAN COPELAND

BLACK
ODYSSEY
MEDIA

WWW.BLACKODYSSEY.NET

Published by
BLACK ODYSSEY MEDIA

www.blackodyssey.net
Email: info@blackodyssey.net

OUTRAGED. Copyright © 2024 by Brian Copeland

Library of Congress Control Number: 2023919233

First Trade Paperback Printing: May 2024
ISBN: 978-1-957950-43-3
ISBN: 978-1-957950-44-0 (e-book)

Cover Design by Ashlee Nassar of Designs With Sass

10 9 8 7 6 5 4 3 2 1

Manufactured in the United States of America

Distributed by Kensington Publishing Corp.

Dear Reader,

I want to thank you immensely for supporting Black Odyssey Media authors, and our ongoing efforts to spotlight more minority storytellers. The scariest and most challenging task for many writers is getting the story, or characters, out of our heads and onto the page. Having admitted that, with every manuscript that Kreceda and I acquire, we believe that it took talent, discipline, and remarkable courage to construct that story, flesh out those characters, and prepare it for the world. Debut or seasoned, our authors are the real heroes and heroines in *OUR* story. And for them, we are eternally grateful.

Whether you are new to Brian Copeland or Black Odyssey Media, we hope that you are here to stay. We also welcome your feedback and kindly ask that you leave a review. For upcoming releases, announcements, submission guidelines, etc., please be sure to visit our website at www.blackodyssey.net or scan the QR code below. We can also be found on social media using @iamblackodyssey. Until next time, take care and enjoy the journey!

Joyfully,

Shawanda Williams

Shawanda "N'Tyse" Williams
Founder/Publisher

DEDICATION

For my sister, Heather Copeland Freeman,
who always believed that I could write this book.

ONE

*W*HAT WAS IT *Forrest Gump had said?*

"It felt like something jumped up and bit me in the buttocks." Was that it?

Mickey Driscoll couldn't remember exactly, but that went through his mind as the first bullet tore into his hip. Funny the things you think about when you're being shot. All he'd wanted to do was cover the car. He'd taken his black '57 T-bird out for a spin before tomorrow's big car show at the fairgrounds in Pleasanton. He loved the month of May when it wasn't the cool of spring nor the unbearable heat of the inland summer.

He'd taken the hardtop off the Black Beauty, as he called the car, and cruised her up I-680, the wind whistling through his graying hair as he gunned the engine in the northbound direction toward Concord. He hadn't taken her out for a few months, so he listened carefully for any clicking in the valves. That would mean that the few drops of oil he'd wiped from the garage floor when he pulled her out indicated a larger leak. He'd hoped not. It had been over a year since he'd had the 312 engine rebuilt, and the warranty had just run out.

1

Wasn't that always the way?

He got off at Treat Boulevard, turned around, and headed back home toward San Ramon, waving at an exuberant older man frantically honking his horn and giving a thumbs-up to the Beauty.

Ah, old guys and their cars . . .

He took the Crow Canyon Road exit, followed the side streets to his sleepy little cul-de-sac, pulled into his driveway, and was getting out of the car to open the garage when a sledgehammer hit him in his right hip, folding him across the top of the open car door.

Forrest Gump was full of shit. This was no bite. The pain was excruciating.

Mickey Driscoll didn't have time to contemplate how badly it hurt because a second shot caught him in his right shoulder. He tried to reach the glove compartment of the Beauty before remembering that his Sig was in the Range Rover, which was his daily driver.

He could feel the wet stickiness of his blood drip down his right leg and ooze into his sock. Then came another shot. This one to the left shoulder. He was a sitting duck, and he knew it.

He thought about Janet and the girls. Thank God they weren't home. Shannon had basketball practice, and Janet was picking Schuyler up from ballet.

He felt a fourth bullet enter his left leg, obliterating his hamstring. So much for the 10K he'd been training so hard for. The thought almost made him smile. He hated running. He was only doing it for Janet. She was the runner in the family.

He felt the fifth and sixth shots enter his back between the shoulder blades as he slid off the car door onto the cool pavement.

Does your life really flash before your eyes? he thought.

And then . . . blackness.

TWO

IN BROADCASTING, IT is known as "The Inevitable Friday Afternoon."

Everyone who works in television and radio will have one. They live in denial about its eventual arrival, but it will come. "The Inevitable Friday Afternoon" is when you finish your Friday broadcast and you're told to report to the general manager's office immediately. There, depending upon disposition and comportment, the GM either gently or callously tells you that you're being let go.

The following Monday, a new person sits behind your mic or in front of your camera.

These events occur on Fridays because management believes viewers and listeners will forget you over the weekend and instantaneously embrace your replacement. Generally, such abrupt changes, especially if the person being fired is a beloved personality, are so jarring that the audience, at least temporarily, scrambles to the competition.

My name is Topher Davis, and for the past sixteen years, I've been with Channel 6 in San Francisco, where I started as a feature reporter. I did stories on things like the circus. The jugglers and knife throwers taught me life-altering skills like the key to juggling is to throw the balls in an arc instead of straight up in the air and that a knife needs to make one complete revolution when thrown in order to stick in its target. Feature reporting also taught me that an inexplicable number of old ladies find potatoes they think are the spitting image of Elvis and trees with trunks that sprout the face of Jesus. That was my beat.

After seven years of such earth-shattering reportage, I talked the station into letting me create an investigative bureau. "Topher Davis Reports" has become an institution of sorts.

I've uncovered jewelry scams where diamonds are certified and sold as high grade when, in actuality, they're closer to the mineral composition of a drinking glass. I've caught city officials in "pay for play" relationships with firms they've awarded government contracts. I even brought down an ice cream company who's lax vetting resulted in the hiring of numerous registered sex offenders to drive their ice cream trucks to parks and schools.

It has been rewarding work that's brought me sixteen local Emmy Awards. More importantly, it harkened back to when local news was considered a public service instead of a profit center.

My "Inevitable Friday Afternoon" came in early May. I was at the Six O'Clock News desk presenting my big sweeps exposé on violations of the Ellis Act. San Francisco's rent is among the nation's highest, thanks mainly to the tech boom. Techies worldwide have flocked to town, hoping to grasp their share of the gold that is Salesforce, Airbnb, or whatever the hot startup du jour happens to be.

This has created a housing shortage.

Simple supply and demand have made rents skyrocket, turning landlords into instant Powerball winners. They evict current, long-time tenants, throw a coat of paint on the place, and then rent again (at multiples of five or ten times what they had previously been charging) to the first techie who can come up with first, last, and a hefty security deposit.

California's Ellis Act says that tenants cannot be evicted without cause unless the landlord (or a family member of the landlord) will live in the unit for at least two years. I caught landlords claiming they were evicting current tenants for family housing, only to discover that the "family member" was actually a newly flush tech bro who could regularly make the exorbitant rent.

I sat on the set next to Katie Robards, the current blond "anchor babe" (as the crew derisively called her behind her back), who had recently been hired to be part of the Channel 6 News Team. Local television is a very sexist business. On TV, a guy who graduated high school with Methuselah can anchor the news, but he must have an aspiring supermodel sitting next to him at the desk.

Channel 6 had all the demographic boxes checked: Katie, the pretty, young, blond anchorwoman; Phil Wagner, the distinguished older anchorman; Charlie Wu, the Asian weatherman; Latino sportscaster Chris Hernandez, and yours truly, their African American investigative reporter.

After my package on the evictions ran, the audio feed of the live broadcast in my earpiece was interrupted.

"Captain Queeg wants to see you upstairs," Phil Silva said in my earpiece, referring to the senile commander in the movie *The Caine Mutiny*.

"Thanks, Bilko," I whispered.

Phil had been directing the six o'clock show for five years. His name, "Phil Silva," sounded a lot like that of the great comedian Phil Silvers, who'd played Sergeant Bilko in the '50s, so I always addressed him as such.

"Captain Queeg" was Curt Weil, our general manager. Curt was a fifty-something man who often made decisions that seemed to defy logic. Hence, his nickname.

I walked off the set, down the hall to the glass elevator, and pushed the button for the third floor. As the elevator rose, I watched a crowd of tourists mesmerized by a juggling stilt walker at Pier 39 below.

Our studios are located on the Embarcadero, one of the city's busiest tourist areas, with attractions including restaurants, magnet stores, T-shirt shops, street vendors, Ripley's Believe It or Not, and The Wax Museum.

It was a busy Friday evening on the wharf as herds of families walked along, munching popcorn and giant pretzels. A jogger ran by, weaving his way between groups of teens out for a night on the town and a mom pushing a very unhappy toddler in a stroller.

A jam-packed ferry shuttled sardined passengers across the bay to Alcatraz for tales of Al Capone and Machine Gun Kelly. Thirty bucks to visit a prison. For fun. Only in America.

I got to the third floor and entered the spacious lobby leading to the general manager's office. One of the secrets to longevity in television is keeping your head down. To that end, I hadn't been up to the third floor in months. I had heard that the outer office had been redone, but I wasn't prepared for what I saw.

Apparently, Queeg and company were going for some kind of faux, avant-garde look. Everything was white—the walls, the carpeting, and the furniture were all the color of bleached vanilla ice cream. It was a sterile atmosphere. I felt like I should scrub in for surgery.

A white, high-back couch sat against a back wall behind a pale, oval-shaped coffee table. White oil paintings hung on the walls in white frames above the couch. Each painting consisted of white paint meticulously slathered on canvas with a single black speck of a dot strategically placed in the center. The dots and the magazines on the coffee table, including *Variety*, *The Hollywood Reporter*, and *Vanity Fair*, bore the burden of providing the only color to the snowy ambiance.

Ethyl, a slight woman nearing retirement (come on . . . Who else would have a name like Ethyl?) furiously pecked away at the keyboard on the Dell desktop computer that sat in front of her on a flat white console reminiscent of the deck of the *Starship Enterprise*.

Does anybody still use Dell? For that matter, does anybody still use a desktop?

A bank of television monitors carrying live air from all the other San Francisco television market stations was adjacent to her desk.

"Hi, Ethyl," I said with my best TV grin. I was proud of that grin. It had taken me years to perfect.

"Hey!" she smiled. "Great piece on the Ellis Act stuff."

"Thanks. Like most of these kinds of stories, it was hard to prove . . . but once I did . . ."

"I'm glad you did. What those greedy bastards are doing to the long-term residents of this city is disgraceful."

Ethyl was a third-generation San Franciscan. She was right. The whole demographic of the city was changing.

"Pretty soon, nobody but twenty-five-year-old tech millionaires will be able to afford to live here."

"It's looking that way," I said. "I got word that The Man wants to see me."

"He's waiting for you in his office."

"Thanks," I said, heading for the inner office door. "And chin up. We won't let the bastards win."

Her lips curled into a reassuring smile as she returned to her Dell.

I strolled jauntily into Weil's office, where he stood gazing out the window, his back to me.

"You wanted to see me boss?" I asked. I assumed that it was to congratulate me on the Ellis Act piece. It had the makings of Emmy number seventeen written all over it.

He turned to face me, and I could see that he was in mid conversation, a wireless headset connected to his ear, the mic protruding inches from his mouth.

"I don't give a flying fuck what they say we agreed to on price. There is a contract that they signed with all the figures in black and white," he bellowed into the headset.

Weil was a slender, middle-aged man who stood five foot eight on his best day. He looked much younger than his fifty-plus years by eating well and keeping a strict gym regimen. Taking care of himself had paid off. So had the dark brown plugs covering his thinning pate.

In stark contrast to the virginal sterility of the outer office, Weil's place was classic masculine overcompensation. It was all done in dark brown wood tones. A large mahogany desk sat in front of the window with its picturesque view of the Bay Bridge. Though two brown leather chairs sat in front of the desk, Weil motioned for me to sit on the leather couch against the opposite wall under his portrait of Napoleon. That's right . . . Napoleon.

Little man conquers the world. A metaphor or an aspiration?

How many strawberries were missing from the mess hall again, Captain Queeg?

"Yeah?" he screamed. "Well, I've got lawyers too. A whole bunch of them just sitting on their asses waiting for me to give them something to do."

He looked at me, pointed to the earpiece, and did the "they're crazy" revolution with his index finger circling his temple.

"What part of 'I don't give a fuck' is unclear?" he said, pausing to take a swig from a bottle of sparking water on his desk. "As I see it, he has two choices. He can pay us to advertise . . . or he can just pay us."

He violently tapped the side of his head, turning off the wireless earpiece.

"Sorry," he said. "Pete's Carpets is trying to weasel out of their ad buy."

Pete's was one of the station's biggest local advertisers. They often sponsored my investigative reports.

Weil pressed a button under his desk, and the heavy wooden door that led to Ethyl's office slowly shut. Didn't Matt Lauer get in trouble for having one of these?

He walked over and sat on the leather sofa beside me. His body angled so that he was personally engaged with me, yet he could be out the door in ten seconds if someone yelled, "Fire."

"I watched the Ellis piece," he said. "Nice work."

"Thanks," I said with all the false modesty I could muster. "We worked really hard on that story."

"It shows," he said. "You work your ass off on everything you put on our air . . . which is what makes this so difficult."

Uh-oh.

"What exactly," I asked, "is so difficult?"

"Corporate has ordered a 15 percent cut across the board," he said. "We're closing the investigative bureau."

I felt the wind kicked out of me.

"You're what??" I managed to spit out. "It's sweeps."

In February, May, July, and November, sweeps are the months that ratings determine ad rates. The higher the ratings, the more that can be charged for commercials. Sweeps months are "all hands-on deck" periods with no vacation or sick time allowed. It's when the most nonsensical scare stories are on the air. It's when you hear things like, "Can your dishwashing liquid lead to a stroke? We'll tell you at eleven."

Firing me during May sweeps would be sheer insanity. Then again, there's a reason we called him Captain Queeg.

"We're letting you go in three weeks when your contract is up, Topher."

He glanced away, no longer looking me in the eye. I could tell that he felt badly about the situation. Fuck him. He should.

"We're the last investigative team on TV in the market. We do important work," I said, unable to process what he was telling me.

"I know," he said. "And I also know you built that organization from the ground up. You should be proud of it. I sure am."

He got up, walked over to his desk, twisted the cap from his bottle of sparkling water, and took a long drink. Destroying careers is a thirsty business.

"What happens to Mandy?" I said, speaking of my producer. "And Stu?"

Stu Simons was my cameraman.

"Mandy will be reassigned," Weil said between gulps of water. "Stu . . . is sixty-eight. He should have retired a year or two ago."

I put my face in my hands. That damn place had been my life. Weil came over and sat back down next to me.

"Normally, you'd have no notice. You know that," he said. "I couldn't do that to you. You deserve better. You've always been a class act, and I know you'll continue to be a class act in your final weeks with us."

"Will there be a memo or an announcement?"

"Not from me," he said. "You handle this however you want. Tell people. Don't tell people. It's 100 percent up to you. I trust you."

I nodded.

"Think you've got one more sweeps story in you in the next three weeks?" he said, standing up, signaling that the meeting was over.

"I'm sure I'll come up with something," I said, rising from the couch.

"I'm sure you will," he said with a half smile.

He walked back over to his desk, pressed the button, and the door opened. I walked out to find Ethyl still furiously stabbing away at her keyboard.

If I was going out, it was going to be in style. I needed an idea. I glanced over Ethyl's head at the bank of monitors, and there it was, clear as day on Channel 7. A bold lower third graphic that read "COP KILLING."

THREE

I PULLED MY Lexus into a space against the curb about fifteen yards from the last police barricade. I checked my hair and teeth in the rearview mirror and then got out. Without turning around, I heard the chirp as I pressed the button on my key fob, setting the car's alarm.

It was a nice cul-de-sac. Upper-middle-class people, usually going about their upper-middle-class lives, stood in their yards and doorways awash in the red, yellow, and blue disco lights of the law enforcement and emergency vehicles, necks uncomfortably craned to get a glimpse of the police activity. Open garages were adorned with an array of late-model Mercedes, BMWs, and Teslas for the well-heeled and environmentally conscious.

I could already hear the refrain we'd get once we began collecting sound bites from the neighbors.

A chorus of, "I can't believe this happened here."

Translation: These things only happen where "those people" live.

I hate to break it to them that murder happens everywhere. Oh sure, the motives and means may differ, and some may be

12

more adept than others in their attempts to evade justice, but a big bank account and an ethnically homogenous neighborhood don't guarantee safety or security. They only guarantee that the media will show up. And that the murder will actually be investigated.

This was the kind of neighborhood the press loved.

The court was ringed by an array of homes built in the eighties, not quite on the McMansion spectrum but close enough to run in the multimillion-dollar range. The houses were all different yet strangely the same. The same postage stamp-sized front yards backed by the same stucco-encrusted homes. Most had two stories. One even sported a third. There was the feel of a black-and-white sitcom about the neighborhood. The set of *My Three Sons* preserved in amber.

I walked up the cul-de-sac to a cop standing in front of the yellow crime scene tape keeping the lookie-loos at bay. He was a young rookie I didn't recognize. Then again, I didn't know most of the cops in San Ramon. He was a handsome six-footer with jet-black hair shaved into a buzz cut. I'd guess recent military experience. He had that "Uncle Sam Wants You" demeanor.

"Officer Whitmeyer," I said, reading his silver nameplate, "I'm—"

"I know who you are, Mr. Davis," he said, cutting me off. "I'm sorry, but my orders are to let no unauthorized personnel into the restricted area. Unfortunately, that includes you."

Looking past Private Pyle, I saw a human-shaped figure lying under a sheet in the driveway. Pools of blood stained the pavement. A gorgeous black '57 Thunderbird sat parked adjacent to the body. The driver's-side door was open, and the red interior was marred by what appeared to be bullet holes, one piercing the side of the driver's seat. The other was in the dash.

"Look," I said to Whitmeyer, "I understand you're just doing your job. Only following orders. I get that. But you see, I have a job to do too—"

"Let him through," came a woman's voice. "Otherwise, you'll get a twenty-minute lecture on the First Amendment."

Detective Lynn Sloan appeared behind the young officer.

"It's okay," she said, gently touching his shoulder. "I'll take responsibility."

Whitmeyer stepped aside. I lifted the crime scene tape and slipped under.

"What are you doing here?" I said. "You're SFPD. San Ramon is a little out of your jurisdiction, isn't it, Detective?"

The detective was a tall, lean, African American woman. She was thin and attractive in a "runway" sort of way, but something about her demeanor conveyed a "don't even think about it if you want your limbs to remain intact" vibe.

"Driscoll was SFPD," she said. "One of ours. This will be a joint investigation."

"What do you know so far?"

"Just because I let you in here doesn't mean I'm spilling my guts on an open investigation into a cop killing," she said. "Brother or no brother."

Even though we're siblings, Lynn has always been clear about setting boundaries.

"Then why let me back here?" I asked.

"Like I told the kid, to spare him from one of your long, boring-ass civics lessons."

I chuckled. Lynn didn't. She was always deadly serious at a crime scene.

"You've got to give me something. A cop who is generally despised by every person of color in the nine Bay Area counties gets gunned down in his own driveway. People are gonna want to know what happened," I said. "Or shall I instruct you in the nuances of the First Amendment?"

"Oh God, no," she said, rolling her eyes. "Look . . . off the record?"

"For now," I promised.

"He took six bullets," she said, releasing an exasperated breath.

"Wow," I said. "Six slugs."

"This was a revenge killing," she said. "Pure and simple."

"Doesn't surprise me a bit," I said.

Lynn shook her head.

A thick, middle-aged Latino San Ramon cop with snow-white hair and a beard approached Lynn.

"Detective . . ." he said, clamming up as soon as he saw me.

"Detective Morales, this is my brother, Chris. Chris, Detective Jose Morales. He caught the case for San Ramon PD."

Morales extended a meaty hand.

"You're the TV guy," he said with recognition.

I nodded.

"I thought your name was Topher or something," he said.

"It is, professionally," I said.

"The name on his driver's license is Christopher Robin Davis," Lynn said. "He uses 'Topher' for television because it sounds whiter."

"Christopher Robin?" Morales said.

"Our mom was a big fan of the Pooh books," I told him. "My sister narrowly escaped being named Piglet."

Morales laughed heartily.

Lynn is the only person who still calls me Chris. While her explanation oversimplified things a bit, when I was starting out, I discovered that "Topher Davis" on a résumé got me a lot more interviews than "Christopher Davis" did. You do what you've got to do.

"You can speak freely in front of Chris," Lynn said. "We're off the record."

A young, redheaded evidence tech approached the T-bird and opened a leather case. She pulled out a silver tool and began extracting a bullet from the dashboard.

"No shell casings anywhere," Morales said. "The shooter apparently used a revolver. We'll know more once we get the slugs over to ballistics."

"I'm sure that a neighborhood like this is especially paranoid and security conscious," I said. "Have you checked for private security cameras?"

"Everybody's got a camera or one of those Ring things for a doorbell," Morales said. "My guys are canvassing the neighborhood right now. We'll get pictures of something."

"I can't see how we wouldn't," Lynn said. "Jesus, he was blown away in broad daylight."

A coroner's van pulled up to the curb, and Officer Whitmayer cleared the growing crowd out of the way. Two officers from the Coroner's Office got out of the van and put the sheet-covered body on a stretcher that they placed in the back of the vehicle.

"Have you talked to the family?" I asked.

Lynn nodded.

"Shittiest part of this gig. I didn't know Driscoll well, but I had met his wife at a few department family events over the years," she said.

"How's she taking it?"

"About as well as can be expected, I suppose."

My turn to nod. "I can imagine," I said.

"I'll let you know what we find as soon as we round up and review footage from the neighbors and the street cameras in the area," Morales chimed in.

"Thanks. And thanks for your cooperation," she said.

"Nice meeting you, Chris," he said, walking over to the T-bird.

"Topher," I hollered after him.

"Topher," he repeated apologetically.

Lynn looked at me and rolled her eyes again. Sisters.

I was walking back to the Lexus when I heard, "Mr. Davis, Mr. Davis," in a loud whisper. I turned to see a seventy-ish woman standing behind me. She had her hair in a bun and wore what my auntie used to call a blue "housecoat." Though she was older and apparently dressed for bed, she looked good for her age. Botox and face-lifts are prerequisites for residence in these parts. God, I'm glad I'm a man. Society will allow me to age gracefully if I so choose.

The skin on the woman's face was so taut you could bounce a quarter off it.

"Mr. Davis," she said again as I faced her.

"Yes," I said.

"I thought that was you. Vera Vance," she said, extending a French-manicured hand with skin much looser than that on her face.

Is there such a thing as "hand lift"? I'll have to ask a cosmetic surgeon next time I run into one.

"It's nice to meet you, Ms. Vance." I figured I'd sign her autograph and get out of there.

"It's Vera."

"Then I'm Topher," I said.

"I live in the house across the street," she said, pointing at a two-story, colonial-style home diagonally from the Driscoll house.

"I saw the whole thing," she told me.

"You did?"

"My kitchen window looks out onto the court. I was watering my African violets. Do you like African violets? They're my favorites," she said. "Purple is the color of royalty, you know."

"They're lovely flowers, Vera. Go on, please. You were watering the African violets . . ."

"I was watering the flowers and noticed Mr. Driscoll pull his old car into his driveway."

"The Thunderbird," I said.

"I really don't know cars."

She pointed to the T-bird in the Driscoll driveway. "That one," she said.

"Okay."

"Well, he parks and gets out when a little white car comes flying into the court."

"Any idea what kind of car?"

"No. Like I said, I don't know cars, but I do know it was one of those new electric ones. It didn't make a sound. I wouldn't have noticed it if I hadn't been at the window when it drove up."

"What happened next?"

"I heard what sounded like firecrackers," she said. "We're two months from the Fourth of July, and I already hear firecrackers going off all the time."

"Go on," I said, my patience running thin.

"I see Mr. Driscoll's body slam against his car. That's when I knew it wasn't a firecracker. I could see blood staining his shirt. Then there were five more shots. *Pop, pop, pop, pop, pop.* And he fell to the ground. The white car then turned and zoomed away."

"Did you get a look at the driver of the white car?"

"No. He was wearing a dark hood or . . . ski mask. That was it. A ski mask."

"What happened next?"

"I called 911 and went over to see if I could help. I used to be an RN. He was already dead by the time I got there."

"Did you get a license plate number?"

"No, I'm sorry I didn't. It all happened so fast."

"Have you told this to the police?"

"Yes," she said. "As soon as they got here. I'm guessing I'll have to give a formal statement of some kind."

"How would you like to be on TV?" I asked.

"Really?" she exclaimed with excitement.

"Really. I can have my producer and cameraman here in half an hour. Will you tell them on camera what you just told me?"

"Of course! I need to change clothes and fix my hair," she said, running a hand down the length of her housecoat to smooth it.

"Any thoughts on who the shooter might have been?"

She shrugged her shoulders. "There's been so much trouble around here since his incident that I've lost track. It could be anybody."

"Trouble?"

"Vandalism mostly. His house was egged. Somebody egged my house once, apparently mistaking it for his," she said. "Somebody even spray painted 'Murderer' on the side of his house. Can you believe that? He had to paint that whole side of the home. Took him a week." She took a breath.

"No painting over this," she said, sadness creeping into her voice. "Those poor girls. He has two daughters, you know."

"That's what I hear."

I thanked her for the information, and she went into the house to freshen up. I pulled out my cell and called Mandy. I told her to grab Stu and get over here pronto. I didn't tell Lynn. Figured she already knew what Vera Vance had to say. If not, I could fill her in later. The important thing was getting the story on the air.

I jumped in the Lexus and headed home, anxious to get started on my final story.

FOUR

NIGHT FELL AS I drove the Lexus down I-680 for the ride home. I was so deep in thought that I almost missed the I-580 West junction that would take me toward Oakland. I mentally tried to download everything I could remember about the Driscoll case.

It had been six months since he'd been dispatched to investigate a noise complaint in San Francisco's Sunset District. Some dumb mom and dad had left their "responsible teenager" in charge as they left for the weekend. The kid, of course, immediately decided to stage a revival of *Animal House*. His folks' car wasn't even out of the driveway, and he was buying red Solo cups, sending out Evites, and posting on Facebook and Instagram—big mistake.

In the preinternet days, news of a house party got around by word of mouth, which kept most gatherings manageable regarding size. With the advent of social media, word of a kegger party travels worldwide at the speed of light to millions of people. Within a few hours, the modest home had been turned into a den of booze, pot, and raging adolescent hormones.

Upon arriving at the house, Driscoll saw the size of the crowd and immediately called for backup. Two other cops, whose names escaped me, were there within minutes. When the police presence was noticed, the teenagers scattered.

A young Black kid, apparently the only African American at the party, ran for the door, which happened to be in the direction of where Driscoll was standing. Driscoll saw the kid running at him with something in his hand that appeared to be a gun. He drew his weapon and fired six shots, hitting the boy in the chest and killing him instantly.

Once the chaos subsided, Driscoll discovered that he'd shot Jamal Williams, a seventeen-year-old honor roll student carrying a black Samsung Galaxy.

The story played out as these stories usually do. Someone at the party recorded the incident and posted the video on Facebook, where it quickly went viral. It showed Driscoll issuing a "drop the weapon" command and firing simultaneously without giving the kid a chance to comply.

Driscoll was placed on paid administrative leave while an investigation was conducted. He said he "feared for my life and the lives of my fellow officers." The SFPD found the shooting to be justified. The grand jury declined to indict. The DA declined to prosecute. There was fury in African American communities throughout the Bay Area and around the country, expressed by three nights of civil unrest, vandalism, riots, and looting.

When these things happen, I've never understood why we, as Blacks, retaliate by tearing up our own neighborhoods.

The violence ended when the DA relented and charged Driscoll with voluntary manslaughter. The trial took two days. The acquittal took less than two hours. More civil unrest followed the verdict as Jamal Williams became #JamalWilliams and #JusticeForJamal.

Eventually, the rioting subsided, Driscoll quietly returned to work, and the story faded from the news as mass school shootings and police killings in other parts of the country grabbed the headlines. Six months later, it was as though the story had been forgotten. At least, it seemed that way until today, when Mickey Driscoll took the same number of slugs as the kid he'd shot. As Lynn always says, there are no coincidences.

I got off the freeway at the Eden Canyon/Palomares Canyon Road exit, and ten minutes later, I was pulling into my gated driveway. Home is a 5,000-square-foot ranch-style house on a two-acre parcel in Palomares Canyon.

Unlike many of my peers in local television, I don't live in the upscale homogenous bubbles of Pleasanton, Danville, Dublin, Alamo, or San Ramon. I just never really felt comfortable there. I need at least some diversity around me. Not that Castro Valley hasn't had its own problems in the past. The unincorporated town had an active Klan chapter well into the 1990s.

Lynn and I had been raised by our aunt Jessie in nearby Piedmont, a wealthy enclave southeast of Oakland. Our mother was killed when we were kids, and Auntie took us in. Jessie was a secretary who worked her way up to vice president at one of the big multinational corporations in San Francisco and did quite well for herself and, thus, for us. We had private schools and advantages, but Auntie made sure that we never lost sight of who we were.

As for our father's whereabouts, your guess is as good as mine. He took off when Lynn was a baby. I was three and barely remembered him.

I had been in Castro Valley for the previous six years. It's a beautiful home that's really too much house for one person and a Bichon Frisé. It hadn't always been that way. When I built the house, Sophie (the Bichon) and I lived with my girlfriend, Sarah. That was then. Six months ago, Sarah left us for greener pastures. She'd "lost her identity," she said. She felt that my life was too "big" for her. That her life had been absorbed by mine. I felt that was utter and complete bullshit. So now, it's me and my fluffy little white dog.

It's a bit isolated, but I love where I live. However, driving the winding road to get there may not be everybody's idea of a leisurely drive home, especially at night when a total lack of streetlights turns the roadway into an inky abyss. It can be dangerous, especially on rainy nights. Head-on collisions are always a concern.

I drove over the small bridge that crosses the creek bed that runs through most of the properties in the canyon. It's pretty and soothing when there's water. An extended California drought has left it dry and dusty as of late.

I parked the Lexus in the garage and entered the house through the kitchen, much to the excitement of Sophie, who was so glad to see me she piddled on the linoleum floor—the perfect end to the perfect day.

"How ya doin', girl?" I asked, scratching behind her left ear.

She wagged her tail furiously and stood tall on her hind legs, propping her front paws on my Armani slacks, begging me to pick her up. I was the one who'd wanted a lap dog.

I obediently complied, holding Sophie cradled in my left arm while I used a paper towel to clean up her accident with my right. I could hear the echo of my footsteps on the hardwood floor as I carried the dog into the living room. It was too quiet without Sarah. The situation sucked. At least I'd had my work to distract me. In a few weeks, I wouldn't even have that.

What the hell was I going to do?

I was set financially. I was lucky enough to have had some cash on hand when the real estate market crashed a few years back, and as a result, I scooped up distressed properties around the Bay Area that have increased in value exponentially.

I never had to work another day in my life if I didn't want to. The problem was I wanted to. I was too damned young to retire. I couldn't see myself rattling around alone in that big empty house without Sarah. My heart was in so many pieces that all the king's horses and all the king's men . . . well, you know.

I fed Sophie the chi chi fresh organic food she eats and tossed a Lean Cuisine into the microwave. Jesus, the dog's eating better than I am. What a pathetic Friday night.

Fifteen minutes later, I sat at the kitchen counter, nibbling on shrimp and pasta, thinking about the murder. There was so much outrage about Jamal then that I could see somebody seeking some sort of "street justice." The notion surprised me a little bit because it appeared that things had calmed down some. Tensions seemed to have eased.

Who kills a cop? Let alone in broad daylight? Either a fool or a psychopath. Or both.

I finished the pasta, tossed the plastic dining dish into the blue recycle bin, and then went to the bar cart in the living room. I picked up the crystal decanter containing Johnnie Walker Blue and poured a neat triple. It had been a rough day. I quickly drained the glass and poured another. I took the fresh drink and decanter out onto the redwood deck in the back of the house, where I looked at the stars and drank lonely sips of scotch until I fell asleep on one of the patio chairs.

FIVE

I WAS AWAKENED the following day by the bright Saturday sun, the empty decanter at my side, and Sophie snoring lightly at my feet. It was not a pleasant awakening. My mouth felt like I'd been licking stamps all night. A construction crew in my skull pounded and jack-hammered at my frontal lobe. Johnnie Walker Blue is not a forgiving mistress.

The theme from *I Love Lucy* cut through the scotch fog. I fumbled in my pocket for my phone and croaked a groggy, "Hello."

It was reciprocated with Mandy's chipper, "Good morning, sleepyhead."

"What time is it?"

"It's 11:30," she said.

"Christ."

"Late night?"

"Something like that."

"Fall asleep in your clothes again?"

I said nothing.

"You hungry?" she asked.

I thought for a moment. "I guess I probably should eat something," I finally said.

"Meet me at The Egg in an hour."

I belched a sour, scotch-fueled burp. Gross.

"Let's make it an hour and a half," I told her.

I swallowed three ibuprofen and washed them down with a full bottle of Evian water. I then took a thirty-minute hot shower and shaved. Once I was dressed, I gave Sophie her breakfast and hopped in the Lexus.

Mandy started as my intern right out of college and has since become my producer, assistant, gofer, friend, and, at the most inopportune times, my conscience.

With Sarah gone, Mandy, Lynn, and Sophie were the three most important women in my life. What would I do without Mandy when I left in three weeks?

I took the two-lane Palomares Road as it snaked through the canyon, turned left on East Castro Valley Boulevard, and followed it into the heart of town. A strip mall sat on the corner of the intersection at Castro Valley Boulevard and Redwood Road with a Lucky's grocery store, a dry cleaner, a new Asian Fusion restaurant, and various sundry establishments. Some were part of chain operations like Pizza Hut; others were individual proprietorships.

The Cracked Egg was located in the corner of the strip mall, nestled snugly between the Lucky's and a small antique shop.

The Egg, as we called it, was an institution in town. It had begun as a simple diner in the 1960s. The kind of place with a blue plate special and waitresses with beehive hairdos who called you "Sweetie." It served good, hearty American food.

Jared Sloan bought the place about twelve years ago, expanded it, spruced it up a bit, and made omelets the focus.

They are multiple in variety, reasonably priced, and served with a side order of the best home fries you'll ever eat. Those, and the Brazilian coffee Jared serves, soon made the place a hangout for local law enforcement. That's how he met Lynn and eventually became my brother-in-law.

I found an empty spot in the crowded parking lot, parked the Lexus, and walked in precisely one hour and forty-five minutes after hanging up with Mandy, who I found sitting at our usual corner table by the window. The sun shimmered off her short blond hair.

"Sorry I'm late," I said, sliding into the booth across from her. "I'm moving kinda slowly today."

"No worries," she said, looking at her iPhone. "For you, this is early."

"I'm not late all the time," I protested.

She laughed.

"All right, a lot of the time," I said. Fessing up is hard to do.

I glanced around the crowded restaurant to see a mix of California Highway Patrol, Alameda County Sheriff's deputies, and officers from nearby Hayward and San Leandro mixed among civilians munching on eggs and toast.

The Egg had a rustic look, with brown wooden walls adorned with photos and posters of James Dean, Marilyn Monroe, Elvis, and Gina Lollobrigida. What is this fascination that white people have with the 1950s? I expected Fonzie to come walking in at any minute.

For Black people, the fifties aren't cars, music, the beach, and girls. They're Emmett Till, Rosa Parks, the Montgomery Bus Boycott, and George Wallace—not a period we look back on with nostalgia.

"Looks like you really tied one on last night," Mandy said.

"What makes you say that?"

"The bags under your eyes and the smell of . . ." she sniffed deeply, "I'd say scotch."

"Damn," I said. "You should ask Lynn if the department needs any new bloodhounds."

"What's going on?" she asked.

I told her about my impending career setback.

"That's just ridiculous," she said, shaking her head with disgust. "A ridiculous, crazy, stupid decision."

"It is what it is," I said.

I was about to tell her the idea I'd come up with for our final story when Jared walked up to the table wearing the black shirt, slacks, and apron all of The Egg's servers wore. He glanced at his Apple watch.

"Thought you said he'd be here in an hour and a half," he said to Mandy with a wink.

"Don't you start on me too," I said. "I had a late night."

He looked me over for a moment, and then his demeanor changed.

"What's up?" he asked.

I told him.

"Well, that's just—"

"Ridiculous," Mandy said, cutting him off.

"Yeah, ridiculous," he said, brushing aside sandy hair from in front of cobalt-blue eyes. "You told Lynn?"

"Not yet," I said. "I saw her, but she was a little preoccupied."

"I know, the Mickey Driscoll thing," he said.

"Did you know him?"

"Not well," Jared said. "He'd come in here for Sunday brunch occasionally with his family. Wife and three . . . no, two daughters. Sad."

"Anything else you know about him?" I asked.

"Not really. We'd make small talk. He knew Lynn casually. As far as I know, she never worked on any cases with him."

"Lynn coming in this morning?" I asked.

"Who knows? She's supposed to be off today, but—"

"Fat chance," Mandy laughed. She turned to me and said, "She's as big a workaholic as you are."

"I won't be for much longer," I said.

"I wish there were something I could do," Jared remarked.

"There is," I said. "Bring me an omelet with crab meat, avocado, and Swiss cheese. And home fries. No onions."

Jared pulled an order pad and pen from his apron pocket and began writing.

"And for you, madam?" he said with a faux French accent.

"Two scrambled egg whites and a cup of honeydew melon," she said. "And black coffee. Some for scotch boy over here too."

"Thanks," I said.

"It'll be out in a few minutes," Jared said, walking toward the kitchen.

"Egg whites?" I said. "Fruit cup?"

"Trying to lose ten pounds. I'm not eating carbs."

Mandy looked at me and let out an exasperated sigh. "Now what?" she asked.

"Now," I said, "we go out with a bang."

"What do you mean?"

"I get one more story and know what it is."

"Okay," she said. "Care to elaborate?"

"The Driscoll case has been out of the news for a while. That's how all of these things go. Shooting of an unarmed person of color …"

"What's the difference between a person of color and a colored person?" she asked.

"The Civil Rights Act of 1964," I said. "Focus, please."

She nodded and giggled.

"As I was saying, these stories all follow the same template: shooting of an unarmed Black person, the cop is placed on paid administrative leave, there's outrage in the Black community, no accountability for the cop, more outrage in the Black community, things calm down, and in a few months, the whole thing is forgotten, and the cop goes back to work."

"And . . ." she added, "the city ponies up a wrongful death settlement to pacify the family. That pretty well sums it up."

"Why don't we find out what happens *after* that narrative?"

"I don't follow you," she said.

"Using the Driscoll murder as a backdrop, I want to do a piece on what life is like for all those involved in these kinds of shootings," I told her. "Once the camera crews leave and it's all 'over,' what happens to the cop and his family? The family of the person killed? How do they fare after a tragedy like that? What do you think?"

"I love it," Mandy said. "I got to know Jamal Williams's mother a little during that whole thing. I think I can get her to talk to us."

"Did you get a sound bite from that neighbor last night? Vera Vance?"

"Told us exactly what she told you about how the shooting went down."

"Lynn knows Driscoll's wife," I said.

"Casually," Mandy corrected.

"Okay, casually," I said. "I can see if she'll give us an introduction."

As I finished my sentence, Lynn walked in, pulled up a chair, and sat between us.

"Speak of the devil," I said.

"My ears were on fire." Lynn smiled.

I filled her in on my impending unemployment and my story idea.

"I'm sorry about your job," Lynn said, shaking her head. "That's just—"

"Ridiculous," Mandy chimed in.

"Actually, 'bullshit' is the word I was going to use," Lynn stated.

"Can you help us with the Driscoll family?" I asked.

"They're planning a funeral. Now's not the best time to go sticking a camera in their faces," she replied.

I thought a moment. "How about just a conversation?" I asked. "No cameras. I just want to talk to her."

Lynn ran her fingers through her short-cropped hair.

"I've got three weeks until my contract's up. We can start with Mrs. Williams on camera and go from there," I said.

Jared returned to the table and placed steaming breakfast plates in front of us. He put a cup of chamomile tea in front of Lynn.

"Thanks, baby," she said.

"But of course," he said, resuming his bogus French. He gave her a quick kiss and hurried back toward the kitchen.

Mandy picked at her egg whites as Lynn sipped her tea.

Lynn has always been weight- and fitness-conscious, even more so after her two tours as an Army Ranger in the Middle East. For Mandy, it's been a little more of a struggle.

"Anything on the shooter yet?" I asked, cutting and forking a piece of my crab omelet.

Mandy took her fork and speared one of the golden-brown home fries on my plate.

"You know there are carbs in those," I said.

Mandy shrugged as she put the piece of potato into her mouth and chewed. An orgasmic look washed over her face.

"Leave her alone," Lynn said. "Egg whites are bland."

"Driscoll," I said.

"Are we off the record?" she asked.

I nodded and repeated, "Off the record."

"Driscoll was shot six times with a .38-caliber revolver. Hollow-point bullets."

"Jesus," Mandy said, taking another one of my potatoes.

"Neighborhood cameras pick up anything useful?" I asked.

"We're still combing through the footage. We know he was driving a white Prius."

"Good luck tracking *that* car down," Mandy said. "In the Bay Area, throw a rock, and you'll hit a white Prius."

"Did any of the cameras get a shot of the plates?" I asked.

"Nothing readable," Lynn said. "Probably stolen anyway."

"How about the driver? Anything?"

"In the few shots of him the neighbors' cameras picked up, he's wearing a black ski mask."

"So, a masked man driving a white Prius with likely stolen plates. Not much to go on," I remarked.

"I've started with less, big brother. This is a cop killing," she said. "We'll catch the bastard."

"I have no doubt," I said.

"Neither do I," Mandy added, looking at my plate and eyeing my potatoes. "Are you gonna eat the rest of those?"

SIX

SHEILA WILLIAMS LIVED in a small house near the South Hayward BART station not far from the old Kaiser Hospital. Modernity declared the facility subpar, so a beautiful new Kaiser facility was built in nearby San Leandro.

As we drove through the neighborhood, we noticed that the houses were older, the development having been built during the housing boom that followed the Second World War. Although modifications had been made by some, all the homes had the same slant roof, long on the left side and shorter on the right. Picture windows adorned the fronts of the homes.

It was a warm day, and the ample front yards were being put to good use. We drove past a muscular, tan man playing Frisbee with a white pit bull. Next door, three Latino boys wearing swim trunks frolicked in the sprinklers. In the house next to them, a septuagenarian in a floppy orange sun hat planted four-o'clock flowers along the side of her garage.

The Williams home sat near the end of the block. The outside looked as though it had been badly neglected. The lawn

33

was overgrown and brown. Paint chipped from the garage and the front of the house along the picture windowsill.

We parked the Lexus in front of the house. Stu parked the ENG truck behind us. Mandy and I walked to the porch with Stu on our heels, his camera resting firmly on his shoulder. He held a folded tripod in his free hand. Stu was a tall, lanky fellow in his sixties with a pronounced Texas twang from his upbringing in Odessa. He'd shot my stories since the days of jugglers and knife throwers. When I told him about my pending departure, he said, "Well, hell, I was gon' retire next year anyhow. I'll go when you do. We can go fishin' together."

Now, I love Stu and have nothing against fishing per se, but I don't see myself spending the rest of my life in a rowboat watching a red and white bobber float in Lake Chabot.

Mandy rang the bell, and Sheila answered. She was both younger and older than I was expecting. Chronologically, I'd put her in her mid-thirties. One of those single, young, African American mothers busting her tail to care for a child she had when she was still a child herself.

She wore a frilly beige blouse with a herringbone skirt cut off a few inches below the knee. Her hair was a fashionable, well-groomed display of dreadlocks that draped her petite shoulders. That was the "younger" part I didn't expect.

The age was in her face. There was a weariness in her eyes. It was a look I'd seen in many Black people much older than us. They had seen and endured so much that they carried a pall in their eyes. That pall was a database of a lifetime of pain, indignity, and humiliation. A database they didn't dare access for fear of what would happen once the floodgates opened and years of injury and grievance were unleashed upon an unsuspecting world.

Sheila Williams was too young for that. She was also too young to be the mother of a dead son.

"Hi, Ms. Williams," Mandy said.

"It's nice to see you again, Amanda," she said in a voice that had an air of culture and dignity.

"This is Topher Davis," Mandy said, gesturing toward me.

I extended my hand, and she took it in both of hers. Her hands were lotion smooth: her grip, that of one holding on for dear life.

"It's nice to meet you, Ms. Williams," I said.

"I admire your work, Mr. Davis," she said. "And please call me Sheila."

"In that case, I'm Topher," I continued. "This is my photographer, Stu."

"Ma'am." Stu nodded.

Sheila Williams smiled and returned the nod.

"Thanks for agreeing to talk with us," I said. "I know it must be difficult."

"I don't know what else I can tell you," Sheila replied. "But—"

"Not very much," said a sharp voice behind her.

A forty-something African American woman appeared in the doorway behind Sheila. She was professionally dressed in dark slacks and a dark blazer over a light blue blouse. She clutched a tan leather attaché case in her left hand and a coffee travel mug in her right. She had a thin face with brown eyes bisected by a long, thin nose. Her skin was the color of caramel corn. Highlighted brown ringlets hung over her left eye.

"This is Kendra Robbins," Sheila said. "My attorney."

"We have a civil suit pending against the City of San Francisco in the wrongful death of Jamal Williams," Kendra informed us.

"She's here to make sure I don't say anything stupid," Sheila said with a faint smile.

"I'm here," Kendra said, "to ensure that my client isn't tricked or pressured into saying something inaccurate or out of context."

I introduced myself and my team.

"I know who you are, Mr. Davis," Kendra said with exasperation. "To be honest, with pending litigation, I've advised my client not to talk to you, but she insists."

"I do indeed," Sheila said, eyes moistening. "People need to know about Jamal. They need to remember him and the way he lived, not just the way he . . . Please, come in."

The house was much neater and well-kept inside than outside. It was a small, two-bedroom home, tastefully furnished with a leather couch, matching ottoman, a love seat, and a spit-shined mahogany coffee table in the living room. The walls and coffee table were covered with framed photos. Jamal as a baby. Jamal with the gap-toothed grin of a seven-year-old. Jamal in Little League gear.

"I like to keep him near me," Sheila said as Mandy and I examined the pictures.

"You have a lovely home," Mandy said.

"Thank you," Sheila replied. "I must apologize for the condition of my yard. You see, that was Jamal's job. He took care of the outside; I kept the inside. I have allergies and can't pull weeds myself."

She paused and took a deep breath.

"I know I should probably hire someone to keep things up, but . . . I haven't been able to. It would almost be as though I was replacing my son. But . . . I need to put my big-girl pants on and do what needs to be done."

"You always do," Kendra said, placing a French-manicured hand on her shoulder. "You always do."

"Ma'am," Stu said, "is it okay if Topher does the interview on your couch?"

"Wherever you'd like is fine," Sheila responded.

Mandy and I studied our surroundings as Stu set up his tripod, camera, and lights and directed them toward the couch. One photo on the coffee table showed Jamal blowing out candles with the numerals one and seven, Sheila standing over his shoulder, beaming with pride. Little did they know that would be the kid's last birthday.

Even though the photo was only a year old, Sheila looked as though she'd had fifteen birthday cakes of her own since then.

Once Stu was set up, Mandy clipped lavalier mics on me and Sheila.

Kendra sat on the love seat across from us out of frame, her attaché case on the floor beside her as she took generous jolts of caffeine from her travel mug.

"We can start whenever you're ready," Mandy said.

"Go ahead," Sheila said, taking a deep, nervous breath.

"Okay," I said. "Let's start here. Most people know Jamal primarily because of the tragedy. Tell us about him and who he was."

Her eyes moistened again.

"Jamal was a kind, sweet, hardworking young man who loved to read, especially about science and space. His dream was to be an astrophysicist. He also liked sports . . . Excuse me, may I please have a drink of water?"

"I'll get it," Mandy said.

"The kitchen is over there," Sheila told her, pointing behind us to the left.

A few moments later, Mandy returned with a Mickey Mouse coffee mug filled with water. She handed it to Sheila, who sipped daintily.

"Jamal loved Disneyland," Sheila said. "We were supposed to go the Christmas after he . . ."

She took another sip.

"Thank you," she said, regaining her composure and returning the mug to Mandy. "Where were we?"

"Sports," I said.

"Jamal loved sports. Especially baseball. The A's were his life. He collected baseball cards and played on the Varsity team in high school. He also played the trumpet in the school band. Louis Armstrong was one of his heroes. He went to Moreau Catholic and graduated valedictorian with a 4.3 GPA."

"Was he a student at USF when he died?" I asked.

"No, a freshman at Cal. He had planned on transferring to Stanford or USF for his graduate degree. He had barely started his freshman classes when . . ."

She held back a sob.

"I think that this is a bad idea. You're only upsetting her," Kendra interjected.

"Would you like to stop?" I asked.

"No, let's continue," Sheila said, composing herself.

"Are you sure?" I asked. "We can come back another—"

"Let's continue," she said, a firmness finding its way into her voice. "He had barely started classes when he went to that damned party."

"Some have painted Jamal as a party kid. Do you know if that was his thing? To the best of your knowledge, did he drink or do drugs?"

"Don't answer that," Kendra interjected.

"Why not?" Sheila said. "If he did, those aren't crimes punishable by death. You have white frat boys getting blasted out of their heads seven days a week who aren't shot dead by police. What difference does it make?"

"I'm not trying to besmirch Jamal's character in any way. I'm just trying to get a full picture of the young man," I said.

"You want a full picture?" Sheila asked. "Follow me."

Mandy looked at me and shrugged.

Sheila led us through a narrow, carpeted hallway into a small bedroom with a twin bed and dresser. A video game controller and console sat on a little desk in the corner, a small flat-screen TV mounted over it.

"This," she said, "is Jamal's room. It's just like he left it."

It was a typical teenage boy's room filled with baseball trophies and video games. The adjacent wall had posters of Drake, Lil Wayne, Albert Einstein, and Stephen Hawking. That's a combination you don't see in every teenager's bedroom. The kid had been gone for over six months, and it was as though his mother had preserved his room as a shrine.

"He was living at home and commuting to Cal. An academic scholarship covered his tuition, but we couldn't afford for him to live on campus during his freshman year. He was working after school as a courtesy clerk at Safeway to save up enough for room and board his sophomore year," she said.

"He was a good kid," Kendra said.

"But I'm not naïve," Sheila added. "Do I think he probably had an occasional beer or smoked a little pot with his friends? I don't know for sure, but I wouldn't be surprised. He wasn't a saint. None of us are."

"He was a teenage boy, Mr. Davis," Kendra said. "I'm sure you did a few things when you were a teenager that your parents were unaware of."

"More than a few," I smiled. "If there was one thing you wanted people to know about Jamal, what would it be?"

"That he had a kind heart. Let me give you an example. When he was around eleven, he found a stray kitten. The apartment managers where we lived then wouldn't allow us to keep it because they had a 'no pets' rule. Jamal took it to the local shelter and discovered that it would be euthanized if it wasn't adopted quickly. So he looked around until he found a 'no kill' shelter," she said. "You know Tony La Russa?"

"The baseball manager?" I said, nodding.

"He has a foundation over in Walnut Creek that keeps cats and dogs until they find them permanent homes, no matter how long that takes," she said. "When Jamal saw the work they were doing, he started volunteering. So, besides his baseball, schoolwork, and the school band, he was volunteering at an animal shelter."

Her eyes watered, and she brushed away tears with the back of her right hand.

"I'm sure by now you've heard about Mickey Driscoll," I said, changing the subject.

"Yes, I watch the news," Sheila replied.

"Do you have any feelings about his death that you'd like to share?"

"I am a Christian, Mr. Davis," she said in a clipped tone. "I hate that Mr. Driscoll felt the need to murder my son, but I did not wish him any ill will. I can't forgive him. Not yet. It's still too fresh. Too raw. But I never wanted to see him dead. I wanted to see him held accountable."

Sheila wiped her eyes again and said, "I know what his family is going through. I don't wish that hell on anyone."

"Out of curiosity," I said, "where were you at around five on Friday evening?"

Kendra jumped in. "Don't answer that."

"Oh? Why not?" Sheila said.

"Are you accusing my client of something?" Kendra demanded.

"No," I said. "Of course not. The cop who killed her son was gunned down in his driveway. I'm not going to be the last person to ask this question."

"I was home. I got off work at four. I do patient intake part time in the ER at Kaiser Hospital in San Leandro."

"She remains too distraught to work full time," Kendra chimed in.

"I got home around 4:30. I made a small salad for dinner, drank tea, and watched the DVR recording of last week's episode of *Survivor*," she said, wiping her eyes. "It was Jamal's favorite show. We started watching it when he was a baby; it became 'our thing' to do together. No matter where he was or what he was doing, he always found time to sit and watch it with me."

"Can anyone vouch for your whereabouts around five that day? Did anybody see you? A neighbor, maybe?"

"Not that I'm aware of," she said. "I'm not very social these days."

"Happy? I think you've upset my client enough for one day," Kendra said. "This interview is over."

"One last question," I said. "How are *you* doing?"

Sheila paused. It was as though no one had asked her that particular question before.

"I buried my only child, Mr. Davis. That's how I'm doing," she said.

"My client has had a difficult time. She was bedridden with depression for weeks after her son was murdered. She only recently returned to work," Kendra interjected. "She couldn't eat. She couldn't sleep. She couldn't work."

"Tell me about the lawsuit," I said to the attorney.

"We're suing for wrongful death, intentional infliction of emotional distress, lost wages, and loss of the companionship of her son," Kendra said. "We're seeking unspecified damages."

"What about Jamal's father?" I asked.

Sheila motioned for Mandy to hand her the Mickey Mouse mug, and she took a sip of water.

"He was killed in a car accident when Jamal was three," she answered.

I paused for a moment, letting her words linger in the air. Sometimes, the world just piles on.

"I'm sorry," I said. "You've suffered a lot of loss."

"Too much loss," Sheila said. "Too much."

Half an hour later, Stu drove the ENG truck back to the station with his footage. Mandy rode in the Lexus with me.

"What do you think?" she asked.

"Well, she's obviously still distraught," I said. "Christian or not, she had every reason to want Mickey Driscoll dead. Lynn will want to follow up on her alibi."

"I don't know," Mandy said. "I just don't see her putting on a ski mask and shooting somebody. Then again, I'm a shitty judge of character. Just look at my ex-boyfriends."

I laughed.

"I'll let Lynn know what we found out and give her access to the raw footage," I said. "Hopefully, she'll be a good little sister, and information will flow both ways."

SEVEN

"**D**O YOU HAVE Johnnie Walker Blue?" I asked the waiter before he took Lynn and Jared's drink orders.

"We don't, sir. We carry Johnnie Walker Black, though," he said apologetically.

We were at Mazzola's, a new Italian fusion restaurant in Walnut Creek that Jared had been itching to try. It was one of those spaces that had a jinxed reputation among restauranteurs. It had been six or seven different eateries over the last several years ranging from an Ethiopian restaurant to a brew pub specializing in the service of seventy different beers from around the world to its most recent iteration, a Chinese joint with the carcasses of roast ducklings dangling in the window. None of them had worked.

I'd read that Mazzola's was the vanity project of two Silicon Valley venture capitalists with more money than brains who'd "always wanted to own a restaurant."

The ambiance was dark, with high ceilings and shiny hardwood floors. Partially melted red and green candles filled empty Chianti bottles on the tables, the wax decoratively dripping along the contours of the glass and straw. It gave me flashbacks to my college dorm room.

A violinist cruised from table to table, playing what I assumed were Italian love songs. I wasn't sure. I took Spanish in high school.

"Fine," I said. "I'll take the Johnnie Walker Black then. A double. Neat."

Jared ordered a vodka martini with a lemon twist. Lynn asked for a glass of a Sonoma Cabernet.

"Very good, sir. I'll be back in a moment with your drinks, and I'll take your dinner orders."

I thanked him as Lynn shook her head.

"What?" I asked.

"A double scotch?" she asked. "Slow down, big bro. I know you've got a lot going on, but . . ."

"But what?"

"Don't you think you might be drinking a little too much?"

"I'm fine, Lynn, but I appreciate your concern," I said. "If you really want to help me, tell me about Driscoll's autopsy."

She sighed a heavy sigh. I couldn't tell if her exasperation was because of the case or because of yours truly.

"Just confirmation of what I told you before. Six bullets. Thirty-eight-caliber hollow points," she said.

"The same number of rounds he put in Jamal Williams."

"This was personal," she stated.

The waiter returned with our drinks and took our orders.

"Did you look into what I told you about Sheila Williams?" I asked once the waiter had gone.

"The security cams in the Kaiser parking lot have her driving away at 4:06 on the afternoon of the murder," Lynn said.

"Plenty of time for her to change cars and drive the fifteen miles to San Ramon for target practice at five," I said.

Lynn shook her head. "I don't think so. Street cams near her house show her driving onto her street at 4:33," she replied.

"Any sign of a white Prius leaving the area?" I asked.

"Nothing. Plus, from what you told me, she couldn't afford her son's college tuition. I don't see her owning two cars."

"She could have rented the Prius," I countered.

"Not with any credit card she's got. Ran both, and they haven't been near a Hertz or an Avis."

"Enterprise?" I said, half joking.

"Her cell phone was pinging off the tower by her house the whole evening."

"You know she could have carried a burner cell and used a debit card for a rental," I said.

"Sheila Williams is *not* our shooter. That doesn't mean she isn't involved, but I just don't feel it," Lynn said. "I've been wrong before, but I don't think she's good for this."

"Are you guys gonna talk shop all night?" Jared asked. "I thought the three of us could go out for a nice, quiet dinner for once."

A twinge of sadness bubbled up inside as I remembered how it used to be the four of us. I missed Sarah. I wondered where she was having dinner that night. And who was she having dinner with? She would have loved this place.

"You thought," I said, "that you could get me out of the house for an evening."

"And what if I did?" Jared said, sipping from his martini. "You only leave your place to work these days, and that's winding down now. You don't wear self-pity well."

"What self-pity?" I said, downing my scotch. "I'm the life of the party."

I motioned for the waiter to bring me another scotch.

"Chris . . ." Lynn said, her forehead resting in the palm of her right hand.

"Lynn, don't start. Just let me be."

Lynn looked at Jared, who had just shaken his head as the waiter set down another double.

"There is one interesting thing about your Sheila Williams. She owns a gun," Lynn informed us.

"Let me guess," I said. "A .38-caliber revolver?"

"No more calls; we have a winner," she exclaimed. "Think she'd let us test it voluntarily? For purposes of elimination?"

"You just said you don't think she's the shooter."

The waiter returned with our meals. Jared dug into his food. I washed mine down with scotch.

"I said that I don't think she's the shooter, but until we catch whoever did do this, everybody's a suspect," she stated as I gestured for the waiter to bring me another drink.

"Would you like me to call her about testing the gun?"

"Would you?"

"If you let me have an exclusive on what you find," I said.

"Chris . . ."

"Come on. It'll get out eventually, anyway. Nobody keeps a secret in this town."

Lynn thought for a minute. "Get her to give up her gun for a ballistics test voluntarily, without a warrant . . . and we'll see," she said.

The waiter set another double Johnnie Walker Black in front of me.

"Chris . . ." she said, "SLOW DOWN."

I pulled out my cell phone and texted Mandy. Since she had a relationship with Sheila Williams good enough to get her to go on camera with us, I figured she'd be more persuasive than I would. Mandy agreed and texted that she'd call her. I shut off the phone and put it in my coat pocket.

"Done," I said. "Mandy will call her."

"I'll have to send an officer with her to retrieve the gun. Mandy is a civilian and—"

"I know," I said. "Chain of custody. What about the Driscoll family? Have you talked to the wife about giving me an interview?"

"The funeral is tomorrow," Lynn said. "Janet Driscoll says that you can come by in the afternoon during the reception."

"How'd you manage that?" I asked.

"She wants Mickey's killer caught as badly as we do. She knows your work and figures talking to you might help."

"Interesting," I said.

"What?" Lynn asked.

"Are you looking at Janet Driscoll?" I asked.

"Why do you ask that?"

"Well, when a married person is murdered, isn't the spouse usually suspect number one?" I inquired. "Don't you watch *Dateline*?"

"If only it were as easy as an episode from that show," she remarked. "Some dumb ass husband uses his home computer to Google, 'How to murder your wife.' He then goes to Walmart, where he buys a shovel, bleach, and duct tape that he pays for in front of their surveillance cameras, putting the whole thing on his credit card."

"The perfect crime," I said.

Jared laughed with a piece of meat in his mouth. It apparently went down the wrong pipe, and he began to cough. Lynn patted his back firmly as he took a few pulls off his martini to dislodge it.

"Thought I was gonna have to give you the Heimlich," I told him. "Then you'd be dead for sure."

"Never make me laugh when I'm eating," he warned.

"Sorry," I said.

The waiter returned to the table.

"Is everything okay?" he asked.

"Everything is delicious," Lynn said.

"Would you like a refill on your drink?" he asked, looking at me.

Lynn gave me a stern look. It was the kind of disapproving stare Auntie gave me if I acted up in church.

"I'm not driving," I told her. "I'll have one more."

"Very good, sir," the waiter said as he headed toward the bar.

"Yes," Lynn said, returning to the topic at hand. "Wives kill their husbands, and husbands kill their wives. And yes, I looked into Janet's whereabouts when Mickey was killed. She was running errands, picking up their daughters from their afterschool activities."

"She could have had it done," I said. "Again . . . *Dateline*."

"Just because you work in TV doesn't mean that life follows a script," she replied, chewing on a mouthful of pasta.

"That," I said, "is painfully true."

The waiter returned to the table and set a fresh drink before me.

"Janet Driscoll will talk only to you. No cameras. She doesn't want to be the grieving widow on television."

"That's okay. For now," I said. "We've talked about Sheila Williams and Janet Driscoll. LOTS of people wanted to kill Mickey Driscoll after he walked away scot-free for shooting that kid. Got your eye on anybody else?"

"I've got my eye on everybody else. And it ain't easy."

"I'll drink to that," I said, raising my glass to my lips.

EIGHT

I AWOKE THE next morning with a nasty hangover. Maybe Lynn was right. I should have slowed down a bit.

I brushed the glue out of my mouth and took a hot shower. Then I dressed, downed a chocolate-premixed protein shake, and took Sophie for her morning walk. I usually walk her twice a day. Morning and whatever time I get in at night. Guess I'll have more time for afternoon walks and games of fetch soon.

I fed and watered her, then hopped into the Lexus and headed to the station. I found Mandy in the editing bay going over the Sheila Williams footage.

"Did you call her?" I asked.

"Yeah. She says we can pick up the gun today."

"Just like that? No push back?"

"None," Mandy said. "She's happy to cooperate."

"I'm sure her lawyer's thrilled about that," I said. "Had dinner with Lynn and Jared last night. Lynn's with you and doesn't think she's involved."

"Then why test the gun?"

"It's like Reagan said about the nukes in the old Soviet Union. Trust but verify."

She nodded without taking her eyes off the video screen of the footage.

"How's the video look?" I asked.

"There's some good stuff here, especially where she talks about Jamal and his interests and aspirations. Powerful and . . . sad."

"Why don't you put that on pause, swing by Sheila's house, and pick up her .38?"

Mandy pressed a button on the console, and the digital video image of Sheila Williams froze as she was in midsentence.

"I'll call Lynn, and she'll arrange for one of her officers to go with you. Get the gun and take it over to her. She'll be in her office at the Hall of Justice. The more we can do for my sister in this investigation, the better it'll be for us when we need something. Sheila knows and likes you," I said. "It's better to have a friendly face deal with this than some lone, random cop. I'm guessing police aren't her favorite people right now."

"That's an understatement if I've ever heard one," she said. "And what will you be doing?"

"I'm going to San Ramon to talk to Janet Driscoll. She wants to speak to me alone. No cameras."

"We ran some video of the funeral on the morning show. Every available cop in the Bay Area was there. Color guard. Flag-draped coffin. The whole nine yards. The department is treating it as though he were killed in the line of duty."

"In a way," I said, "he was."

"You really think Sheila might have been involved?" Mandy said.

"Probably not. But let's see what her gun has to say."

A little after one, I hopped on the lower deck of the Bay Bridge at Battery Street and headed toward the East Bay. Traffic is getting worse and worse around the Bay Area. The freeways are jammed day and night. It's starting to look like L.A. Too many cars and not enough road.

I took I-80 West to I-580 East, continued until I hit the 580/680 junction in Pleasanton, and then took I-680 North to Crow Canyon Road. I made my way through side streets courtesy of the Waze app, and soon, I was on Janet Driscoll's street. Black-and-white police SUVs, CHP patrol cars, and police vehicles from San Francisco, Oakland, Hayward, San Ramon, Pleasanton, Dublin, and the Alameda County and Contra Costa County Sheriff's Departments lined the curb for blocks. I parked behind an SFPD cruiser five blocks away, walked to the house, and rang the bell.

A skinny girl of about fifteen answered the door. She wore a black dress and a string of pearls with a pinkish tinge. Long, blond hair draped over drooping shoulders. Her eyes were red from crying, and tracks, where tears had recently streamed, were evident on her cheeks. I was immediately reminded of Smokey Robinson's "*Tracks of my Tears.*"

"Hi," I said. "I'm Topher. I'm here to see your mom."

"Aren't you on TV?" the girl asked.

"Sometimes," I said with a smile. Her lips furled into a faint grin.

"I'm Schuyler Driscoll," she said, extending a hand. I took it.

"I'm very sorry for your loss."

"Thanks," she said. "Did you know my daddy?"

"I never had the pleasure of meeting him."

"He liked to watch your show."

"I'm flattered. I'm sorry I didn't get the opportunity to know him," I said.

Her eyes welled up with tears that she wiped with a sleeve before they fell to her cheeks.

"You'd have liked him," she said. "Please, come in."

I thanked her and entered. The floor of the entryway was shiny marble. A large painting of a Spanish conquistador hung on the wall adjacent to the front door. I followed Schuyler into the living room. It was beautifully decorated and had a hardwood floor accentuated with an oriental rug. Cops sat on the French provincial-style sofa and love seat, drinking coffee and balancing paper plates of cold cuts on their laps.

"Let me see if I can track down Mom. Help yourself to the food," she said, gesturing toward a table nestled against the far wall.

I thanked her, and she made her way through the throng of uniforms toward the rear of the house.

I scanned the room. There were more than a few members of law enforcement I recognized from The Egg.

I was saying a few perfunctory hellos when I felt a meaty hand on my shoulder. I turned to find a tall, burly man with thinning gray hair and remnants of potato salad in the corner of his mouth. He wore civilian clothes, a dark suit, white shirt, and a black tie. He held a paper plate piled high with a sandwich Dagwood Bumstead would have envied.

"Topher Davis?"

"Who's asking?" I said.

"I'm sorry. Where are my manners?"

He removed his hand from my shoulder and extended it for me to shake.

"Sergeant Phil Curtain, SFPD. Retired."

"Nice to meet you, Sergeant Curtain," I said, shaking his hand.

"I generally keep the sergeant part quiet these days. Like I said, I'm retired. Call me Phil."

"Well, in that case, I'm Topher."

He nodded and took a bite of the behemoth sandwich on his plate.

"How'd you know Driscoll?" he asked once he swallowed.

"I didn't," I said. "I'm here in a more or less professional capacity."

"Six o'clock news stuff, huh?" he said, taking another bite of his tower of meat, pumpernickel, and Swiss cheese.

"Something like that. How about you? Did you know Officer Driscoll?"

"Oh yeah," he said. "Knew Mickey for years. Worked out of the same station for a while. Even rode together for a minute."

"I'm sorry for your loss," I said.

"Thanks," Curtain said, taking another bite of the sandwich.

I was going to ask his thoughts on Driscoll's killer when Schuyler reappeared.

"Mom's in the kitchen. She wants me to bring you back."

"Nice meeting you," Curtain said, grasping my hand again.

"You too," I replied. "Sorry that it was under these circumstances."

Curtain nodded and went back to his Dagwood.

I followed Schuyler through a dining room with a teak table and chairs for eight. The walls were lined with more paintings—a Spanish ship and what appeared to be a portrait of Hernán Cortés this time. Somebody apparently had a thing for European colonialism.

Schuyler led me into the large kitchen. Shiny silver appliances, a dishwasher, a refrigerator, and a trash compactor surrounded a large island with a black marble countertop. Mickey Driscoll had done well for himself. This was a really nice place.

A woman dressed in black with long, brown hair up in a bun stood at the island, robotically spooning ground coffee into the paper filter of a silver coffeemaker.

Janet Driscoll was a petite woman barely five feet tall. I'd be shocked if she weighed a hundred pounds soaking wet. She was dainty like a doll made of porcelain. You'd avoid touching her for fear she'd break. Her cheeks were rosy. The skin on her face had the windburned look of a competitive runner.

"Mom," Schuyler said, causing Janet to look up from her side hustle as a barista. It took her a moment. She was in a sort of daze.

"Mr. Davis," she said with a flash of recognition.

"Mrs. Driscoll," I said, extending a hand. She took it and wrapped it in both of hers. Like Sheila Williams, her hands were a living lotion commercial with their softness. Unlike Sheila, Janet Driscoll's hands were tiny. Both hands barely encompassed one of mine.

"Thank you for coming," she said. "And it's Janet."

"I'm Topher," I replied. "I'm very sorry for your loss."

"Thank you," she said. "Schuyler, will you and your sister see if we need to put out more food?"

The girl turned and headed back toward the living room without saying a word.

"How is she doing?" I asked.

"As well as can be expected, I guess."

"And your other daughter?"

"Shannon. She's thirteen," Janet said. "She and her father were very close. She's taking Mickey's death exceptionally hard."

"I'm sorry to hear that," I said.

"They'd argued that morning. She was in a mood. You know how adolescent children can be."

"I don't have children, but yes, I know. Difficult," I said.

"The last thing she said to her father was, 'I hate you.'"

"Ouch," I said.

I thought about some of my adolescent snits with Auntie. I'm lucky to be alive.

"We found him, you know?" she said.

"I didn't," I said. Actually, I did.

"I had just picked up Schuyler from ballet and Shannon from her CYO basketball practice. We pulled up to the house and found him lying in the driveway. Schuyler screamed. Shannon completely lost it."

"That's awful."

"I've got both girls starting therapy tomorrow," she said.

"How are you holding up?"

"It hasn't really sunk in. I've been so busy taking care of the funeral arrangements and looking after the girls I haven't really had a chance to process yet."

"Maybe some therapy would be good for you, too," I commented.

"Maybe," she said with a nod.

"I appreciate you agreeing to talk with me."

"I just want to know who did this. We need closure. These girls need to know who killed their father and why. So do I."

"How long were you married?"

"Married eighteen years. Together, a little over twenty."

"That's a long time."

"Especially to be married to a cop," she said. "I had always worried that someday he'd be out on patrol somewhere, and I'd open the front door to find two solemn, uniformed officers standing there."

She began to tear up and brushed her eyes with the back of her hand.

"I never thought he'd go like this."

I handed her one of the cocktail napkins stacked on the countertop.

"Thank you," she said, taking the napkin and dabbing at her eyes.

"Do you have any thoughts about who might have done this?"
I asked.

"You saw the mob scene after the acquittal in that shooting.
Mickey got death threats. Our home was vandalized after
somebody posted our address on the internet. It could be anyone.
Mickey stopped telling me about the threats after a while. Things
died down, but I know he was still getting them."

"Six months later?"

"Crazy, isn't it? As if he didn't feel bad enough."

"How do you mean?" I asked.

"Mr. Dav . . . Topher . . . Contrary to what some people want
to believe, my husband was not a monster. He killed a kid not
much older than his own daughters, and he did it by mistake,"
she said. "The guilt and depression he had as the result of that
shooting . . . It nearly destroyed him. It came close to destroying
our marriage," she told me, eyes watering again as she wiped them
with her napkin. "These people assume that since there was no
criminal conviction, Mickey just skipped away, and everything was
hunky dory."

"It must have been tough. How do you live with something
like that? Other than his administrative leave, did Mickey take any
time off?" I asked.

"Yes," she said. "The last month. He had decided to go back
to work long enough to be able to retire and collect his pension.
He was scheduled to go back on active duty next week. Had he
lived, he would have retired early next year."

"What was he gonna do then?"

"He loved classic cars. He restored that old Thunderbird he
was killed in," she told me. "He planned on restoring others once
he retired."

"Speaking of the T-Bird, I didn't see it in your driveway."

"The police impounded it. It's now evidence in a homicide."

"Of course," I said.

"I'll probably sell it."

"Is money going to be a problem?"

"No," she said. "Mickey had about two million dollars in life insurance. We'll be fine on that front. I just don't want that damned thing around since they killed him in it."

"They?" I asked.

"Yes. The public. The activist groups. The media." She paused. "No offense."

"None taken," I said. "The press can be difficult when it's on a feeding frenzy."

"They might not have actually pulled the trigger, but they all killed my husband."

"I understand," I said. "So, why did you agree to see me? I *am* part of the media."

"I've seen your work, and I know your reputation. You were always fair to Mickey in your reporting," she said. "And your sister's a cop."

"I do have a little insight into those on the job. I know that there are good cops and bad ones. I tend to start off by assuming an officer is on the up and up until they show me otherwise," I told her. "I guess my sister is one of the reasons."

She closed the filter compartment of the coffeemaker, filled the carafe with water, and poured it into the top.

"Forgive my manners," she said, putting the carafe in the coffeemaker and pressing the ON button. "Can I offer you something to eat or drink?"

"No, thank you," I replied. "And your manners are just fine. I can't believe you're doing all of this today."

"Some of the neighbors offered to help, but I wanted to handle all the funeral and reception arrangements myself. It takes my mind off . . ." she said, her voice trailing off. "It gives me something to do."

"I understand. You mentioned groups threatening Mickey. Which ones?"

"You name it. African Americans Rising, Take Black America, Freedom Now."

"Any he was especially concerned with?"

"There was one called The Sentinels for Black something or other. They were advocating the killing of policemen."

I made a mental note to look into the group.

"Do you know of any recent threats he might have received?"

"No, as I said, he stopped telling me about them. He may have been threatened recently. It's certainly possible. I'd better get back to my guests."

"Of course," I said. "I'll see myself out."

"Thank you for listening. The girls and I have a long road ahead."

"If there's anything I can do, please don't hesitate to call," I said, handing her my business card.

"Thank you," she replied. "I may take you up on that."

I thought about what I'd learned on the drive back to the station. Mickey Driscoll got lots of death threats. He'd had marital problems. His wife said that the shooting almost destroyed their marriage. Add to that a two-million-dollar life insurance policy, and that's a lot of motive.

I activated the hands-free phone function in the Lexus and called Mandy. I told her about my chat with Janet Driscoll.

"So, you suspect her?" she asked.

"Well, Lynn won't be too keen on the idea, but I don't think it's beyond the realm of possibility."

"She's got an alibi. She was picking up her daughters," Mandy reminded me.

"Ever hear of murder for hire?" I asked.

"Killing her husband and leaving his body for her teenage daughters to find? No mother would do that."

I thought for a moment. It was a good point. Janet Driscoll appeared to be deeply concerned about the girls' mental well-being. Mandy was right. I couldn't see her deliberately subjecting them to that.

"Did you pick up Sheila Williams's .38 for Lynn?"

"No."

"What happened? She change her mind?"

"No," Mandy said. "The gun is missing."

NINE

I RETURNED TO the city about four o'clock and realized I hadn't eaten much that day. I tend to get a little cranky when my blood sugar is low, so I need to keep myself fed regularly. I stopped at the Waterfront restaurant on the Embarcadero and picked up two crab salads I brought back to the station. I found Mandy in the editing bay working on the Sheila Williams piece.

"How's it looking?" I asked.

"Coming along," she said. "You need to write and record your voice-over."

I handed her one of the salads, a napkin, and cellophane-wrapped plastic utensils.

"Thank you," she said. "I'm starving."

She removed the plastic lid from her salad and popped a piece of crab meat into her mouth.

"The Waterfront?"

"Where else?" I replied.

"They have the best seafood there."

"Tell me what happened with Sheila Williams."

"Lynn's officer and I went to her house as scheduled. She invited us in, and we went to get the gun. She keeps it in the drawer of the nightstand next to her bed. She said she bought it for protection, being a woman living alone and all."

"Go on."

"We open the drawer . . . and no .38."

"How'd she react?"

"She seemed genuinely surprised that it wasn't there."

"When did she say she saw it last?"

"She said she'd cleaned it about a month ago."

"She owns a gun the same caliber as the murder weapon, and when we ask for it, it's suddenly gone missing. That sure is convenient."

Mandy thought for a moment. "I'll tell you, Topher, you didn't see the look on her face," she stated. "I believe her. She really was surprised. We checked the house to see if anything else was missing. Turns out somebody stole the few nice pieces of jewelry she owns. A nice coat and her grandmother's silver were also gone."

"Does she have any idea when this burglary took place?"

"None. The thieves were very neat. It was almost like they knew exactly where the valuables were. They didn't ransack the place. It could have happened days ago. We called the police. They came, dusted for prints, and took a report. They said not to expect much. Over the last several months, there has been a rash of burglaries in that area. Local fentanyl addicts looking for anything they can trade for money or drugs."

"So, somebody steals her gun and uses it to murder the man who killed her son, and she knows nothing about it? Come on," I said.

"You don't know it was her gun that killed Mickey Driscoll," Mandy countered, picking at the avocado in her salad bowl.

"I'll bet you another crab salad that when that gun is finally recovered, *if* it's ever recovered, it turns out to be the murder weapon," I said.

"You're on."

"I'd better let Lynn know what's going on. She's not gonna be happy." I pulled out my cell phone and called Lynn, whom I keep on speed dial.

"Hey," I said. "I've got some news on Sheila Williams's .38."

"I can't talk now," Lynn replied. "We've got another cop killing."

TEN

ALAMEDA IS AN island city about sixteen miles south of San Francisco, adjacent to San Leandro and Oakland. For years, it had a strong military presence due to the Alameda Naval Air Station built just before the Second World War. The military closed the installation a little over twenty years ago, and the city has been trying to devise a plan to develop the fifteen hundred acres ever since. It's been used for a few television and film projects like *The Matrix* in the ensuing years.

I took the Bay Bridge to I-880 South until I got to Fruitvale Avenue and followed it to the High Street Bridge that funneled me onto the island. I eventually made my way to Park Street. Park Street is the hub of Alameda, with cute little shops and cafes. I found an empty parking spot, a rarity in the afternoons and on weekends, and parked the Lexus. Then I walked a few blocks past boutiques, a bookstore, and an Italian restaurant named in honor of Al Capone, and soon, I approached The Angler.

Yellow crime scene tape blocked the entrance and the sidewalk. Alameda police officers held back a large crowd fronted by a Black man with a much too-large Colin Kaepernick-style Afro. A white man with a blond crew cut stood beside "Kap," craning his neck to get a look. He wore a tank top that exposed beefy arms with tats of Warner Brothers cartoon characters, including Tweety Bird and Porky Pig. Loony Tunes *does* realize those are permanent . . . I hope.

As with the Driscoll shooting, Lynn was on the scene working with local law enforcement. She saw me and waved me in.

The Angler was a high-end boutique filled with various fishing accoutrements. It was the kind of place Stu would love as soon as he and Mandy arrived. Racks along the walls displayed the latest rods for freshwater and saltwater bait fishing as well as fly fishing. There were aisles with waders, inflatable inner tubes, and tackle boxes. In the front of the shop sat a glass counter that displayed high-end reels and hand-tied trout flies.

On the floor behind the counter lay a bloodied man. His face was a disfigured mass of swollen crimson. His right hand was missing the ring finger that lay three to four feet behind him. I guessed he'd held up his hands to defend himself before the shooter opened fire, the round having taken the digit clean off. I counted three rounds in the blood-soaked Pendleton shirt he wore. A fourth was lodged right between his eyes.

A tearful woman in her mid-sixties stood in the corner of the shop talking to an Alameda cop who stood scribbling in a notepad.

"What have we got?" I asked Lynn.

"Phil Curtain. Retired SFPD."

Sergeant Phil Curtain, the cop I'd met at Mickey Driscoll's memorial. He was unrecognizable.

"Multiple gunshot wounds," she said. "We won't know until the autopsy, but it looks like a revolver was used. Again, no shell casings."

"How do you know the killer didn't just pick them up?" I asked.

"He didn't have time. He shot this man on a busy street in the middle of the day. Someone could have walked in at any minute."

"I met him," I said.

"When?" she asked, surprised.

"A few hours ago, at Mickey Driscoll's memorial."

"What can you tell me about him?"

"He liked big sandwiches."

Lynn gave me her patented "This is no time to fuck around" look.

"We only spoke for a minute," I said. "He told me that he and Driscoll used to work at the same station and were partners for a brief time."

She gestured toward the woman in the corner. "That's Edna Curtain. She and Phil opened this place after he retired. Curtain had just changed clothes after returning to the store from Mickey Driscoll's funeral. She went out to pick up some lunch, and when she returned twenty minutes later, she found him like this," Lynn said.

"Robbery?"

"Nope. About six hundred dollars untouched in the register."

"Six hundred bucks? That's a lot of trout flies," I said.

"We're clearly in the wrong business," she added.

I noticed a security camera in the corner of the ceiling behind the register.

"Will that tell us anything?" I asked, pointing at the camera.

"It doesn't work. The wife says it's there as a 'deterrent.'"

Lynn sighed. There had recently been a killing on a BART train that had a security camera that wasn't operational for the same reason.

"What do you know about the vic?" I asked.

"He was SFPD for thirty years before retiring seven or eight years ago. I didn't know him, but I knew of him. He was on his way out the door when I graduated from the academy."

"Think it's connected to Driscoll?"

She thought for a moment. "I don't know."

"You're the one who always says, 'There are no coincidences,'" I reminded her.

She nodded.

"This was pretty brazen," I said. "Besides all the people on the street, there's the camera. The shooter had no way of knowing that it didn't work. He either didn't see it or didn't care."

"Or he was somebody Curtain knew who was aware of the camera situation," she said. "There are street cameras and security cameras at other businesses. Hopefully, some of them are functional and will tell us something," Lynn said.

"Ever hear of a group called the Black Sentinels or something?" I asked.

"The Black Sentinels for Justice," she confirmed. "They're a radical group of militants that sprang up after Ferguson. They advocate killing cops. Why do you ask?"

"Janet Driscoll says they threatened her husband. She said he took it seriously. Two dead SFPD cops in less than a week . . ."

Lynn ran a hand through her dark hair and let out an exasperated breath. "Then I guess we'd better go talk to these assholes," she muttered.

"We?" I asked.

"You're working this case too," Lynn said.

"What's the catch?"

"Just promise me you won't broadcast anything without running it by me first."

"You know me better than that," I said.

She smiled. "Yeah, I guess I do." She drew in a deep breath.

"I need you to do what you can to keep the media from putting out the information I don't want disseminated to the public. Information that could jeopardize this case. You're the press gatekeeper," she told me. "In exchange, I'll give you exclusives. Agreed?"

"Agreed," I said.

Stu drove up in the ENG truck with Mandy and entered the store.

I explained the situation, and Stu started shooting B-roll. I was right about the shop. Stu's eyes got big when he came in and looked around. He suddenly became a nine-year-old at Toys R Us.

"They've got some mighty fine rods here," he exclaimed. "Mighty fine."

Mandy got a few sound bites from the Alameda Homicide cop who caught the case, a veteran homicide detective named Barry Weiss. She then got a few clips of the crowd echoing the folks in San Ramon with the "I can't believe this happened here" mantra.

I taped a standup report for the six o'clock show in front of the store. Something like this wouldn't normally be my job, but I was there with my crew. Noblesse oblige is not dead, even when you're being fired in two and a half weeks.

What I wanted was to talk to Edna Curtain, but she was otherwise engaged in giving her police interview. I'd get to her once things calmed down.

After we wrapped, I went home to think.

ELEVEN

At ABOUT SIX, I got home and was greeted ecstatically by Sophie, who bolted to me, tag wagging furiously. There was something in her mouth that she proudly dropped at my feet. It was a dead gray rat. I thought only cats did that.

The acreage my house sits on is filled with critters. There are rattlesnakes, skunks, raccoons, deer, possums, the occasional fox, field mice, and, of course, rats. Rats totally creep me out. When I was a kid, back in the Mesozoic Age and local stations still had a *Late Late Show*, Auntie allowed me to stay up one night to see the movie *Willard*. The scene where the kid sics the rats on Ernest Borgnine gave me nightmares for days. I've had a rat phobia ever since.

I gently patted Sophie on the head and went into the garage, where I got her pooper scooper. I brought it into the house, swept up the deceased rodent, and tossed it in the trash bin around the back.

"The next time you want to give me a present," I told her, "think more along the lines of a gift card."

She wagged her tail and put her front paws on my leg to lift her up. I did and took her into the kitchen where I mixed a cup of kibble with her fresh gourmet dog food and poured it into her bowl. While she ate, I went into my den.

My den is really my home office, but I call it a "den" because I always liked the fact that Mike Brady and Ward Cleaver had them on TV. I hoped that someday, I'd have a son who needed "a serious talking to," and I could say, "Come into my den."

I sat at my desk, fired up my MacBook Pro, and went to Google. I wanted to see what I could learn about the Black Sentinels for Justice. Five minutes later, I was reading a profile piece on the group's founder in *San Francisco Magazine*.

Taronte Rogers was an Oakland computer tech who became radicalized after the Michael Brown shooting in Ferguson, Missouri, and, renouncing what he called his "slave name," changed his moniker to Malik Otumba. He described the Sentinels as a "paramilitary organization" whose mission is to protect people of color from police brutality by force, if necessary. He had given himself the title "Field Marshal." They sounded like a cross between the old Black Panther Party, Malcolm X, and a Tea Party militia.

Otumba talked about encouraging African Americans to "stop relying on the white man to protect our lives and civil liberties" and to "take up arms and protect those rights yourself." He encouraged Black people to carry guns in their vehicles in order to "defend themselves" during traffic stops. He declined to say precisely how many members the organization had, but he claimed it was in the hundreds.

Great, hundreds of idiots driving around with guns in their cars. No chance of a violent escalation with law enforcement there at all.

I went to the Sentinels website, which contained a "defense manual" written by Otumba in which he said that police shootings of unarmed Black people should be punishable by death.

And this group sent threats to Mickey Driscoll. Somebody just bolted to the top of the suspect list.

I Googled Phil Curtain.

I found an old *San Francisco Examiner* story from 2001 about him. He had stopped a vehicle with three Black men carpooling from their jobs on a construction site for allegedly running a stop sign. Curtain said he saw the man in the passenger seat reaching for a gun in the glove compartment, so he drew his weapon and opened fire. The passenger was killed, and the other two occupants of the vehicle were seriously wounded. Turned out that the man was just reaching for the car's registration and insurance card.

Later stories chronicled how Curtain was put on paid administrative leave and that some of the men in the car had priors, including one on parole after doing a stretch for armed robbery. The shooting was deemed justified. The victims and their families received a settlement from the city, and Curtain returned to work.

There are no coincidences.

I called Lynn to tell her what I'd found on the web.

"So, we've got two dead cops, both of whom have killed unarmed Black people without any real consequences," she said.

"Actually, ex-cops," I informed her. "Curtain was retired, and Mickey Driscoll was planning his exit."

"Good point," Lynn replied.

"And we have a group that's practically telling people to do just this sort of thing. I'm betting that if the Sentinels didn't do this, they know who did," I stated. "Or, at the very least, they inspired the shooter."

Lynn paused for a moment, thinking. "When you called me earlier, what did you want?" she asked.

"I almost forgot. It was about Sheila Williams's .38. It's missing."

"How convenient."

"That's what I said."

"Does she have any idea when this gun allegedly vanished?"

"She claims she cleaned it about a month ago and then put it in the drawer of her nightstand. She took Mandy and Officer Reynolds from your department to get it and said it was gone. She and Mandy checked the rest of the house and found some valuables missing. According to the report filed with Hayward PD, the thief broke in through the garage. The stolen items were not things she'd miss immediately, so there's no telling when the burglary occurred."

"Lovely."

"Just for giggles," I said, "let's assume she's telling the truth."

"Okay," Lynn agreed.

"Jamal Williams was a high-profile case. Suppose somebody from the Sentinels broke into Sheila's house, took the gun, and used it to kill Mickey Driscoll with the same number of shots Driscoll fired to kill her son. Poetic justice."

"Okay, just for giggles," Lynn said, "tell me why they killed Phil Curtain. He had nothing to do with the Driscoll case, and from what you tell me, his shooting was twenty years ago."

"Maybe Otumba is gunning for all cops in the area who've killed unarmed Blacks and gone 'unpunished.'"

"I'm on the force, and I didn't know about Curtain's shooting; it was so long ago. How would the shooter?"

I thought for a minute. "I haven't figured that part out yet," I said.

"Let me know when you do," Lynn replied with sisterly sarcasm. "In the meantime, let's go see Field Marshal Otumba."

"How you gonna do that? You gonna call and ask for an appointment?"

"Yes," she said. "I'll have my scheduling secretary call his, and we'll set something up. Either that or I'll just kick his fucking door in."

"I love it when the Army Ranger in you comes out."

"We'll go tomorrow," she said before clicking off.

The *I Love Lucy* theme kicked in just as I was putting the phone on my desk. I answered it.

"Hello?"

"Mr. Davis?" came a sharp voice on the other end.

"Yes."

"This is Kendra Robbins. Sheila Williams's attorney."

"Oh yes. What can I do for you, Ms. Robbins?"

"You can stay away from my client," she snapped.

"Excuse me?"

"Didn't you send one of your producers to Ms. Williams's residence today to obtain a weapon she owns?"

"Yes. Ms. Williams voluntarily agreed to surrender her gun to the authorities to eliminate it as a murder weapon."

"I was not aware that your producer was a member of the law enforcement community."

"She isn't. An SFPD officer accompanied her. My producer and Ms. Williams have a friendly relationship, and being the gentlewoman that Ms. Williams is, we thought that it might be less stressful for her to turn the gun over to my producer. It's a moot point anyway because the weapon is missing."

"Nevertheless, I am Ms. Williams's attorney. I should have been consulted," Kendra Robbins said, the anger in her voice palpable.

"With all due respect, wouldn't it have been up to your client to consult with you if she wanted you in the loop on this?" I said in a soft voice, hoping to calm her down.

"From this point forward," she said, "if you wish to communicate with my client, you do it through my office."

"I'm sorry if we—" was all I got out before she hung up.

TWELVE

THE BLACK SENTINELS for Justice were headquartered in Oakland on San Pablo Avenue in a red brick building that had once been the site of a Black-owned bakery. The building had a radical history. The bakery had been part of a chain that started in Santa Barbara to promote Black entrepreneurship, independence, and cooperative economics. Three decades later, it was closed, and its proprietors were incarcerated after being convicted of a series of crimes that culminated in the assassination of an African American journalist.

With housing prices in San Francisco rapidly escalating due to the tech boom, many tech companies and their employees headed south for Oakland's lower prices. This had caused prices to rise in that city as well. Homes in formerly "undesirable neighborhoods" were going for double and triple their asking prices. Commercial and retail spaces boosted rents beyond the means of long-term tenants to survive. Whole blocks of mom-and-pop establishments were razed to make way for glitzy tech offices and living spaces that were economically far out of reach of native Oaklanders.

A joke spread, that went, "Look up the word 'gentrification' in the dictionary, and you'll see a picture of Oakland."

San Pablo Avenue had been spared the tech invasion momentarily, although most believed it was a temporary reprieve. The nondescript red brick building was sandwiched between a pawn shop and Popeye's Fried Chicken on a street filled with small businesses, franchise operations, and mom-and-pop stores. A few tents marked the beginning of a homeless encampment on the sidewalk.

This is America. People shouldn't have to live like this.

We parked Lynn's unmarked directly in front and headed up the short walkway. The building had no signage. The windows and the front door were fortified with sturdy black bars. A copper doorbell centered by a small black button was embedded on the left side of the front door, and Lynn pressed it. The door was opened by a young Black man in his early twenties. He sported a white wife beater that exposed his muscular, tattoo-covered arms. He had a bodybuilder's physique with broad, sloping shoulders and cantaloupe biceps. The Nike shorts he wore only partially covered his tree trunk-sized legs. A diamond stud accessorized his right ear. Lynn pulled out her badge.

"I'm Detective Sloan with the SFPD. We want to speak with Mr. Otumba," she said.

"He's busy," the ebony Charles Atlas said as he started to close the door.

"Well, I'd suggest he extricate himself from his busy schedule and talk to me. Or I can come back with a warrant and a bunch of my friends. I'll bet we would find all sorts of interesting things here."

The man thought for a moment and then shut the door. We could hear muffled voices, and then the door opened again.

"Field Marshal Otumba will see you," he said, unlocking and opening the bars in front of the door.

Lynn and I entered a dark place. Shades were pulled down over the closed windows, and the unmistakable smell of cannabis permeated the air. They hadn't done much with the place. The ovens and equipment from when it was a bakery were still in place, although the dust and dirt on them made it clear that they weren't being maintained.

We followed the man through what had apparently been a reception area at one point. It was dirty and unkempt, with a couch that a thrift store would reject. We walked by a group of young Black men passing a blunt back and forth between them. They were surprisingly well dressed in uniforms that consisted of neatly pressed dark suits, crisply starched white dress shirts, and black bow ties—a stark dichotomy to the disarray of their surroundings.

Lynn looked at them and then said to the muscleman in the tank top, "You get a free dress pass today?"

We were led into a back office where Otumba sat behind a battered wooden desk. He wore the same uniform as the men smoking pot we'd just passed, the only difference being the gold epaulets he wore on his shoulders. He glared at us as we entered the office. Two large, muscular Black men who had previously been at his side made their way directly behind us.

Otumba's glare transformed into a sarcastic smile. He was a young, thin man who looked like a little boy playing dress up in his father's clothes.

"What can I do to be of assistance to you pigs?" he asked.

"She's the pig," I said, gesturing toward my sister. "I'm just here for moral support."

"You're too fine to be a pig," the man directly behind Lynn said, patting her ass with his right hand.

In what seemed like a fraction of a second, Lynn grabbed his hand, twisted his arm behind his back, and slammed his head on Otumba's desk.

The man behind me walked toward my sister and took a swing at her. She ducked and returned the favor with a fist to his Adam's apple. The man grabbed his throat as Lynn kicked his legs from under him. He fell to the floor beside the other man, gasping for breath.

The swiftness with which she dispatched the two men prevented me from stepping in and helping her. That and the fact that I'm a wuss when it comes to fighting.

"You want a go at me?" she said to Otumba.

The men who had been smoking the blunt gathered in the doorway behind us.

"Not on your life," he said, raising his hands as if to surrender.

"Then answer some questions before I show you what I can *really* do," she warned.

"This is police brutality," he protested.

"Call a cop," she said. "Given the way you threaten the lives of the police, I'm sure one will be right over to give you a hand."

"What do you want?" he said, lowering his arms.

"Where were you last Friday and yesterday afternoon?"

"Why?"

Lynn glared at him. I'd seen her like this many times. She was not in the mood for any of his bullshit.

Otumba thought for a moment. "Is this about those pigs that got smoked?" he asked.

"Just answer the damn question," Lynn said, her patience growing thin.

"I was here with my boys," he said. "We're organizing a march."

"Let me guess," I said. "A nonviolent march using Dr. King's tactic of passive resistance."

Otumba laughed. Spittle flew out of his mouth and onto his desk. The man Lynn had slammed into it sat up and began massaging his forehead.

"We're marching to tell Black people we need to police ourselves. We don't need the pigs. We need to take care of our own shit. We also need to defend ourselves against police violence," he said.

I looked at the two men on the floor. "How's that working out for you?" I asked.

His attention returned to Lynn.

"I'm assuming that all of these fine, upstanding citizens will vouch for you," she said.

"Ask my boys. I was here from Friday morning until eleven or twelve at night. Same thing every day for the last two weeks."

"Do you own a white Prius?" she asked.

"Bitch," he said, "do I look like I drive a Prius?"

"Call me a bitch again, and you'll be driving a wheelchair," she said.

He paused. "No, I do not drive or own a Prius."

"You advocate the killing of police," I said.

"I advocate self-defense. We have the right to defend ourselves against police aggression."

"By any means necessary?" I asked.

"If you mean by killing pigs after the fact," he said, "I never told anybody to do that. We're about self-defense, not revenge."

"You aware of anybody who might have taken your online 'self-defense' manual a little further than you intended?" Lynn asked.

"Now, how in the hell would I know that? I can't help what people do after they read what I post online."

"Mickey Driscoll got death threats signed by the Black Sentinels for Justice. Want to tell us about that?" I asked.

"Do I look stupid?" he asked.

I decided not to answer that.

"Why would I threaten a cop and then put our name on it?" he asked. "Somebody is trying to set us up."

"Who'd want to do that?" Lynn inquired.

"Your brothers in blue for a start," he said.

"So, cops sent death threats to another cop and put the name of your organization on them?" she asked. "Why would they do that?"

"I don't know why pigs do what they do," he said. "You'll have to ask them."

"Let's go," she said to me.

We turned and headed for the door. The men standing in the doorway looked as though they were considering trying to block us but thought better of it, parting like the Red Sea to make a path for us to walk through.

"Thanks for the hospitality," Lynn said, looking over her shoulder as we exited the room.

"Fuck you," Otumba screamed.

"My, my, such language from a man in such a lovely suit," I said.

We hopped in Lynn's unmarked, and she took off in the direction of 880 North toward the Bay Bridge.

"You know," I said, "what he said made sense. If the Sentinels did send Driscoll those threats, they sure wouldn't have put their name on them."

She said nothing.

"Maybe he's telling the truth," I said.

"Just because he didn't pull the trigger himself doesn't mean that he didn't order or inspire somebody else to do it," Lynn replied.

I nodded.

"It's scary how the web can radicalize people," I said. "He's right. He has no idea who's reading his garbage."

"Or acting on it," Lynn added.

"We're seeing perfectly normal, young, suburban kids being radicalized by a steady diet of online white supremacist and Isis bullshit," I said. "Anything's possible."

"That," she replied, "is unfortunately true."

"What now?" I asked.

"We see if Phil Curtain's widow can tell us anything, and we check the street cams and business security footage for Park Street at the time of the shooting."

THIRTEEN

LYNN DROPPED ME off at the station, where I filled Mandy in on our chat with Otumba and my phone call from Kendra Robbins. She showed me the edited footage of the Sheila Williams piece, and I recorded my voice-over. It looked and sounded good. A nice opening to our upcoming series . . . our final series. We ran it on the six o'clock show, and I announced that more reporting would come.

Once we finished working, I decided to grab dinner at the House of Prime Rib on Van Ness Street. The Hopper, as regulars call it, is one of my favorite restaurants. They do one thing, and they do it well. Prime rib wheeled around in shiny metal carts, carved to order, served with a side of creamed spinach and Yorkshire pudding. Beats the hell out of the Lean Cuisine I had waiting for me at home. I invited Mandy to join me, but she had a date, so I went alone.

I was seated immediately upon arrival and without a reservation— one of the perks of being on television. I wondered what would happen once that was no longer the case. I used to be able to gauge the trajectory of my career by how one maître d' at another restaurant in town seated me. When I was doing well and had a high-profile job, he'd seat me near the front of the restaurant. During dry spells, I'd be seated in the back, out of sight. If my current gig were somewhere in between, he'd seat me in the middle of the dining room. I'd been seated at the front of that restaurant for quite some time now.

I sat at my favorite table and ordered a double Johnnie Walker Blue. As the waiter brought my drink, I noticed a pretty, caramel-colored woman alone at the bar. I'd seen her somewhere before. It took me a moment to place her. It was Kendra Robbins, Sheila Williams's attorney, sipping a solitary Cosmo. I got up and walked over to her.

"You know, drinking alone is the first step," I said.

"To what?" she replied with an icy tone. I felt the temperature in the room drop ten degrees.

"Standing in the street on a median with a cardboard sign that says, 'Will work for booze.'"

She reluctantly smiled.

"'Jesus Loves You' is another popular one," I said.

"You forgot, 'Will litigate for food,'" she added.

I suddenly felt a pang of guilt. San Francisco's massive homeless problem is not something I should be joking about.

"What makes you think I'm drinking alone?" she asked.

"Well, I suppose you could be having a quiet tête-à-tête with Claude Rains."

"Who?"

"An old-time actor. He played the Invisible Man."

"I'm not drinking alone . . . well, not exactly," she said. "Not that it's any of your business, but I appear to have been stood up."

"Boyfriend?" I asked.

"Tinder date. Was supposed to be here half an hour ago."

"His loss," I said. "I have a table right over there. Would you like to join me?"

She paused for a moment, deep in thought.

"Come on," I pressed. "It beats standing at the bar alone."

She looked me over as if she were sizing me up.

"I don't bite," I said. "Honest."

"What the hell," she finally said, getting up and following me to my table just as the waiter served my scotch.

"Would you care for another?" I said, gesturing toward her near-empty Cosmo.

"Sure," she said.

"The lady will have another Cosmopolitan," I told the waiter.

She finished the cocktail in her glass.

"Funny seeing you here. I never would have figured you for a carnivore," I said.

"I'm a lawyer," she replied. "Red meat helps me keep my edge."

"I appreciated your client's cooperation the other day. Thank you."

"No need to thank me. I told her not to do it. I still don't think she should have done it, to be perfectly honest with you."

"You think she said something that might hurt your wrongful death case?" I asked.

Kendra Robbins smiled. "Is that why you invited me over?" she asked. "To pump me for information?"

I decided not to mention the missing .38. Why antagonize her?

"We're off the record," I said.

"Good. I've had a long day."

"Then enough shop talk. Let's talk about you. How long have you been a lawyer?" I asked.

She thought for a moment. "Ten years in October."

"Did you always want to be a lawyer? Did you grow up watching reruns of *Perry Mason* or something?"

She laughed. "Nope. Believe it or not, I wanted to be a cop. Circumstances pulled me to the bar."

"What an odd coincidence. Me too!" I said, taking a healthy sip from my glass. "See, common ground already."

She laughed again. I can be pretty damned charming when I want to be.

"How about you?" she asked. "How'd you end up in television?"

"My mom was killed when I was a kid."

"I'm sorry," she said. "What happened?"

"That's a tale for another day," I said, taking a pull from my cocktail. "I always wanted to do something to help people who were being victimized, and, even though I've always been into comic books, I wasn't going to dress up like a bat to fight crime."

She laughed again.

"So, I figured broadcast journalism. Went to SF State and got my degree, then interned until I got hired to be on air."

"And the rest is history," she said with a slightly sarcastic tinge in her voice.

"I suppose that's one way of looking at it."

The waiter came and set down Kendra's drink. He then took our orders. I got the house cut with the bone in. Rare. Kendra got the petite cut. She specified "blood rare."

"Just put a Band-Aid on it," she said.

Once the waiter had gone, the interrogation began anew.

"Brothers and sisters?" she asked.

"One sister. Lynn. She's SFPD. She fights crime more directly than I do," I said. "You?"

"I'm an only child."

"That's a shame. I don't know what I'd do without Lynn in my life."

I drank the last of my scotch and motioned again for the waiter.

"Would you like some wine?" I asked.

"A glass of red would be lovely."

"Rare meat and red wine. If you like dogs, I think I'll marry you."

I ordered a bottle of French Bordeaux.

"What kind of dog do you have?" she asked.

"A Bichon Frisé. Her name is Sophie."

She giggled.

"What?" I asked.

"I just can't imagine you walking around town with a little fluffy white dog," she said.

"What can I tell you?" I replied. "I am a twenty-first-century guy. I may look all tough on the outside, but I have a gooey nougat center."

We ate dinner and had a pleasant conversation. A few drinks melted her usually tough demeanor, and she actually became . . . flirty. We passed on dessert in favor of after-dinner drinks. I had Cognac. Kendra drank a port.

After dinner, we headed outside, where I gave the valet my ticket for the Lexus. Kendra pulled out her phone.

"No car?" I said as the valet pulled up with mine.

"Took an Uber here. Didn't feel much like driving. Traffic when I got here was bad."

"It always is," I said. "Can I drop you somewhere?"

"I don't think so. I'm all the way out in Montclair."

"Really? I'm in Castro Valley. It's on the way. Hop in."

She looked me over. "You sure you're okay to drive?" she asked.

"Not my first rodeo. I'm fine. Really."

The valet opened the door to the passenger side of the Lexus. Kendra got in and buckled up. I slipped the valet a twenty and hopped behind the wheel.

I took Van Ness to I-80 West, crossed the Bay Bridge, and then headed to I-580 East.

"Look," I said, "I'm sorry about my producer approaching Sheila Williams about the gun. You were right. We should have coordinated with you."

"Thank you for that," she said.

"So, how'd you end up representing Sheila Williams?"

"I thought we had a moratorium on shop talk."

"Just wondering. Don't want you to violate attorney-client privilege or anything."

"I was outraged when I heard the details of her son's shooting, so I reached out to her. Too many of us are being killed for no reason, and there's no accountability. This shit has got to stop."

I nodded.

"This your first case like this?" I asked.

"Yes. I generally handle class-action suits against big corporations. Fighting for the little guy. Tilting at windmills. That kind of thing," she said. "Now, my focus is on police accountability for the killing of Black and brown bodies."

I took 580 to Highway 13, and Lynn directed me to her place.

Montclair is an upscale community at the foot of the Oakland Hills. It's technically part of the City of Oakland, but the community tends to live by its own set of rules.

We drove down the main drag past boutiques and upscale mom-and-pop shops. Everything was ritzy. It was like the community was saying, "Yes, we're Oakland, but we're not *that* part of Oakland."

At the rate gentrification was happening, there would soon be no "*that* part of Oakland" left.

Kendra directed me to a side street with remodeled Victorians dispersed randomly between custom-built homes, and soon, we approached a rustic-style building not far from Montclair's shopping district.

"Here we are," she announced.

I pulled over and brought the Lexus to a stop at the curb in front of her building.

"I've really enjoyed talking to you," I said.

"You sound surprised."

"You're not what I expected at all."

"What's that supposed to mean?"

"Well, let's get real here," I said. "Our first two encounters were far from lovefests."

"I can be tough when I have to be," she said. "Does that bother you?"

"I get it," I said. "My professional and personal sides are not always in sync."

She paused and looked me over like an army sergeant conducting an inspection. Finally, she said, "Do strong women intimidate you?"

I laughed. "Wait'll you meet my sister."

She nodded.

"Would you like to come up?" she asked.

My turn to pause.

"You sure that's a good idea? I wouldn't want you crossing ethical boundaries or anything," I said. "And I'm a journalist working on a story you're tangentially involved in."

"I think we're all right," she said. "Up to you."

I took another minute to think.

"As you said earlier . . . What the hell?"

She smiled.

We got out, and I pressed the button on the key fob locking the car doors and followed her up a walkway lined with neatly trimmed bushes. As soon as we approached the porch, sensor lights came on. Kendra fumbled for her keys, opened the door, and turned on the light. The inside of her condo was much larger than I imagined, looking at the building from the street.

A burgundy three-piece sectional sat in front of a large picture window with curtains that matched the couch. A glass coffee table was neatly positioned in front of the center of the sectional. A bookcase stood against the adjacent wall. I walked over and looked. *Little Women. Moby Dick. The Odyssey. A Tale of Two Cities.*

"You read all of these?" I asked.

"I like the classics. It's still the best writing around," she said. "You?"

"I read a lot of nonfiction. For escapism, I read comics and graphic novels."

It started when I was a kid. I used to imagine growing up and being the hero who solved the mystery surrounding my mother's killing.

"Can I offer you a drink?" she asked.

"No, thank you," I said. "I think I've had enough."

"Coffee? Tea?" she asked.

"No, thank you."

She walked closer and stopped inches from my face.

"How about me?" she said, placing a mocha-colored hand behind my head, pulling me to meet her lips.

The kiss was long and deep. Her lips were soft.

The kiss broke, and we stood looking into each other's eyes. Kendra's were deep brown. Almond colored.

"Here's to flaky Tinder hookups," I said, leaning in for another kiss.

FOURTEEN

I LEFT KENDRA'S bed at about 5:30 the next morning. Never in a million years did I ever imagine I'd end up here. The universe plays some strange tricks sometimes. Kendra was a sound sleeper, and my stirring didn't wake her. I found a pen and scratch paper on her bedside table and jotted down that I wanted to see her again, along with my cell number.

For the first morning in months, I wasn't thinking about Sarah. Maybe that old saying is true. "The fastest way to get over somebody is to get under somebody."

I didn't have a toothbrush, so I went into her bathroom and fumbled through the medicine cabinet, looking for some mouthwash. It was well stocked. Theraflu, NyQuil, Ambien, Diazepam, Ibuprofen, and Oxsoralen. Auntie would get psoriasis from time to time and use the latter. I eventually came across a small bottle of Scope, took a swig, and gargled. I then borrowed a comb to drag through my nappy hair, and fifteen minutes later, I was in the Lexus headed home. I entered the door at about 6:30 to find Sophie gently snoring at the foot of my bed.

I went into the kitchen, scrambled a couple of eggs, put on a pot of coffee, and placed a couple of strips of turkey bacon in the microwave. When everything was done, I ate at my kitchen counter, reviewing what I knew about the case. I think best on paper, so I wrote down everything on the pages of my reporter's notebook.

Two cops murdered within a week. Both had shot and killed unarmed Black people and received no consequences beyond paid administrative leave. Mickey Driscoll was shot with a .38-caliber revolver the same number of times he shot Jamal Williams. Sheila Williams owns a .38 that's supposedly gone missing. Mickey Driscoll had a two-million-dollar life insurance policy with his wife Janet as beneficiary. Neighborhood cameras show a white Prius and a ski-masked driver in the area at the time of his murder.

Malik Otumba and his Black Sentinels for Justice advocated killing cops in "self-defense."

Driscoll's widow had an alibi. So did Otumba, although it's questionable. Sheila Williams was on a Kaiser security camera leaving work and another coming home shortly before the time of the Driscoll killing. Her house had apparently been burgled of valuables, including her pistol.

Phil Curtain killed an unarmed Black man and was retired. He was shot to death in his store. The killer wouldn't have had time to remove shell casings, and there were none at the scene, so he . . . or she . . . probably used a revolver. If it turns out to have been a .38, chances are it's the same murderer.

None of this made any sense. My gut told me the killings were connected, but why go after these cops now? Driscoll shot Jamal Williams six months ago. Curtain's shooting was twenty years old. Who waits two decades to exact revenge?

What's that old saying about the serpent with a long memory?

I finished breakfast, pulled out my phone, and called Lynn at her office.

"Got the Curtain autopsy back yet?" I asked.

"Looking at it right now," she said. "Shot five times with a .38. Probably a revolver. The slugs in the two slayings came from the same gun."

"Let me guess . . . Curtain fired into that car five times twenty years ago."

"You got it," she said. "I pulled up the police report from his shooting. He discharged his weapon in that car five times. He hit one of the passengers with three shots and killed him. Severely wounded the driver and the other passenger."

"How so?"

"The other passenger was hit in his spinal column. He's paralyzed from the waist down."

"We should talk to him," I said. "Anything useful from Curtain's wife?"

"Not beyond what we already know. She goes out to get some sandwiches, comes back, and he's dead."

"Did he get death threats? Like Driscoll did?"

"Not that she's aware of."

"You know," I said, "that makes me think that Driscoll was the premeditated target and Curtain was an afterthought."

"I was thinking the same thing, Big Bro."

"Learn anything from the street cam footage?" I asked.

"Gonna look at it this morning. Want to come watch with me?"

"I'll be there in an hour," I said. "Should I bring popcorn?"

Lynn clicked off the phone.

I fed, watered, and walked Sophie, then grabbed a quick shower. Was Phil Curtain an afterthought? The killer, confident that he'd gotten away with the Driscoll shooting, going after another "unpunished" cop? And would Curtain be the last?

Not all police shootings are high profile, but many departments have officers who have made these tragic and often careless mistakes. Yes, some jump to conclusions based on the race of the person they shoot. More often, they genuinely believe that the person has a weapon in hand or is reaching for one. If somebody is out to kill all cops who've killed unarmed Blacks, we will be looking at a lot of bodies.

Which brings me to another question . . . The murders didn't take place in San Francisco. One was in San Ramon, the other in Alameda. Why target SFPD cops? And one on leave, the other retired? Why nobody on active duty? Could it be because a cop on duty has a weapon to shoot back?

Lynn worked out of the SFPD Headquarters at 850 Bryant Street in San Francisco. Its official name is the Hall of Justice Building. I have trouble calling it that. It reminds me too much of watching *Super Friends* as a kid.

Meanwhile, at the Hall of Justice . . .

850 Bryant is a one-stop shop. Over 400 cops, a jail, a traffic court, and a superior court are headquartered there.

I entered and made my way through the metal detectors and security, then the lobby, where I walked past the Spiral of Gratitude, a beautiful piece of art mixing light and glass that stands as a memorial to San Francisco's fallen officers. A plaque engraved with the names of the dead is part of the piece.

I wondered if Driscoll and Curtain would make the cut.

I took the elevator to the fourth floor and went to room 455. Homicide. I found Lynn sitting at her desk, sipping from a steaming mug, her eyes fixed on the open laptop in front of her.

"Hey," I said.

"Hey. Want some tea?" she asked.

"Have you met me? No, I don't want any tea. I'll take black coffee if you have some."

"I'll have to go down the hall to get it," she said. "In the meantime, take a look at this. It's from the security camera at the jewelry store across the street from the Curtain crime scene at the time of the murder."

Lynn went to get my coffee, and I plopped behind her desk and pressed the "play" icon on the screen.

Grainy footage. Various shoppers walk by. Curtain's wife leaves the store, presumably to pick up lunch, as she said. A white Prius pulls up in front of the fishing store. The driver parks, then gets out of the car. He's a stocky blond man with a crew cut. I recognized him immediately. He's the guy with the Looney Tunes tattoos I saw police holding back with the crowd of gawkers.

Looney Tunes goes into the shop and comes back about two minutes later. He hops in the Prius and takes off. I fast-forward and see Curtain's wife return to the store with a brown paper bag, apparently the sandwiches she went out for. Fifteen minutes later, the police are on the scene, and a crowd begins to form outside the store. Looney Tunes returns on foot and joins the crowd.

And here I thought all of that "the murderer always returns to the scene of the crime" stuff was just Agatha Christie bullshit.

Lynn returned with a steaming mug that she handed me. I took a sip. The coffee was scalding and bitter. It tasted like hot mud. I made a face to that effect.

"You're the one who wanted it black. We aren't exactly Starbucks around here," she said.

"I recognize the shooter."

"You do? From where?"

"He was standing in the crowd at the crime scene," I said, pointing him out on the video.

I explained how his tats made me notice him.

"Well, that clears Sheila Williams and Janet Driscoll," she said.

"How do you figure? He could be a hit man for all we know. Or he could be an innocent bystander who just walked in, saw the body, and left."

"True," she said. "The plates are visible. I'll run them, but I'm betting they're stolen."

"Don't you guys have that facial recognition software? Can't you run a still shot of him from this video and try to get an ID? See if he's in the system?"

"You're watching way too much TV, brother," she said. "We don't have access to that technology yet."

"He's possibly killed two people," I said. "Something tells me that this isn't his first offense."

"I'll see what I can find out," she said. "I pulled the file from the 2001 shooting. Lamont Jackson was the driver killed at the scene. The passenger in the backseat was Michael Woods. He died of leukemia back in 2010. That leaves Odell Watkins. He's the one with the spinal cord injury. He lives in a nursing home in San Leandro."

FIFTEEN

I WAS HALFWAY across the lower deck of the Bay Bridge when my *I Love Lucy* ringtone went off.

"Hello?" I said, using my hands-free device. I had to stop using the handheld while driving because Lynn actually gave me a $250 ticket for that practice. Sometimes having a cop in the family is a real pain in the ass.

"You know, I never pegged you for a guy who would make love to a girl and then creep out in the dead of night," said a woman's voice.

"Creep?" I asked. "How about quietly slipped out the back door?"

Kendra laughed.

"You have an adorable laugh, you know that?"

"Why, thank you, sir," she said.

"How'd you sleep?" I asked.

"Like a baby . . . until I rolled over and you weren't there."

"I had to get to work, and you were sleeping so soundly, I didn't want to wake you," I said.

"And he's a gentleman to boot."

"Just doing what my auntie taught me to do."

"She schooled you in the etiquette of one-night stands?"

"Is that what this was?" I asked. "A one-night stand?"

"If you don't take me out tonight, it was," she said, a coyness in her voice.

"Seven o'clock," I said. "My place. I'll make you dinner."

"And he even cooks. I've hit the motherload!" she exclaimed. My turn to laugh.

"Seven thirty. I have a late meeting with a client," she said. I gave her my Castro Valley address.

"Do you want me to bring anything?" she asked.

"Just what you brought last night," I said.

"See you then," she said with a smile in her voice.

San Leandro, California, is approximately twenty miles from San Francisco. The city of 90,000 borders Oakland to the south. From the 1950s through the 1980s, the town had a reputation as a "whites-only" enclave. Through redlining and housing discrimination, the city could circumvent Fair Housing Laws and keep people of color from buying or renting.

Multiculturalism eventually won the day, and by the turn of the twenty-first century, San Leandro could proudly boast that it had become one of the most diverse suburbs in the country.

Mercy Hospital is a long-term care facility just west of the city's upscale Bay-O-Vista neighborhood, above Interstate 580. It began as a standard care hospital before changing hands several times over the last thirty or so years, finally morphing into a nursing home.

I pulled into the parking lot just as Lynn got out of her unmarked.

"Ready?" she asked.

"I hate nursing homes and hospitals," I said. "They always remind me of death."

"Says the man investigating a double homicide," she shot back. "I can do this by myself if you want."

"No," I said. "In for a penny, in for a pound."

As we reached the building entrance, sliding glass doors automatically opened to welcome us into the lobby. It was a fairly large lobby with a seating area composed of a few dozen connected orange chairs made of what would have been touted as "space-age" plastic when we were kids.

The right corner of the room was cordoned off by folding yellow signs reading CAUTION WET FLOOR as a rotund African American woman toiled away with a mop and pail. Her labor gave the room an antiseptic smell. That smell was one of the reasons I hated hospitals so much. It brought me back to the day Auntie died. She had suffered a massive stroke. All Lynn and I could do was sit in the waiting room as the doctors worked on her. I felt so helpless just sitting there. Sitting there with Lynn . . . and that smell.

People say that music is a time machine that brings you back to wherever you were the first time you heard it. Funny how odors can do the same thing.

We walked up to the information desk and found a twenty-something woman perusing the latest *People* magazine. Do they ever publish an issue that doesn't have Kate Middleton on the cover?

We stood at the desk and watched the young woman immersed in her magazine for several seconds before Lynn loudly cleared her throat. The millennial leaped to attention as Lynn displayed her badge.

"We're here to see Odell Watkins."

"Why?" she asked. "Is he in trouble?"

"None whatsoever," Lynn said. "We just want to talk to him."

"I'll have to check with his doctor," she said as she picked up the phone on her desk and punched in an extension.

She softly whispered something into the receiver and then hung up.

"The doctor will be out in a minute," she said. "Please have a seat."

Lynn and I sat on a pair of space-age seats. They were hard and uncomfortable. I wondered if they had a chiropractor on staff.

A few minutes later, a white-haired doctor in his mid-sixties appeared at the desk. He was of average height and build and wore the requisite white coat and stethoscope around his neck.

"I'm Dr. Andy Stevens," he said. "I'm Mr. Watkins' primary care physician."

Lynn and I rose to meet him.

"What can I do for you?" he asked.

Lynn flashed her badge. "I'm Detective Sloan. This is my associate Chri . . . Topher Davis," Lynn said, correcting herself.

"Ah, Mr. Davis. I recognize you from the TV," he said.

"We'd like to speak with Mr. Watkins," I said.

"May I ask what this is regarding?" he said, impatiently shifting his weight from one foot to the other. For some reason, the man was clearly uncomfortable.

"Routine police matter, Doctor," Lynn said. "We need to ask him a few questions."

"I'm afraid that he's not up for that right now," Stevens said, still shifting his weight back and forth. "He's recovering from a bout of pneumonia."

"I'm sorry to hear that," I stated.

"Unfortunately, it's not his first go-round. Bouts of pneumonia are common with his kind of injury."

"And what type of injury is that?"

"I really shouldn't be discussing my patient's condition. HIPPA laws and all that," Stevens said.

"I hear he's paralyzed," I said.

Dr. Stevens looked at me without speaking.

"Come on, Doctor," I said. "It was in the papers. You're not giving anything away."

He let out a heavy sigh. "The bullet severed his spinal cord between S1 and S2. He's paralyzed from the waist down. He's a total invalid."

"The shooting was over twenty years ago," Lynn said. "What's he doing living here? People in wheelchairs can be pretty self-sufficient."

"Mr. Watkins's condition requires long-term care. He prefers to live here."

Why not? I thought. *I'm sure the settlement he got as the result of the shooting was more than adequate to cover the medical costs.*

"Any idea when he'll be up to visitors?" Lynn asked.

"Hard to tell," said Stevens. "He's recovering well from this latest bout. Why don't you come back in a few days?"

"Are you sure we can't ask him a few questions now?" Lynn said. "We won't be long."

"I must insist that you allow my patient to rest," Stevens said. "A few days. Now, if you'll excuse me, I have other patients to check on."

He turned around and headed back down the hallway.

Lynn and I sat in the unmarked in the parking lot.

"Did that feel weird to you?" I asked.

"Yeah," Lynn replied, "Like this doctor didn't want us talking to Watkins at all."

"Remember when I had pneumonia when we were kids?" I asked. "I was as sick as a dog, but talking for a few minutes wasn't so taxing it impaired my recovery."

"Talking for a few minutes? You *never* shut up," she laughed.

"It just doesn't smell right," I said. "So, what's this doctor hiding?"

"I guess we'll give him a few days and find out," Lynn said, firing up her car's engine.

SIXTEEN

"**Y**OU HAVE GOT to be kidding me," Mandy said.

"She's really sweet once you get to know her," I said.

"She's an obnoxious barracuda, is what she is."

"Actually, I think lawyers prefer the word 'shark.'"

I left the nursing home and returned home—no need to drive back into the city and then double back to East Bay. I called Mandy from my den, where I was trying to find out more about the Phil Curtain shooting online. There wasn't much beyond what Lynn had already uncovered. Back in the early 2000s, when the internet was new, a lot of news didn't make it online.

"So, you're seeing her again?" Mandy said.

"Jealous?"

"Please."

"She's coming over for dinner tonight," I said.

"You're actually cooking for that . . . 'See you next Tuesday'?"

"My, such language."

"Seriously, Topher . . . I just get a bad vibe from the woman," Mandy shared.

"Well, she didn't make the best first impression, that's for sure," I replied.

"You're not over Sarah. You do realize what you're doing here, right?"

"And what am I doing?"

"You're rebounding."

"I am not!" I snapped.

"As I said before . . . please."

We were both silent for a moment.

"You have so much going on . . . Sarah. The situation at the station," Mandy said. "Seeing you hurt even more would really break my heart."

"I'll be fine," I said. "I'm a grown-ass man."

"Who often acts like a petulant little boy," she replied.

"Say that again, and I'll hold my breath until I turn blue."

"I'm being serious here."

"Mandy . . . Kendra and I have this . . . connection . . ." I said, trying to explain the inexplicable.

"BE CAREFUL," she said before hanging up.

I thought about what she said. Kendra and I did have a connection. A connection . . .

I picked up the phone and dialed Lynn's cell.

She answered with an exasperated, "Yeah."

"I just thought about something. We've been looking for a connection between the deaths of Driscoll and Curtain. Maybe we've got it backward. Maybe we should be looking for a connection to their lives."

"I'm listening."

"Is there a way you can find out if Driscoll and Curtain ever worked together on anything? If their names appear on any police reports together. Stuff like that."

"You think that this may be connected to a case?"

"You always say, 'never rule anything out,'" I said.

"Let me see what I can find out. It's gonna take a minute. Curtain's been retired for a while, meaning his old police reports are . . . God knows where," she said. "I'll get back to you."

After she hung up, I Googled both victims' names to see if they came up together in any searches. There was a plethora of articles on Driscoll's shooting of Jamal Williams but very little on the Curtain shooting of Odell Watkins. As for anything with both officers' names, I came up blank. I was about to call Mandy back and ask her to do a LexisNexis search at the station to see if Curtain and Driscoll came up together in any old news stories in that database when I noticed the time. Kendra would be by in an hour and a half.

I jumped in the Lexus and drove to Galvan's Market in San Leandro, where I picked up two nicely marbled ribeye steaks. I then went across the street to Estudillo Produce, where I got salad fixings and a nice bottle of cab.

I'm a decent cook—not a chef. There's a difference. A chef can create multi-ingredient, multistep dishes. A cook can prepare simpler things. Any moron can grill a steak. Lynn would say that I'm living proof of that.

I went home, washed the steaks, patted them dry with a paper towel, and put them on a platter to let them get to room temperature. I opened the bottle of wine and decanted it to give it time to breathe. I then took Sophie for a short walk and a brief round of fetch. Once I fed the dog, I hopped in the shower and changed into my tan slacks and black turtleneck. I looked in the mirror and felt like Steve Jobs. I was thinking of changing when Kendra rang my doorbell promptly at 7:30. I opened the door to find her on my porch in a tan business suit and black blouse, her briefcase in hand.

"Seven thirty on the dot," I said, looking at my Rolex. "This isn't a billable hour, is it?"

"It depends on how dinner goes," she smiled and kissed me on the cheek. She looked at my tan slacks and her tan business suit.

"Look at us, all matchy-matchy," she said.

"Great minds . . ." I said. "Please, come in."

She walked in and was immediately accosted by Sophie, who ran up to her and barked, tail wagging.

"Kendra, Sophie. Sophie, Kendra," I said by way of introduction.

Kendra bent down and began scratching the dog behind her ears. Sophie stopped barking and rolled over on her back for Kendra to rub her tummy.

"Looks like you've made a conquest," I said. "Congratulations. You've officially been given the seal of approval from the lady of the house."

Kendra smiled.

"Just don't get on her bad side," I warned.

I took Kendra's jacket and mixed her a Cosmopolitan at my bar cart. I poured myself a double Johnnie Walker Blue. She sat at my kitchen counter and watched as I chopped lettuce, tomatoes, radishes, walnuts, and scallions for my salad.

We made small talk as I seared the steaks in my large cast-iron skillet. I then placed the meat skillet in the oven to broil for two minutes on each side. I put the meat on a platter and covered it with foil. Next, I put a stick of butter and a splash of the cab I'd opened in the skillet and mixed it with the meat's juices. I brought it to a boil, tossed it in a tablespoon of peppercorns, and poured the butter sauce over the ribeyes.

"Look at you, all Food Network," she said.

I laughed. Maybe I did have the makings of a chef.

"I wish," I said.

I poured two glasses of Cabernet and handed her one.

"Would you like to eat here at the counter or at the table in the dining room?" I asked.

"Here is just fine. I like your kitchen. Hell, I like your whole house. It's beautiful."

"Thanks."

I tossed the salad with a bottled vinaigrette, divided it into two wooden bowls, and then plated the steaks.

"Blood rare," I said. "Just like you like it."

Kendra cut into her steak, closed her eyes, and made an expression that looked like she'd just discovered Nirvana.

"You like?" I asked.

"Mm-hmm," she said as she nodded and chewed.

She swallowed her steak, put her arms around my neck, and gave me a peck on the lips that evolved into a deep kiss.

"Mandy says I should be careful when it comes to you," I whispered.

"Mandy?"

"My producer. You met her at Sheila's."

"Why does she say that?"

"She's very . . . protective," I said. I broke free from her embrace.

"Do you think you need protection from me?"

"I was in a relationship for four years. It ended badly."

"I see," she said. "Are you over her?"

"I wasn't, but now . . . I'm not so sure."

"Let me know when you figure it out," she said, cutting a small piece of steak and putting it into her mouth. "I'm not going anywhere."

SEVENTEEN

THIS TIME, IT was Kendra's turn to slip out of bed in the early morning. She kissed me on the cheek and woke me up.

"Good morning," she said a satisfied smile on her face.

"Good morning," I said, wiping the haze from my eyes. "What time is it?"

"Six. Gotta go—long day. I'm due in court at nine. I need to go home and freshen up."

"Will I see you tonight?"

"Do you *want* to see me tonight?" she asked.

I paused and then said, "You're sort of growing on me."

She kissed me on the mouth, hard.

"I have morning breath," I said. "Yuck!"

"How about drinks at that place by your station?"

"The Waterfront?"

"Yes. Seven?"

"Seven it is," I confirmed.

She ran her fingers through my hair, gently kissed my lips again, and departed.

I was just pulling into the station garage when the *I Love Lucy* theme blared on my phone.

"Hey, Lynn."

"Where are you?"

"Just getting to work," I said.

"Can you come over to my office? I want to show you something."

"I'll be there in fifteen minutes."

I took the Embarcadero to Bryant Street and followed it to the Hall of Justice, where I found Lynn sitting behind her desk sipping hot tea.

"Coffee?" she asked.

"After the last time? Not on your life."

"Snob."

"What have you got?" I asked.

She tossed a time-worn manila case file in front of me.

"What's this?"

"Your hunch was right. Driscoll and Curtain do show up in one report together," she said. "And the case was race related."

I perused the file.

"In 1998," Lynn said, "four officers, Driscoll, Curtain, Joseph Martin, and a rookie named Carla Isherwood, responded to a domestic violence call in the Bay View district."

"Predominantly Black," I noticed.

Lynn nodded.

"Why so many cops sent on a DV call?" I asked.

"This was right after the O.J. trial. Law enforcement finally began taking domestic violence seriously," she said, sipping her tea.

"Driscoll and Isherwood, the rookie, were partners," she informed me. "So were Curtain and Martin. Upon arrival, they find Isaac Wilson beating the shit out of his girlfriend, Sharica Jones. According to the police report, Driscoll, Curtain, and

Martin subdued and handcuffed Wilson. Isherwood tends to Jones and calls for an ambulance to take her to the hospital.

"At some point before the ambulance arrives, Wilson, who has been ranting and raving the whole time, refers to Isherwood as 'a cunt.' Isherwood loses it, pulls out her baton, and beats the handcuffed suspect. When the other officers restrain her, Wilson has a broken nose, cheekbone, eye socket, and skull fracture."

"Jesus," I said.

She took a big swig from her teacup as if to wash the taste of the whole affair out of her mouth.

Lynn continued, "The ambulance takes both suspects to the hospital. Wilson is charged with domestic battery and resisting."

"No way that holds up," I said.

"You're right. Wilson and Jones sue the department for excessive force, denial of due process, and violating their civil rights."

"How'd it shake out?"

"During depositions, Driscoll, Curtain, and Martin threw Isherwood under the bus."

"So much for the thin blue line," I said.

Lynn rolled her eyes.

"Well, if what you're telling me is accurate, she did severely beat a handcuffed suspect," I stated.

"The city settled. Isherwood, who was still in her probationary period with the department, was fired," Lynn said.

"Well, she sure as hell should have been."

"Probably."

"What do you mean, 'probably'?"

Lynn said, "She was a young cop who made a mistake."

"You're my little sister, and I love you, but if you call beating a handcuffed suspect to within an inch of his life 'a mistake,' you're on Oxy."

"She was a young female cop who hadn't had time to develop the thick skin you need to do this job," Lynn said. "I've been called 'a cunt,' and worse, throughout my career."

"Yeah, but you never cracked the skull of a handcuffed suspect because of it."

"She needed more training. I'm betting if she were a man, the department wouldn't have kicked her to the curb so quickly."

"Did they charge Isherwood with anything?"

"I haven't found any record of that."

"She's lucky," I said.

"Lucky? Police work remains a good ole boys' profession," Lynn stated. "Civilians like to talk about 'the thin blue line.' That's generally true when there's a threat from the outside. There's also a gender line all women in law enforcement deal with internally. Believe me, there are some skulls I'd like to crack in this building."

"Be that as it may, as one of those civilians you mentioned, I don't want a cop I'm paying with my tax dollars walking the streets with a baton, a gun, and a short fuse. She shouldn't need training to teach her not to abuse somebody who's already been restrained. That's a convenient excuse we always hear in these cases," I remarked. "She should have gone to jail."

Lynn gave me her "You don't get it" look.

"I'm not anticop," I said. "You know that. What you do is brave, difficult, and necessary. I sure as hell couldn't do it. Neither could most people who criticize the department and the profession."

"Okay," she said, "although I feel a 'but' coming."

"But," I said, "the problem is that, in my humble opinion, there is insufficient accountability. Mickey Driscoll kills a kid holding a cell phone and gets administrative leave. Basically, a paid vacation. Ditto Phil Curtain, who fires into a car full of unarmed men. Carla Isherwood beats a guy to within an inch of his life and at least gets fired. If I did any of those things, I'd be 'under the jail,' as Auntie used to say."

"You don't understand," she said. "You can't. You're not a cop. When I kiss my husband goodbye every morning and walk out the door, we both know it might be the last time we see each other."

"I know that. Cops always say that, and it's true," I said, "but no cop was drafted into the police force. There was no conscription here. This is the life they chose. The life *you* chose."

"And people like you are damned lucky we did," she snapped.

"Little sister, I am not slamming law enforcement. I know how everybody hates cops until they need one. I'm not one of those people. I have a deep respect and admiration for what it is you do. Like I said . . . I couldn't do it. I'm just saying that there needs to be some accountability."

She drank the rest of her tea.

"And . . . face it, there are some people who have no business being cops. Sounds like Carla Isherwood was one of them."

She thought for a moment and then reluctantly nodded.

Lynn and I still fight like we did when we were kids. Cats and dogs. We also still admit when the other person has a good point. Auntie taught us that too.

"Do you think there's a connection between this case and the murders?" I asked, thumbing through the file.

"I don't know," she said.

Near the back were police photos of the officers involved. Driscoll was young and fresh faced. Curtain, not so fresh faced, but much younger than the grizzled old man I'd met at the funeral reception. Martin was older with a tired face that looked like it had seen enough.

Lastly, there was Carla Isherwood. A blue-eyed twenty-something with a thin face, narrow aquiline nose, and broad smile.

Her blond hair was apparently in a bun under her uniform police cap.

"We've got an incident with four cops that resulted in one of them getting fired. Two of them have been murdered . . ."

"Yes," Lynn said. "But all this happened over twenty-five years ago."

"It did," I agreed. "What do you know about Martin?"

"He's retired and living up in the gold country somewhere. Twain Harte, I think."

"Road trip?"

"Way the hell up there? Why?"

"Maybe he can tell us something. I don't know what, but if there's any connection between that incident and the murders . . ." I said. "What about Carla Isherwood?"

"Nobody knows," Lynn said. "It's like she fell off the face of the earth after her firing. Her driver's license expired in 2001 and was never renewed. There's no cell phone in her name. Credit cards—Nothing."

"Maybe she got married and changed her name."

"There'd still be some trace. I had friends in the Social Security office and the Franchise Tax Board look up the number we have on file. She came up blank. No withholdings from any job since she left the department. No state tax returns filed."

"You got a last known address?"

"It's there in the file," she said, gesturing toward the papers I held. I rifled through them until I found it.

"A place in the Mission District," I observed.

"She and Driscoll were working out of the Mission station then."

"A San Francisco cop actually living in the city. Those were the days," I said.

"Hell, cops can barely afford to even commute to the city now," Lynn remarked. "If you think there might be a connection, why don't we start here in the Mission before going way the hell up to Twain Harte."

"That makes sense. Twain Harte is over two hours away. The Mission District is ten minutes."

I wrote the address in my reporter's notebook and shoved it in my vest pocket.

"By the way," she said, "I ran the plates from the Prius."

"Stolen?"

"From another white Prius. The owner of the Prius, who was actually issued those plates, is a dentist in Emeryville. He reported them stolen the day before the Curtain killing. The thief also took the registration and insurance card from the glove box."

"Clever," I said. "If a cop runs the plates, he'll come up with a white Prius, and the registration would match."

"Exactly," she said. "Looks like we're not dealing with an idiot here."

I handed the file back to her.

"Why don't you swing by that place in the Mission and see if you can learn anything about Carla Isherwood? I'll meet you at the Mission District station in about an hour," she said. "We'll see if anybody over there remembers her."

EIGHTEEN

I GOT IN the Lexus and headed up Bryant Street toward the Mission District. As I drove, something kept nagging at me about this case. Suppose Carla Isherwood was in some way connected, who was Loony Tunes? Was *he* the shooter? If so, what's his relationship with Isherwood and Martin? And what's Martin's role if this is connected to that old DV incident?

For decades, the Mission, as locals call it, was known for its Latino roots and Mexican culture. In recent years, taquerias have been replaced by trendy, upscale noodle houses, cafes, and shops specializing in things like candles and copper cookware. High-rise buildings with condos priced in the seven-figure range now stand where small Mexican stores once were. It's a hipsters' paradise that gets less and less diverse daily. Latinos whose families have lived in the neighborhood for generations have been pushed out by the likes of workers for Salesforce and Google.

The address Lynn had given me was in a residential area off Guerrero Street. Guerrero was typical of gentrification, although the residential areas surrounding it remained mostly intact.

San Francisco has always been expensive. Not insane like today, but never really affordable either.

Back in the late '90s, the Mission District would have been one of the few places in the city where a cop could afford to live. A blond, white cop residing in that neighborhood would have been a unicorn of sorts in those days. Demographics aside, most police I know don't like to live in the areas where they serve. Lynn says the reasons are twofold: they can become targets of retribution, and everybody in the neighborhood with a problem is knocking on their doors at all hours of the day and night.

I found the building. It was a steel-gray Victorian that had been converted to a triplex. I parked the Lexus, walked up to the door, and knocked after noticing a small white piece of paper with the words OUT OF ORDER taped above the doorbell.

A skinny, white kid in his early twenties opened the door wearing a black T-shirt for the band Weezer draped over baggy jeans. A black, wireless headset protruded from his right ear, the microphone close to the corner of his mouth. A pork pie hat completed the ensemble.

"Greetings," he said.

"Hi," I said. "I'm looking for Carla Isherwood. Is she around?"

"Who?" Pork Pie asked.

I repeated the name.

He looked over his shoulder and yelled to someone unseen. "Anybody know a girl named Carla?"

The response came in a chorus of "noes."

"Sorry, dude," he said.

"You live here?" I asked.

"Yeah."

"How long?"

He thought for a moment. "About a year. Since right after graduation."

"From where?"

"Chico," he responded.

"Work in tech?" I asked.

"I don't code if that's what you're asking. I'm a gamer."

"A gamer?"

"I play video games professionally."

I was incredulous. "You can do that? How's that pay?" I asked.

"I live here, don't I?"

Point taken.

"Do you or any of your friends own the building?" I asked.

"No," he said with a chuckle. "But I can give you the landlord's number."

"That would be great," I said.

He left for a few minutes, and when he returned, he handed me a business card for a property management firm in the financial district.

"Gotta get back to work now," he said.

"What are you playing?"

"The new *Call of Duty*," he told me. "It's pretty sick."

I recently learned from some of the kids at the station that "sick" is a good thing in the twenty-first century. Who knew?

"Play on," I said as he closed the door.

Making a living playing video games . . . If only I'd known that during my *Ms. Pac-Man* and *Galaga* days. My whole career trajectory might have been different.

Lynn pulled up in the unmarked just as I descended the stairs of the Victorian.

"Thought you were meeting me at the Mission District Station," I greeted her.

"I was able to get out of the office sooner than I thought. What'd you find out?"

I filled her in on my conversation with Pork Pie.

"Okay," she said, "I'll have somebody check in with the property manager to see if there's a current address on Carla Isherwood. I doubt it. That place has probably changed hands four or five times in the last twenty years.

"In the meantime, let's pop into the Mission station and see if anybody remembers anything about her."

I hopped in the passenger seat of the unmarked. We made our way to Valencia Street and headed south past Indian restaurants, trendy new tea shops, and record stores that sold albums on actual vinyl. Soon, we reached the Mission Police Station, a brick building that seemed out of place with the new direction and architecture of the neighborhood. Lynn parked, and we went inside where several officers of varying ranks warmly greeted her as they passed us while going about their business.

Lynn asked around, but we found no one who had been at that particular station over two decades ago. We decided to bag the idea and get some lunch.

On our way out, a middle-aged police sergeant stopped us.

"Detective Sloan?" the sergeant asked.

Lynn answered in the affirmative.

"I'm Bill Whitaker. I'm a desk sergeant here. I understand you're looking for information on Carla Isherwood."

"Yes, we are."

He looked at me. "I see you have Mr. Davis with you. Is this for the news?"

Lynn said, "We're looking into a case. Gathering info. That's all."

"We are all aware that you caught the Driscoll case. Now Phil Curtain . . . What's all this got to do with Carla?"

"Probably nothing," Lynn said. "We'd just like to talk to her."

"You know her?" I asked.

"Not well. We were at the academy together."

"What can you tell us about her? We're trying to locate her," Lynn said.

"It's been a long time," he told us, rubbing his forehead as if it were an Aladdin's lamp that could conjure memories.

"I can tell you that she was driven. Anything male recruits did, she had to do better. If I did one hundred push-ups, Carla did a hundred and one. Stuff like that," he said. "Real gung ho."

"Too 'gung ho' based on what ultimately happened," I said.

"Not everyone is built to be on the job," he said.

"Carla was one of them?" I asked.

He nodded.

"It was like she was always trying to prove something," he said.

"I'll show you. I'll show you all!" Lynn said, doing her best bullied teenage girl impression.

"Who do you think she wanted to 'show'?" I asked.

"Your guess is as good as mine."

"Did you socialize with her?" Lynn asked.

"A little. A group of us would go out for a few beers after classes from time to time. That sort of thing."

"Anything else you can tell us?" Lynn said. "Did she have any family?"

"There was a brother, as I recall," Whitaker said. "He wasn't all there."

"In what regard?" I asked.

Whitaker thought for a moment.

"He was . . . slow. 'Special needs,' I guess you'd call it. Carla talked about him a lot, though. She was the big sister. Really looked after him."

"Do you remember his name?" I asked.

Whitaker scratched his head.

"You're talking over twenty years ago," he reminded us. "I barely remember my own name. I only met him once at our graduation from the academy. He was probably in his late teens then. Big kid. Husky."

"We'd appreciate it if you'd holler if you should remember anything else," Lynn said, handing him her card.

"You're trying to catch a cop killer," Whitaker said. "You bet your ass I'll call you if anything comes up."

"Thanks," Lynn said.

"You really think Carla might have something to do with this?"

"Like I said, we'd just like to talk to her," Lynn stated.

"If you ask me, you're barking up the wrong tree," Whitaker said. "You need to look at these Black anticop groups. They're the ones advocating violence against police."

Lynn shook her head as we walked out of the station. "When can you go to Twain Harte with me?" she said with resignation.

"I guess tomorrow will work," I answered. "What exactly is it we're looking for up there? What do you think Martin can tell us that we don't already know?"

"Carla Isherwood's name and his are the only other ones that turn up in the police report with the two dead cops. There's a thread here. Let's pull on it and see what happens."

We walked a couple of blocks to a cozy little Indian place nestled between an auto body shop that I didn't figure was long for the neighborhood and a new ice creamery. We went inside and, to our delight, found it mostly empty. We'd just missed the lunch crowd.

Our entrance interrupted a young Indian woman wearing jeans and a white "#MeToo" T-shirt seated behind a podium at the front door. She appeared to be in her late teens or early twenties and was reading a textbook. She saw us enter, marked her place, and shut the book. *Essential Cell Biology.*

"Some light reading?" I asked.

"Finals coming up. This is my parents' place; they've got me multitasking."

She grabbed a couple of menus and seated us at a table near the window where we could people watch as a menagerie of hipsters, homeless, techies, and Latino men and women paraded up and down Valencia Street.

Lynn ordered tandoori chicken. I got goat rogan josh with a side of curried rice. The hostess brought a basket of garlic and cheese naan to get us started. I grabbed the Indian bread, tore off a small piece, and nibbled. I offered some to Lynn, who declined.

"You're off carbs now too?"

"Just thinking," she said.

"About?"

"Carla Isherwood."

"Okay?" I said.

"This situation is bad," she said. "Do you have any idea how much worse it gets if it turns out that a cop is somehow involved?"

"You're the detective," I said, "but aren't you jumping the gun here a bit? No pun intended."

"How so?"

"You have nothing to tie her to this case at all. You've got a name on a twenty-five-year-old police report."

"Let's just call her a person of interest," she said.

"Still, nothing but an old police report connects her to the vics," I stated. "I'm betting that our shooter is a blond man with a fondness for old Warner Brothers cartoons."

"Suffering succotash," she said.

NINETEEN

KENDRA'S BRONZE, NUDE body felt like warm silk as I spooned her. She was sleeping soundly with even, rhythmic breathing that matched mine. The full moon beamed through the skylight, bathing us in its luminous glow.

I was wide awake. I couldn't get the name Carla Isherwood out of my head. We needed to talk to Joe Martin and Carla Isherwood, if only for for purposes of elimination. Or was I just avoiding the obvious? It's just some radical doling out vigilante justice against white cops who killed unarmed African Americans.

Sheila Williams was the most obvious person to have a vendetta against the police. If the legal system wouldn't deal with cops who killed people like her son, then she would. She even owns a .38 revolver.

She seems like a warm and lovely mother, but she wouldn't be the first person to snap and seek vengeance. "When all else fails, pick up a gun and settle it yourself" seems to be the American way these days between cops killing civilians and nuts shooting up schools.

Why do we have so many fucking guns in this society?

Lynn owns an arsenal and has been telling me for years that with the kind of work I do and the feathers I ruffle, I should be armed. She even offered to help me get a concealed carry permit.

I've resisted, though. It's not that I'm antigun or anti-Second Amendment. I just feel uneasy about the idea of having a gun in my house.

Auntie had one when we were kids. A silver snub-nosed Smith & Wesson revolver. She bought it after our mother died. She said, "If anybody tries to break in here, I'll be ready for him."

She certainly was ready for me the day she came home from work and found me playing with it. I didn't really understand what the phrase "beaten to within an inch of your life" meant until she took a switch to my behind that day. I never touched that weapon, or any other, ever again.

There was also the matter of Odell Watkins. I wanted to know what he could tell us about his encounter with Curtain.

I finally drifted off to sleep for a few hours. When I awoke, Kendra was still lightly snoring, and I took extra care in extricating my body from hers as I slipped out of bed. I went into the bathroom, shaved, showered, and brushed my teeth.

I then headed into the kitchen, where I put on a pot of coffee.

I took six eggs from the fridge and separated the yolks from the whites. I found some scallions, chives, mushrooms, and a large tomato in the crisper bin, chopped up the vegetables, grated a little piece of Havarti cheese, whisked everything together, and poured the mixture into a hot frying pan coated with cooking spray. It turned out to be a reasonably decent egg white frittata.

When it was done, I put it on a plate with some sliced strawberries and placed it on a tray. I then went outside to my American Beauty rosebush, found the perfect flower, snipped it, removed the thorns, and brought it inside, putting it in a crystal vase that I added to my presentation.

Sarah said that one of the reasons she was leaving was that she felt neglected. I won't make that mistake again.

I poured a mug of coffee, put it on the tray next to the frittata, and carried the whole production into the bedroom, where Kendra was just waking up.

"Good morning," I said, smiling.

"Good morning," she said. "For a moment, I thought you snuck out on me again."

"Not on your life. Just making you a little breakfast. You know, it is the most important meal of the day," I said.

"I can't believe you did this!" she exclaimed, shocked delight overtaking her face. "You are the sweetest man on the planet!"

"I've been trying to tell you that for days," I said, setting the tray across her lap and gently kissing her.

I returned to the kitchen and poured myself a mug of black coffee that I brought back into the bedroom. I sat on the bed beside Kendra and drank it while she ate.

"No breakfast for you?"

"Not this morning. Just a little coffee."

"This is really good," she said, forking a small piece of mushroom.

"I can do a few things in the kitchen," I said.

"You can do a few things in the bedroom too," she said, kissing me.

"So, what's your day like today?"

"I need to go home and freshen up, and then I'm due in court. You?"

"I'm going into the station to work with Mandy on some editing. She got Phil Curtain's wife to give us an interview on camera."

Kendra took another bite of the egg and washed it down with a swallow of coffee.

"Lynn and I are driving up to Twain Harte this afternoon."

"Why in God's name are you going all the way up there?" she asked.

"To talk to a cop involved in a case with Driscoll and Curtain. Probably a waste of time, but Lynn thinks we should see what he has to say."

I took a sip of coffee and then stared into my cup as if looking for answers. Without looking up, I said, "Listen . . . since you're here so much anyway . . . Why don't you bring a few things over? Like some clothes, toiletries. Stuff like that."

"Why, Mr. Davis, are you asking me to move in with you?"

I looked up from my coffee cup and into her eyes. "I'm just thinking of the hassle you have running to your place to shower and change clothes before you can start your day," I said with a coy smile. "I'm only thinking about you."

She took a sip of her coffee and smiled. "I'll think about it," she said.

"I'm not offering to endow you with all my worldly possessions. Just thought you might like a toothbrush here," I said, again staring into my empty coffee mug.

She took a final bite of egg, set the breakfast tray on the nightstand, rolled over, and climbed on top of me. The kiss was long and deep.

This time, I broke it.

"What's the deal with Sheila Williams's gun?"

"What?" she said, a little taken aback.

"She owns a .38-caliber revolver that she agreed to turn over. Now, she says her place was burglarized, and it's missing. I'm going through you, as we agreed. What do you know about it?"

She gave me a look that said, "Are you *seriously* asking me this? Now??"

Kendra climbed off of me and rolled back over to her side of the bed.

"First," she said, "I have no idea. Second, I wouldn't tell you if I did know because Sheila is my client, and I'm not breaking privilege. Even for you."

I nodded.

"And third . . . Is that what this whole thing is about? I'm just another source to you??"

Shit. You're blowing it again, Davis.

"No, of course not," I said. "I like you. A lot."

"But not as much as you like pumping me for information about my clients."

"Now, you know that isn't true."

"Do I? Is that what this whole frittata seduction was all about?" she asked. "Softening me up for an interrogation?"

"I'm sorry. I never should have asked you that. I don't want you to breach attorney-client privilege. Please, forget I said anything."

She angrily climbed out of bed and began dressing, putting on each garment as though it were an act of violence.

I climbed out of bed and gently grabbed her hand.

"Look, I really *am* sorry. Sometimes, it's hard to take off my reporter's hat."

"I thought we had something going here," she said.

"We do. At least, I think we do. We need some time to figure this thing out," I told her. "In the meantime, how about a truce?"

She stopped dressing.

"What kind of truce?"

"This house is 'no man's . . . or woman's . . . land.' We don't talk business once we walk in the door of this place. There are no cases. No clients. No news stories. Just us," I said. "Separation of church and state."

Kendra thought for a moment. "Do you think you can live with that?"

"I do," I said.

She smiled reluctantly.

"Now, come back to bed. I'll get you some more coffee."

She picked up her phone from the nightstand and glanced at it.

"I guess I do have a little time," she said. "No-man's-land?"

"And no-woman's. Sanctuary."

Kendra began undressing as I went into the kitchen to get her a fresh mug of French Roast.

TWENTY

WE DIDN'T LEARN much new from the Edna Curtain interview. She talked about how Curtain had worked his whole adult life for the department, took retirement years ago, and decided to live his dream of making fishing his livelihood. The store did a good business; according to Edna, they were happy. Mandy had conducted the interview and was reminded that the surveillance camera behind the register was just for show. As for suspects, she said that Curtain had made a lot of enemies during his years in uniform.

"Mostly perps who found it easier to blame Philly for going to jail than to accept responsibility for their own actions," she said. "People like that."

Could our blond mystery man be somebody Curtain helped send to San Quentin? But if that were the case, how does it tie in with the Mickey Driscoll killing? Ballistics confirmed both men were killed with the same gun.

Around noon, I picked up Lynn at her office, and we began the trek up to Twain Harte to pop in on Joe Martin.

"What do we know about him?" I asked Lynn as I headed for the Bay Bridge toward Oakland.

"Seventeen years on the job. Lives up in Petaluma but spends most of his time in a vacation house he owns in Twain Harte."

We could have talked to him on the phone, but conversations of this nature are better conducted in person. Sometimes, you learn things you wouldn't discover otherwise when you're face-to-face in a room with somebody.

I took the Bay Bridge to I-580E and followed it for thirty-three miles until I got to Interstate 205, which I took toward Stockton. From there, we headed for the 99/120 interchange and followed Highway 120 to East Yosemite Drive. An hour later, we pulled into Twain Harte.

Twain Harte is a quaint little town about two and a half hours from the Bay Area. Lots of people from the Bay have second homes there. It's quiet and affordable. No surprise that a big city cop who wanted a slower pace of life would opt to escape to the land of Mark Twain and Bret Harte.

Joe Martin had built a small home near the Twain Harte Golf Club. It was a brown, single-story building with a rustic look. It had a "cabin feel," but you could tell from the outside that it had all of the modern amenities, starting with the solar panels on the roof to power the place.

"A green cop," I said. "There's something you don't see every day."

"There are all kinds of people on the job," Lynn said. "I can't believe you don't know that by now."

"I do know that," I said. "But it's just so much fun messing with your head."

I pulled the Lexus into the long driveway and parked behind a Chevy Volt.

"Our man Martin is really walking the walk," I said.

We headed up a red brick walkway to the sturdy-looking oak front door, and Lynn rang the bell.

No answer.

She rang again and got the same nonresponse.

I knocked on the door . . . and it crept open.

What the hell?

Lynn unholstered her Glock, and I followed her inside.

The living room was modestly furnished. A gray sectional couch centered the room, facing a wood-burning fireplace. An antique upright piano was against one wall—a grandfather clock against another. A smart TV hung above the fireplace. The place was neat and tidy. Nothing appeared to be disturbed or out of place.

We went into a small kitchen that was all done in eggshell. I'd have called it "white," but Lynn taught me better. The kitchen was clean. The counters had been freshly wiped down, and no dishes were in the sink.

We went through a small door off the kitchen to find a home office. It was complete with a laptop, landline, fax machine, oak rolltop desk, and chair. Seated in the chair with his bloody head resting on the desk was the body of a man. He had been shot behind his right ear. It would have looked like he had put his head down for a nap if it weren't for all the blood.

Lynn touched his neck and checked for a pulse.

"Stay here," she said as she prepared to sweep the rest of the house, Glock in hand.

"Maybe I'd better go with you," I said.

"Stay here!" she repeated.

"Be careful," I warned her.

"I always am," she said as she exited the room.

Five minutes later, she was back.

"The house is clean," she said, reaching into the hip pocket of the dead man and extracting his wallet.

"Joe Martin?"

"Looks like," she said. "He's been here for a while. Rigor has already set in."

She pulled out her cell phone, dialed 911, identified herself, and explained the situation. Within minutes, the area was filled with EMTs, sheriff's deputies, and a van from the coroner's office.

A paunchy, middle-aged sheriff who identified himself as Theo Long coordinated the operation and controlled the crime scene. A wooden toothpick danced between his lips as he spoke with us.

"Pardon the toothpick," he said. "Keeps me from smoking."

"Is it working?" I asked.

"So far. I had been up to a pack and a half of unfiltered Lucky Strikes a day. Now . . . none."

"When did you quit?"

"Yesterday."

I fought a smile.

"May I ask what your business is with him?" Theo Long asked.

"Part of a murder investigation," Lynn said. "Did you know him?"

Long chuckled. "Everybody knows everybody in Twain Harte," he said.

"What can you tell me about him?"

"Built this place about ten years ago as a weekend getaway. Came up here full time in the last few months. Ex-cop living on a pension. Played a lot of golf but kept mostly to himself."

"Notice any out-of-place visitors in town lately?" I asked.

"You mean besides you?" He chuckled again. "We have all kinds of visitors up here. People coming to golf. People staying the weekends in houses and cabins they've rented through Airbnb. Those of us who live here all know each other, but we do get our share of tourism."

"I don't suppose you'd have street cameras," Lynn said.

"For what? This isn't San Francisco. Twenty-five hundred people live here. There's not a lot of crime."

"You just had a homicide," I reminded him.

"It's the first one we've had in . . . I don't know how long," the sheriff said.

Lynn asked a few more questions, and then she and Long exchanged business cards, promising to keep each other in the loop about further developments.

Lynn was uncharacteristically quiet on the drive back to the Bay Area. After about forty minutes of silence, I broke the impasse.

"Whatcha thinking about?" I finally said.

"Carla Isherwood."

"What about her?"

"We have to find her," Lynn said. "Of the four cops on the case that got her fired, three are dead, and she's in the wind."

"Or dead."

"I think she's either victim number four . . . or our killer."

"As far as you know, was Martin ever involved in the shooting of an unarmed Black person?" I asked.

She drew in a deep breath and then slowly exhaled. "On the day Phil Curtain fired into that car full of people, Martin was riding with him."

TWENTY-ONE

WE MADE IT back to San Francisco shortly after nightfall. We were late getting back, so I called Kendra and canceled our date for the evening.

"Awww," she said, the pout in her voice evident through the phone.

"I know," I said. "I was looking forward to tonight too."

I explained what I could about the situation in Twain Harte.

"Wow," Kendra said. "Of course. I understand. Call me tomorrow, 'kay?"

"I'll make it up to you."

"You bet you will," she said with a giggle. I adored her laugh. It was playful and girlish.

She clicked off.

"Sounds like this is getting serious," Lynn said.

"I don't know. It's only been a couple of weeks. I like her, Sis. She makes me feel . . . I don't know. Maybe 'alive' is the word?"

"Alive?" she repeated. "If you say, 'She completes me,' I'm going to pistol-whip you."

I laughed.

"When Sarah left, something inside of me . . . died," I said. "I wasn't all there."

Lynn looked at me quizzically.

I said, "You know how when you have a cold coming on, you get that hollow feeling in your head? You're pushing through, trying to do what you need to do, but your sinuses feel funny, and you don't feel well, but you push through anyway until you finally admit to yourself that you're getting sick, and your body forces you to take some NyQuil and rest until you get better?"

She thought for a moment before saying, "I think so."

"I've been walking around with that hollow feeling since Sarah walked out. I've been pushing through, trying to do what needs to be done."

"And now? Do you still feel . . . hollow?"

"The hollowness is going away."

"So, you're comparing this woman to cold medicine that puts you to sleep."

"Never mind," I snapped in frustration.

"I'm just messing with you," she said. "I think I understand what you're trying to say."

"Good."

"Friday night work?" she asked.

"Friday night?"

"For you to bring this Wonder Woman to dinner with Jared and me," she said. "You didn't think for a minute you were going to see her for any length of time without my signing off, did you? Unless you really *do* have a head cold."

I sighed.

"Friday night?" she repeated.

"I'll ask her."

I dropped Lynn at her office and headed home. As I approached San Leandro on I-580, I got off on the Grand Avenue exit and headed east toward Mercy Hospital. I wanted to talk to Odell Watkins. I wanted to know what he could tell me about Phil Curtain, the shooting that had crippled him, and Joe Martin's involvement, if any.

I took Grand to Benedict Drive, made a right, and followed it to Mercy Hospital. I parked and went inside, finding a different receptionist than the one I'd seen the last time. This was an older lady in her mid- to late sixties. I pegged her as a volunteer.

"Excuse me," I said. "I'm here to see Odell Watkins."

"Visiting hours are over," she said, pointing to a sign on the wall indicating that they ended at eight p.m.

I looked at the clock on the wall. It was 7:50 p.m.

"It isn't eight yet," I said, pointing at the clock.

She let out an annoyed sigh.

"What was the name again?"

"Odell Watkins."

She tapped the keys on the white computer in front of her, and a look of concern washed over her face.

"Just a minute," she said.

She picked up the phone beside her and punched in an extension. A few minutes later, Dr. Stevens appeared at the reception desk.

"Mr. Davis. I had a feeling it might be you," he said.

"I'd like to speak with Mr. Watkins if he's up to it."

"Unfortunately, he isn't."

"Can you give me an estimate as to when he'll be up to receiving visitors? It's imperative that I speak with him," I said.

"I'm afraid that's impossible," Stevens said. "Mr. Watkins passed away this morning."

I returned to the parking lot, climbed into the Lexus, and called Lynn.

"He said it was complications from the pneumonia," I told her.

"Convenient," Lynn replied.

"The bodies are just piling up, aren't they?" I said. "Now what?"

"Something tells me that this all leads back to Carla Isherwood. We've *got* to find her."

"Any luck with the property management company running her old place?"

"No," she said. "I was right. That building has changed hands five times since she lived there."

"DMV?"

"She has no license or vehicle registration in her name in California. No marriage certificate. No death certificate. No real property—nothing I could find after she left the department. It's like she fell off the face of the earth. Either that . . . or she's under it."

"What about the brother? Maybe we can catch a break and locate him."

"We don't even have a first name," Lynn said.

"Isherwood isn't like Smith. The name isn't that common."

"True," Lynn said. "I'll see what I can find out tomorrow."

I hung up my cell, started the Lexus, and pulled out of the hospital's parking lot. If Carla Isherwood was, in fact, dead, that meant that every cop on that police report was dead. What are the odds of that?

On the other hand, if she's alive ... Why was she the only one left standing?

And in the Curtain and Driscoll killings, the number of bullets they were shot with corresponded directly with the number of bullets they'd pumped into their victims. It was as if the shooter was sending a message.

Martin, on the other hand, was only shot once. Why the discrepancy? Was Joe Martin's shooting not meant to send a message? If not, then why kill him at all? Was somebody tying up loose ends?

Twenty minutes later, I pulled into my driveway to find Kendra's car there. I parked and walked in the front door. The aroma of basil and oregano filled the air.

"Honey, I'm home from the club," I said in my best Ricky Ricardo accent.

Kendra entered the room wearing a low-cut black dress that clung to her body like a second skin. She wore one of my white aprons over her neck and around her waist.

"What is it with you and *I Love Lucy*?" she asked.

"When we were kids, Auntie didn't get home until around dinnertime, and after Lynn and I finished our homework, we'd watch the reruns every day. It reminds me of the fun times we had as kids," I said. "Does it bother you?"

"Not as long as you don't expect me to wrap chocolates on a conveyor belt or something," she said, greeting me with a kiss.

"Ooh," I said. "A conveyor belt could be interesting."

I surveyed her in my apron and took another whiff of the delicious smell coming from my kitchen. "What's all this? What are you doing here? Not that I'm not glad to see you."

"We had a rocky morning, so I decided we needed a nice night," she said, kissing me again. "You couldn't come to me, so I came to you. I found your spare key under that fake rock outside the front door and let myself in. I hope you don't mind. You know . . . boundaries and all."

"No," I said. "It's a nice surprise."

I meant it. It felt good to come home to someone.

Sophie, quietly resting on the couch, jumped down and greeted me. I picked her up, and she kissed my face.

"I finished up at the office early, came over, and made us a little dinner. I hope you like Italian."

"Doesn't everybody?"

I put Sophie down, and Kendra kissed me again. She then took me by the hand and led me to the dining room table, where a glass of Chianti waited.

"Have a drink. Dinner will be ready in about fifteen minutes."

She scurried off to the kitchen as I sipped the wine. It was good. Smooth with a dry aftertaste that lingered on the tongue.

It wasn't all jugglers and knife throwers at the beginning of my career. I did a wine segment or two during those days. I learned just enough enology to be pretentious.

I liked this. The house had felt so empty since Sarah left. It was nice to have someone care for me. Look after me. I'm a very simple creature at heart. It doesn't take much to please me. All I need is what I call FFL: Feed Me. Fuck Me. Love Me.

So far, Kendra has accomplished one F. The steaming platters of pasta, broccolini, and chicken cacciatore she placed on the table before me achieved the second. If she could somehow pull off the L . . .

"This looks and smells wonderful," I said, picking up a warm piece of sourdough bread from a wicker basket Kendra placed on the table.

"You have a great kitchen," she said. "Lots of fun to cook in."

"You'll have to do it more often," I said with a smile.

"Maybe I will," she said. "Maybe I will."

TWENTY-TWO

KENDRA DIDN'T SPEND the night, citing some work she needed to finish for an early-morning settlement conference. After a prolonged goodbye, she headed home.

Once she'd gone, I was too keyed up to sleep, so I went into my den and fired up my MacBook. I wanted to see what I could find on Carla Isherwood.

Lynn ascertained that Carla had been raised in the North Bay town of Fairfield. A Google search pulled up several archived newspaper articles from her high school years.

FAIRFIELD GIRL SUES SCHOOL DISTRICT
SEEKS SPOT ON BOYS' BASEBALL TEAM
By Tom Stiles, Staff Writer
March 3, 1992

Carla Isherwood, sixteen, has filed a civil lawsuit in Fairfield Superior Court against the Fairfield-Suisun Unified School District on the grounds of gender discrimination, claiming she was denied a spot on the Fairfield High School Boys' Junior Varsity baseball team because she is a girl.

"If I can hit and field as well as the boys, I should be allowed to compete with the boys," Isherwood said.

Isherwood claims that she went to baseball tryouts and was told she was ineligible for the team due to her gender. She says she was then directed to "try out for the Fairfield High Girls' Softball Team."

Officials from the Fairfield-Suisun Unified School District had no comment, citing the district's policy of not commenting on pending litigation.

Isherwood seeks a spot on the boys' junior varsity baseball team and unspecified damages.

A few links down, I found:

ISHERWOOD TO BE FIRST GIRL ON BOYS' TEAM
By Tom Stiles, Staff Writer
April 4, 1992

Sixteen-year-old Carla Isherwood will be the first girl on the Fairfield High School Boys' Junior Varsity baseball team when the Fairfield Trojans face the Armijo High Indians this Saturday in the season opener. Isherwood had filed a lawsuit against the Fairfield-Suisun Unified School District alleging gender discrimination after purportedly being barred from tryouts. The suit has since been settled, and Isherwood will take the field in her first outing as shortstop on Saturday. The terms of the settlement are confidential.

This was all right in line with what Sergeant Whitaker had told us. Carla Isherwood was driven to prove she was as good as any man. That said, why in the world would she pick police work? While there have been women on the force for years, it's still a "boys' club" in many ways. She broke one glass ceiling with high school baseball. Was she trying to break another?

A further Google search revealed that she played for the boys' varsity team in her junior and senior years, batting .350 and leading them to two division championships—a young pioneer for women's equality.

After that, she disappeared until March 2002, when a story appeared in the *San Francisco Chronicle*.

AFRICAN AMERICAN MAN ALLEGES SFPD BEAT HIM WHILE HANDCUFFED
By Geoffrey Ross, Staff Writer
March 23, 2002

An African American San Francisco man alleges that he was beaten by a member of the SFPD while handcuffed. On Saturday, Isaac Wilson, twenty-one, was detained by police responding to a domestic violence call in the Bay View District. Wilson alleges that he was searched, handcuffed, and then beaten with a baton by rookie officer Carla Isherwood, twenty-six. Wilson suffered bruises and a cheekbone fracture during the incident. According to Wilson, three other officers, Phil Curtain, forty-five, Joe Martin, forty-four, and Michael (Mickey) Driscoll, thirty, had to pull Isherwood off him and physically restrain her.

Wilson and his girlfriend, Sharica Jones, were arrested and charged with resisting arrest. Wilson was also charged with assault and battery on a police officer and domestic battery for allegedly beating Ms. Jones.

Wilson has retained legal counsel and is suing the department. He is seeking unspecified damages. An SFPD spokesman says that the matter is under review by the department's Legal Affairs and Internal Affairs divisions.

Scrolling further down, I found:

OFFICER FIRED IN ALLEGED
SUSPECT BEATING
by Geoffrey Ross, Staff Writer
July 9, 2002

An SFPD spokesman announced today that the officer involved in the alleged beating of a handcuffed suspect in March has been fired. Carla Isherwood, twenty-six, a rookie with the department, was accused of beating Isaac Wilson, a twenty-one-year-old African American man, while he was handcuffed and in custody on charges of domestic battery and resisting arrest. Wilson had filed a lawsuit against the department seeking unspecified damages.

At a press conference this afternoon, SFPD Public Information Officer Darryl Hines said that the department had fired Isherwood, who was still in her initial probationary period as a new officer. The other officers involved in the incident have been cleared of any wrongdoing and returned to active duty. Hines stated that the lawsuit with Wilson has been settled. Under the settlement agreement, the terms are confidential.

I went to the Fairfield High School website and found the yearbook section. Fortunately for me, the yearbooks had been scanned and posted on the site going back to the 1960s. I found Carla Isherwood's graduation picture from the class of 1993. She was a pretty teenager, thin with high cheekbones, golden-blond hair, and steel-blue eyes. Her senior quote was, "If I can believe it, I can achieve it."

Scrolling through the yearbook, I found that she had been on its editorial staff and the Honor Roll.

Sgt. Whitaker had said that she had a younger brother. I scrolled through the class pictures and found him in the class of 1995. Fred (Freddy) Isherwood Jr. was a stocky kid with his sister's blond hair and blue eyes. He was younger in the photo but still recognizable. Looney Tunes.

I picked up the phone and called Lynn.

"Wow," she said. "So, little brother is settling scores for big sister."

"Settling scores?" I asked.

"I dug deeper into the beating incident. Curtain, Martin, and Driscoll all threw Carla under the bus. They all reported that she was completely out of control and that the victim had indeed been beaten while handcuffed and posed no imminent threat to anyone at the scene. Their statements were instrumental in getting her fired."

"So, the question is, is Freddy Isherwood acting alone, or is he being directed by his sister? Whitaker said that he had a developmental disability. If he and Carla were close, he might be easy for her to manipulate."

"Or he could just be taking revenge against the cops who got his sister fired," Lynn said. "Sibling loyalty. Wouldn't you kill for me, big brother?"

"There have been plenty of times I've wanted to kill you. Does that count?"

"It appears that we're now looking for the Isherwood sibs."

"Looks that way," I said. "Unless . . ."

"Unless what?"

"Unless we're looking at this thing all wrong and brother Freddy took out big sister too."

"That makes no sense," she said.

"None of it makes any sense," I said. "She was fired over twenty-five years ago. If it's revenge, why wait so long? And why have little brother do it? Based on her history, Carla's a self-sufficient woman who can do anything a man can do. Play high school baseball. Join the force."

"We'll ask her when we find her," she said.

"Whatcha thinking?"

"SFPD employment records. Let's see who she lists as next of kin and visit them."

"Would the department keep those records for this long?" I asked.

"We'll know soon enough," Lynn said.

TWENTY-THREE

THE NEXT DAY, I rolled into the studio at around noon. There wasn't much for me to do on the story at the moment. Mandy and Stu drove up to Twain Harte to get some sound bites from Theo Long and some local residents. They also got some sound from a few old-timers who'd worked with Joe Martin.

The story quickly changed from our initial premise of tracking cops and victims after a shooting tragedy to "Who's killing cops and why?"

I went into the station lunchroom to grab some coffee, and Curt Weil walked in.

"How's your story coming along?" he asked.

I updated him on our progress. "It's getting complicated. I'm just hoping that I can finish by the deadline."

He frowned. "I wish there were another way," he said. "If it were up to me, you'd stay here forever."

I could tell that he was sincere.

"I know, Curt. Thanks for saying that."

"I hope you can finish in time. It sounds like one hell of a story," he said.

"That it is," I replied.

With Mandy and Stu in Twain Harte, there wasn't much for me to do, so I headed out for an early lunch. Grumpy's is a little watering hole strategically located within walking distance of all the TV and radio stations in town. It's a bar and grill where you can get a decent breakfast or a sandwich that you can wash down with the latest, trendy IPA. I ordered a hamburger. I was craving a scotch but passed since they didn't have Johnnie Walker Blue. Plus, it was the middle of the afternoon. I generally have a rule that I don't touch a drop until after work. But I had no work today. Soon, this would be the norm.

What was I going to do then? My biggest fear was turning into one of those old, retired broadcasters who filled their days with booze. It's an occupational hazard, and if I wasn't careful, I could easily be well on my way.

I opted for a diet soda and had a salad instead of french fries, the antidote to all the liquor I'd been consuming lately.

I ate my burger in silence and then headed home.

Traffic was light, and forty-five minutes later, I pulled into my garage and closed the door. I walked into the house, where Sophie greeted me with wet kisses. She wasn't used to seeing me home so early on a weekday, so I took her out back, and we played fetch for half an hour or so.

On the way back into the house, I reached inside my country-style mailbox, grabbed a handful of envelopes, and took them inside. I gave Sophie a rawhide chew to occupy her while I sorted the mail. There was nothing spectacular. The electric bill from PG&E. The water bill from the East Bay Municipal Utilities District. A solicitation for a reverse mortgage. Christ, am I that old already?

At the bottom of the stack was a sealed, plain white envelope. It had no writing on its front or back. I opened it and took out a folded white sheet of printer paper. As I unfolded it, something fell into the palm of my hand.

The laser-printed message was succinct and to the point.

LEAVE IT ALONE

I opened my palm to see what was enclosed in the note. It was a .38-caliber bullet.

TWENTY-FOUR

"**Y**OU OKAY?" LYNN asked as she stood in the middle of my living room.

"I'm an investigative journalist. This isn't even close to the first time I've been threatened," I said.

"That may be, but it's the first time a serial killer has threatened you."

"Come on, Sis, he's hardly the Zodiac."

"He's killed three people . . . that we know of. There may be more."

"Three?" I said.

"Ballistics came back on Joe Martin. Same .38 as the others."

"Christ, we've got to find Freddy Isherwood," I said. "Any word on a next of kin for big sister Carla?"

"Not yet. Got a friend in HR working on it," she said. "Chris . . ."

"I know what you're going to say," I said, "and the answer is no. I'm not moving to a hotel. That son of a bitch will not run me out of my own home."

She nodded.

"At least hold on to this," she said, extending her hand. In it was Auntie's old snub-nosed revolver.

"No!" I snapped. "No guns."

"You've got to be able to defend yourself, Big Bro."

"Not that way. I haven't lived in a house with a gun since we were kids, and I don't intend to start now."

"All right," she said. "Can't say I'm surprised."

She walked to my bar cart and filled two glasses with Johnnie Walker Blue.

"Here," she said, handing me one.

"I thought you said I was drinking too much," I said.

"You get a pass on days when somebody threatens to kill you."

We both drained our glasses.

"Now what?" I asked.

"Now we track down this tattooed bastard before he hurts anybody else."

"And Carla?"

"If she's still alive."

"You think he offed his own sister?"

"She's vanished. There's no trace of her. And like I said earlier, I can't find a death certificate anywhere."

"So, you think Freddy either killed her or did something to her?"

"Entirely possible," Lynn said, pouring another pair of scotches. This was weird. She didn't usually drink during the day either. Especially not on duty.

"This bullet thing's really got you spooked, doesn't it?"

"It does," she said. "It should have you spooked too."

"Lynn, I've been getting death threats since I first stepped before a television camera. Like I said, it comes with the territory."

Lynn took a healthy swig from her glass.

"A few years back, there was a guy who wanted to kill me because he said that I was sending him secret messages through the TV," I told her.

"Jeez. What happened?" she asked, refilling her glass and topping off mine.

"Station security notified the authorities, who picked him up. He said he had nothing against me personally. He only wanted me to stop beaming the messages into his head. I told the cops I was clandestinely communicating with him through the tube. I was telling him to fuck off."

I caught Lynn in mid swallow with that. She almost did a spit take.

"I'm going to be okay, Sis."

"Well, if you won't leave and you won't arm yourself, I'm at least going to have the sheriff's department keep an eye on the place."

"Okay," I relented. "If it'll make you feel better."

"It will," she said. "You're a pain in my ass, but you're the only brother I've got."

The vibrating hum of her iPhone punctuated her words. She pulled it out of her jacket pocket and answered.

"What have you got?" she barked. "Good work. Thanks."

She clicked off.

"Bingo," she said. "Carla Isherwood's next of kin is her mother in Fairfield."

TWENTY-FIVE

LYNN FEARED THAT in light of Carla's firing, her mom might not have the warm fuzzies for the SFPD, so I reached out to Martha Isherwood, and she agreed to see us the following afternoon.

Fairfield, California, is about forty miles from the heart of San Francisco. It's the midway point between that city and the state capitol in Sacramento.

It's a military town that's home to Travis Air Force Base. It's also the home of Jelly Belly, the company that made the jellybeans that Ronald Reagan was so enamored with during his presidency.

Martha Isherwood lived in a tract house in one of Fairfield's working-class neighborhoods. Though the house was older, the pride of ownership was evident. It was well maintained with what appeared to be a fresh coat of paint and a neatly manicured patch of lawn that mimicked those of her neighbors, who primarily earned their livings by supporting the military or military families in some fashion, such as retail, restaurants, or personal services. A military base brings a lot of work to a community.

We rang the bell, and it was answered by a slight woman with black hair, much too dark for her pale, aging skin. She was in her mid- to late sixties. Her eyes were blue, like her daughter's, and she and Carla shared the same narrow nose and high cheekbones. Age and gravity appeared to have avoided her waistline and figure. She must have been a striking woman in her youth.

Martha Isherwood wore a floral dress at least twenty years out of style and white low-top tennis shoes. They were the kind that Auntie used to call "tennies." You could find them tied together by their laces in the discount bin at Kmart. It was evident that she was doing her best to present well. Apparently, company didn't come a-callin' very often.

"Mrs. Isherwood?" I asked.

"Yes."

"I'm Topher Davis. We spoke on the phone."

"Yes," she said. "I've been expecting you. I've been following you for years. It's nice to meet you in person."

"It's nice to meet you too," I said, extending my hand for her to shake.

She took it. Her skin was rough. Her hands calloused. I must have reacted in some noticeable way.

"Please excuse my hands. I've been doing a lot of work around the house recently," she said.

"No problem at all," I replied. "Your house and yard are lovely. This is my sister, Detective Lynn Sloan of the SFPD."

"Ma'am," Lynn said, extending her hand.

"SFPD? Has something happened?" Martha said.

"Just a routine investigation."

Martha looked Lynn over briefly before saying, "Please, come in." She opened the door wide.

She led us inside, and we sat on a couch draped with three large, white lace doilies. Martha sat in an easy chair across from us. A silver-plated coffee set sat on a dark brown table between us. Next to it were three china cups with matching saucers. The china pattern consisted of rust-colored flowers, their long stems intertwined against a white backdrop.

"I made us some coffee," she said. "Would you care for a cup?"

"We'd love some," Lynn said, trying to ingratiate herself with the woman.

Martha Isherwood filled two of the flowered cups with coffee.

"Cream and sugar?" she asked.

Lynn and I both declined.

Shaky hands offered us cups of coffee that began to spill onto the saucers. Lynn and I quickly relieved her of them. Once free from the balancing act, she massaged her palms and digits.

"I'm sorry," she said. "I'm a little nervous. I've never entertained a celebrity before."

"Don't worry about it, ma'am," I said. "I put my pants on one leg at a time, just like everybody else."

"I guess I should also let you know that I'm in the early stages of Parkinson's disease. I'm a little shaky today."

"I'm sorry," Lynn said. "How long have you known?"

"I was diagnosed about six months ago," she said, her hands settling as the tremor subsided.

"How are you doing?" I asked.

"Good days and bad," she replied.

I sipped my coffee. It was so much better than what they served at 850 Bryant.

I glanced around the room. Like the rest of the little place, it was neat and tidy. I felt like we were on a visit to Grandma's house. I was surprised that she didn't have a batch of freshly baked Toll House cookies to offer us.

A five-by-seven-inch photo in a silver frame sat at the far end of the coffee table. Two towheaded kids who appeared to be between eight and ten years of age mugged for the camera.

"Those your kids?" I asked.

"That's them," Martha Isherwood said. "Adorable, weren't they?"

"They were. Where are they now?" Lynn said, getting to the point.

Martha, her hands now steady, poured herself a cup of coffee and added a splash from the small silver creamer.

"Your guess is as good as mine."

"I'm sorry," I said. "I don't understand."

Martha Isherwood shook her head. "Our family's story is . . . complicated," she said, taking a dainty sip.

I half-expected her to extend her pinky finger as she drank.

"How so?" Lynn inquired.

Martha took another sip of coffee, frowned, and added more cream.

"It's okay," I said. "We have time. We'd love to hear your story."

"My children's father, Fred Senior, was older than me. Twenty years. Carla was a surprise. I was practically a child myself. Barely out of my teens when she was born. Two years later, Freddy came along."

I nodded and finished my cup of coffee. Martha Isherwood immediately refilled it.

"With older fathers, there is an increased possibility of . . . complications," she said.

"Developmental issues," Lynn said, nodding.

"Among other things," she said. "Carla came out just fine. Exceptional actually. Smart as a whip. As for Fred Junior . . . Freddy had some difficulties."

"What kind of 'difficulties'?" Lynn asked.

"We learned that he was . . . different early on," Martha Isherwood said. "He just wasn't developing like Carla had. He was much slower. As a toddler, he wouldn't giggle or laugh like his sister did at that age. He couldn't form words easily as a toddler. He barely spoke at all until he was almost four. And the tantrums . . ."

She shook her head, finished her coffee, poured another cup, and added cream.

"We really knew he was different when he was about seven or eight. Freddy wasn't much for playing with other kids. He preferred to play alone. Or draw. He was a natural artist. Gifted. He could look at a cartoon on television once and then draw it on binder paper better than the animators."

She took a sip of coffee and added more cream.

"Anyway," she continued, "when he was five or six, I arranged a play date with one of the little boys in the neighborhood. They were here in the living room playing with Lincoln Logs. They were each building their own little cabins. They were playing together but apart. Like I said, Freddy wasn't much for playing with other kids.

"I went to the laundry room to pull some things out of the dryer. I couldn't have been gone for more than five minutes when I heard this . . . bloodcurdling scream.

"I ran back in here to discover that the boys had gotten hold of one of my husband's cigarette lighters and had apparently been playing with it when the neighbor boy's clothes caught fire.

"It was terrible. He had second- and third-degree burns. Ended up needing skin grafts. Awful."

"And Freddy?" Lynn asked.

"That's just it," Martha Isherwood said. "The neighbor boy was on fire. I was hysterical, yet Freddy . . . just stood there watching the flames. He didn't say a word. He just watched this little boy burn.

"I used a tablecloth to smother the flames and then called 911. An ambulance came to take the boy to the hospital. Freddy was indifferent. He just went back to playing with his Lincoln

Logs. It was like nothing had happened. The EMTs are strapping this smoldering kid to a gurney, and Freddy is calmly sitting on the floor playing. My husband and I got him tested after that. Severe developmental issues."

"I looked through your kids' high school yearbook. I see that Freddy went to regular school," I said.

"That was because of Carla," Martha Isherwood said. "Carla was the only person Freddy responded to. He became her shadow. Wherever she went, he went. No brother and sister were ever closer."

Lynn glanced in my direction and gave me a half smile.

"Carla insisted we send Freddy to school with her, so we did. His grades ranged from failing to mediocre, but she got him through his sophomore year. Once Carla graduated, he dropped out. She went to San Francisco State and studied criminal justice. Freddy followed her and audited all of her classes. They lived here. My husband left at the end of Carla's first semester in college. During the holidays, no less."

She cast her eyes on her cup as though looking for answers in her French Roast. Then she raised the cup to her lips and drank its contents.

"He was a supervisor at the Jelly Belly plant. Fell in love with his admin. A woman even younger than I was."

"I'm sorry," Lynn said.

"I should have seen it coming. I was Fred Senior's second wife. We became involved when I was his admin." Martha Isherwood chuckled as she poured herself another cup of coffee. "I guess Karma does indeed catch us all," she said.

"My ex-husband is a real piece of work. He cut off all ties, not just with me, but the kids too. His new girlfriend, excuse me . . . wife, I can't believe he married the bitch . . . wanted no reminders of his past life, I guess."

"How'd the kids take that?" I asked.

"Carla was just devastated, and she blamed me. She adored her father. She was a real daddy's girl," Martha Isherwood said. "She said that he left because of me. That I drove him away. Have you ever heard anything more ridiculous? She and Freddy moved someplace near campus. I haven't seen hide nor hair of either of them since."

"Nothing?" Lynn said.

"Not a peep. I kept up with what they were doing through mutual friends for a while. Kids they'd gone to high school with would tell their parents things, and they, in turn, would tell me," she said, pouring another cup of coffee. This lady liked her caffeine even more than I liked my scotch.

"I, of course, read about her problems with the police department. Beating that poor man. Just terrible," she said.

"Out of character for her?" Lynn asked.

"Well," Martha said, "I understand that the man called her a misogynistic name. Sexism for Carla is like a matador's red cape to a bull. You know she sued to play on the boys' baseball team?"

"I'd read that," I replied.

"If that man said what I heard he called her, the response is vintage Carla."

"What about Freddy?" I asked. "Have you heard anything about him?"

"Not really," she said. "I assume that he's with Carla. He certainly isn't self-sufficient. Carla was everything to him growing up. He wouldn't remember to tie his shoes if Carla didn't tell him to."

"Anything else you can tell us about him?" Lynn asked. "Did he have any hobbies? Was he into anything special?"

Martha Isherwood thought for a moment.

"As I said, he loved to draw. He loved Bugs Bunny. My husband . . . excuse me . . . ex-husband . . . bought him some videotapes of those old cartoons. He'd sit glued to the television for hours. In fact, it's how we'd calm him down if he was throwing a tantrum. We'd put on Bugs Bunny or Tweety Bird, and soon, he was off in his own animated world, watching and sketching them."

"If you should remember anything or hear anything, would you give us a call?" Lynn said, handing Martha an SFPD business card.

"Of course," she said, taking the card and running her fingertips over its raised lettering. "But I don't know what else I can tell you. I haven't heard anything about either of them in years. What's this all about? Why are you looking for my children?"

"Just part of a routine investigation," Lynn said.

"Your card says 'Homicide.' Has someone been killed?"

"Unfortunately, I can't go into details about an ongoing investigation," Lynn said. "But we appreciate your cooperation and any help you can give us."

"It must be quiet around here with it being just you," I said, quickly changing the subject.

"I'll admit that it's lonely at times. I miss my family, but I try to stay busy," she explained. "Like I said, I've been working on the house. I painted it inside and out. Next, I'll put new linoleum in the master bathroom."

"You're pretty handy," I said. "I can't change a lightbulb."

She laughed. "YouTube has a video for everything. I figure it out," she said. "It's challenging sometimes when my Parkinson's is acting up."

"If you don't mind my asking, what do you do for money?" I inquired.

"The one decent thing my ex did was let me have the house," she told us. "It's paid for, so I have a roof over my head. Everything else comes from my business."

"What do you do?" Lynn asked.

"I have an Etsy store selling knickknacks that I drop ship from China. Porcelain figurines. Things like that. I also have an eBay store," she said.

"God bless the gig economy," I said, finishing the last of my coffee.

About half an hour later, Lynn and I cruised the Lexus up I-80 West across the Carquinez Bridge back toward San Francisco.

"So, what do you think?" I asked. "Was she being straight with us? About not knowing where her kids are?"

"I think so," Lynn said.

"I believe her too. I found her information on brother Freddy particularly enlightening."

"I know what you mean. Developmentally stunted. Extremely susceptible to suggestion from his sister."

"Not to mention that fire story," I said. "A complete and total lack of any empathy."

"Would make it easy to gun down a man in his driveway and leave him for his wife and daughters to find," Lynn said.

"So, you think Carla is having her brother do her dirty work? Settling old scores against the cops she blames for getting her fired?" I asked.

Lynn nodded.

"Possibly."

"That still doesn't answer the question of timing. Why now?" I asked.

"I've been thinking about that," Lynn said. "Try this on. Carla beats a handcuffed suspect while in the company of three other officers. They are instrumental in getting her fired for excessive force. Then, throughout their careers, they kill unarmed African Americans and get to keep their jobs."

"Not to mention the months of administrative leave. In essence, a paid vacation," I added. "It would piss me off."

"The Driscoll shooting of that kid in the city is the last straw. So, Carla plots the murders and gives Freddy explicit directions on carrying them out, right down to using a revolver so as not to leave any shell casings that could somehow be traced back to them," Lynn said. "Hell, she probably supplied the gun."

"It makes sense," I agreed.

"She gets him to steal a Prius and license plates, knowing how popular that car is in these parts, which makes it nondescript," Lynn said.

"And she knows that if he ever messes up and gets caught, there's no way her brother rats her out," I surmised.

"And even if he does, with his diminished mental capacity ... Let's just say I don't see the court throwing the book at him. Even for three murders," Lynn stated.

"One thing bothers me," I said. "How does Odell Watkins fit into all of this? It's obvious Dr. Stevens didn't want us to talk to him. Then he suddenly up and dies."

"That part bothers me too. I don't know what the answer is. I think we should look into the background of the good doctor," Lynn said.

We soon found ourselves in Emeryville near the Golden Gate Fields Racetrack. Traffic was at a standstill, as it always is on this stretch of the freeway 24/7.

"How do we find Carla Isherwood?" I asked.

"By somehow tracking down Freddy," she said.

"If it were only that easy. You say there were just those three other cops on that police report?"

"Yep."

"If your revenge theory is correct, then it's mission accomplished. He's done killing and probably in the wind right now."

"Maybe. Maybe not," she countered.

"What do you mean?"

"A few things," she said. "Where have Carla and Freddy been all this time? Why does she completely drop off the grid once she's dismissed from the department?"

Something occurred to me.

"You think she could be dead?"

"That's theory number two. That would explain why there's no record of her after the firing."

"That doesn't make any sense in one regard," I said. "If Carla's dead, that would mean Freddy is acting of his own accord. If Martha is to be believed, he just doesn't have the mental capacity to do that. Can you see him planning these murders alone and being clever enough to elude police?"

"No, I can't," she said. "But that doesn't mean there isn't another Geppetto pulling the puppet strings."

TWENTY-SIX

THAT NIGHT, KENDRA came over with pizza and champagne. We ate, drank, and watched Netflix before she fell asleep on my sofa. I covered her with one of the quilts that Auntie made me when I was a kid.

Auntie was always quilting. It was her one form of relaxation after dealing with work and single parenthood. She'd take my old trousers and jeans she picked up from the thrift store and make these heavy pants quilts. I loved them. There was something comforting about being cocooned in one of those weighty covers. I felt . . . safe.

I quietly walked out of the living room and into my den, where I fired up my laptop and did a Google search for Dr. Andrew Stevens. There were several, including a podiatrist in Los Angeles, a Sacramento orthodontist, and a physicist and lecturer at Stanford. Nothing for Doctor Andy or Andrew Stevens caring for the disabled in the Bay Area.

I Googled Odell Watkins and found a few stories about his shooting and Phil Curtain's exoneration and administrative leave. Joe Martin is mentioned in passing as "another officer on the scene." Odell doesn't appear anywhere else online until his obituary. Nothing there that I didn't already know. The shooting. Ill health. His previous work as a warehouse laborer.

It was the last line of the obit that caught my eye.

Mr. Watkins is survived by two sisters, Mrs. Lillian Russell of Antioch, California, and Mrs. Fern Mason of Glendale, California, as well as two nephews, Mr. Michael Brooks of Akron, Ohio, and Mr. Taronte Rogers of Oakland.

Taronte Rogers aka Malik Otumba.

It explained a lot. Taronte Rogers must have been a teenager when Curtain shot his uncle Odell. He watched the man deteriorate from his injuries for years. Then when Ferguson happens and multiple videos of police killings are splashed across the news and social media, he becomes radicalized, changes his name, and forms the Black Sentinels for Justice.

Otumba's group advocates the killing of cops. We've got video of a masked driver, who is probably Freddy Isherwood, leaving the scene of the Driscoll killing and definitive video of him at Phil Curtain's shop, but there's no way he planned it alone.

Could Otumba be the puppeteer here? Could *he* be planning these killings and making Freddy his personal assassin? It would certainly be in line with his stated philosophy.

If Otumba is behind the whole thing, why target only the cops who got Freddy's sister fired? Was that how Otumba got Freddy on board?

"Cops destroyed your sister. Do it for her, Freddy."

And why keep us from talking to Uncle Odell? He sustained injuries in that shooting that ultimately cost him his life. He'd have every reason in the world to want Phil Curtain dead, yet he lacked the physical capability to do it himself. Could he have somehow been involved in this?

I picked up the phone to call Lynn and tell her what I'd discovered when I was interrupted by a tired, "Whatcha doin'?"

Kendra stood in the doorway of my den, wiping sleepy eyes.

"Just catching up on a few things," I said, putting the phone down. "You were sleeping so peacefully. I didn't want to disturb you."

She walked over to me and kissed my cheek.

"Thoughtful man," she said.

"Want to stay over?"

"May I?"

"Always." I closed my laptop, and Kendra took my hand and led me to the bedroom.

TWENTY-SEVEN

I AWOKE EARLY the next morning to find a note from Kendra that she was due in court and would see me that night. I showered, brushed my teeth, shaved, and got dressed. Then I walked, fed, and watered Sophie, jumped in the Lexus, and headed for The Egg. Lynn was already there, seated at our regular table, sipping tea.

I told her what I'd discovered.

"Wow," she said. "That opens up a whole world of possibilities. So, Odell and Malik decide they want revenge and somehow get Freddy to go along. He commits the murders, and their hands don't get dirty."

"That's what I'm thinking," I said. "And Dr. Stevens is part of this in some way too. He doesn't let us see Odell because the old man is sick, and Malik is afraid he might have an attack of conscience or something and spill the whole plot."

"A couple of things, though . . ." she said. "Revenge against Curtain and Martin, I can understand, but how does Mickey Driscoll fit into all of this? He had nothing to do with the Odell shooting."

"I'm not sure," I said.

"And ..."

"I know," I said. "Where's Carla? Let's assume that Carla is dead. Who killed her? And why?"

"I don't see Freddy offing his own sister, especially as close as Martha Isherwood says they were."

"Who knows," I said. "Maybe she did it herself."

"What makes you think that?" Lynn asked, raising a cup of chamomile tea to her lips.

"I had Mandy go through our station's archives and see what was there on the Isaac Wilson beating. Isherwood was vilified at the time. The press, civil rights groups—everybody called her a racist. That kind of pressure can be too much for anyone to take."

"Then where's her body?" Lynn said.

"People jump off the Golden Gate Bridge and wash out to sea every day," I stated.

Lynn drank some more tea. "Okay, let's go with your theory for a minute. Let's say you're on the nose with all of this. Where's Freddy Isherwood been all this time, and how do we tie him to Malik Otumba?"

"That part I haven't quite figured out yet," I confessed.

Jared walked over to the table and kissed his wife. I shook my head.

"You guys and your public displays of affection," I said. "Sickening."

"My poor cynical brother-in-law. One must work to keep the flame of love ablaze," Jared said, planting another one on my sister.

I rolled my eyes.

"Speaking of which," Lynn said, "Mandy and I talked a little about your new girlfriend. Says that Kendra's the last thing you need in your life right now."

"Mandy needs to mind her own business," I stated.

"Look," Lynn said, "you're just out of a long-term relationship and—"

I covered my ears with my hands. "La La La," I sang.

"Oh, grow up!" Lynn snapped.

I removed my hands from my ears.

Jared looked at the floor. He'd watched us have sibling spats for years, and they always made him uncomfortable.

"It isn't any of your business, either," I snapped back.

She took a sip of her tea. "You've been hurt pretty badly," she said softly. "I'd hate to see you hurt even more."

"I know what I'm doing," I said.

"Do you? You've had some major life changes. Sarah. The station," she said. "Have you thought about what you will do once your job ends?"

"I don't know. Maybe I'll join the circus. I could become a fire-eater or a knife thrower. The carnies taught me skills to fall back on."

Lynn shook her head.

"I appreciate your concern, little sis. Truly . . . I do. Stop worrying. I'm going to be okay," I said with confidence.

"I hope so. At least you've cut back on your drinking since you've been seeing this new woman. Have you checked with her about dinner Friday night yet?"

Shit. I forgot. Or was it that I really didn't want to?

"Not yet."

"Get on it," my sister ordered.

"So, are we going to talk to Malik Otumba again?" I asked, quickly changing the subject.

"Not yet. We've got zero proof of anything. Just conjecture. All we're going to get from him is attitude."

"Well then . . . What now?"

"I'll put somebody on surveillance of both Malik and the Sentinels' HQ," she said. "In the meantime, I want to talk to Dr. Stevens and see what he knows."

"That's a waste of time. He's just gonna stonewall us with that HIPPA bullshit."

"I've got a friend who investigates Medicare fraud. Maybe the threat of somebody looking into his records and billing will loosen his tongue," she replied.

"How do you know he's committing Medicare fraud?"

"I don't. But I *do* know that an audit and a government investigation are real pains in the ass, even if you're as clean as a whistle. *Nobody* wants that kind of scrutiny."

I ordered an omelet with Monterey Jack cheese, mushrooms, and bell peppers. Lynn had more tea with a side of avocado toast.

Whoever came up with the idea of spreading some avocado on a piece of toast and then charging ten bucks for it is a frigging genius.

As we ate, Lynn tried to glean more information from me about my relationship with Kendra. It can be challenging having a sister who's a trained interrogator. It must be tough for her to have a brother who knows how and when to keep his mouth shut—most of the time.

After breakfast, we took Lynn's unmarked to Mercy Hospital. We parked in the lot and entered the reception area, where we saw the same receptionist who'd first greeted us. Her eyes were red as though she'd been crying.

Lynn flashed her badge. "We'd like to speak with Dr. Stevens," she said.

It was a command. Not a request.

"You can't," the receptionist said. "Dr. Stevens is dead."

"What?" Lynn said. "How?"

"Car crash. Last night on 580 near Pleasanton," the receptionist said. "I don't have all the details. They say that he ran into a truck."

TWENTY-EIGHT

WE DROVE THE few miles back to The Egg, and Lynn reached out to Sergeant Dale Harris of the California Highway Patrol. I was on a first-name basis with Dale. He was one of the CHP officers who frequented The Egg and helped me by providing background on more than a few of my stories.

He was a thin man in his early forties with wire-rimmed glasses and a distinguished graying of his brown hair at the temples. He stood a towering six foot five, which is intimidating if you're unlucky enough to be pulled over by him.

We found Dale at a table near the front of the restaurant, about to attack a tower of pancakes. He spotted us as he began to drown the flapjacks in syrup.

"Well, what have we got here?" he said. "What do you hear? What do you say?"

Dale always greeted everybody that way. It was a line from an old James Cagney movie. *Angels with Dirty Faces*, I think.

"Same ole, same ole," I replied. "We need to ask a favor . . ."

"You're right," he said, chuckling with a mouthful of pancakes. "It is the same ole."

"Can you get us an accident report?" Lynn asked.

"Freeway smashup or city?" he asked, adding a dollop of whipped butter to his next forkful.

"Freeway," Lynn said. "Interstate 580 in Pleasanton."

"Give me a day," Dale said. "I'll have it here tomorrow morning. You're buying breakfast."

"I wouldn't have it any other way," Lynn said, scribbling Dr. Stevens's name and the location of the accident in the notepad she carried. She tore off a sheet and handed it to him.

"Thanks," I said as we went out the door and headed to the parking lot.

"So . . . either all of the people surrounding this case are jinxed . . . or somebody is indeed tying up loose ends," I remarked.

"Hold your horses," Lynn said. "Sometimes an accident is just an accident."

"Where you off to?" I asked.

"To see what I can find on Dr. Stevens."

"Good. I'm going into the station to see if Mandy has come up with anything."

I made it into the station a little after eleven and had a brief production meeting with Stu and Mandy in one of the editing bays.

"I don't know where we go from here," I told them.

"Well," Mandy said, "while you were out playing Sherlock Holmes with Lynn, I got Janet Driscoll to give us an interview on camera."

"That's wonderful! How?"

"I don't know what you said when you talked with her, but she trusts you. She says she knows you'll be fair to Mickey."

"Of course I will," I said. "We don't do hit pieces."

A sinking feeling kicked me in the pit of my stomach. Soon, I wouldn't be doing any pieces at all.

"So, we've got Janet Driscoll and Sheila Williams," I said.

"And Edna Curtain," Stu added. "Plus, Theo Long and company up in Twain Harte."

"That's good, but we need more," I told them.

"What now, then?" Mandy asked.

"I'm not sure," I said. "Phil Curtain is dead. Joe Martin is dead. The man Curtain shot is dead, and so is his doctor."

"His doctor?" Mandy said, putting a hand over her mouth in surprise.

"The dead bodies sure are piling up, ain't they?" Stu said, shaking his head.

"That they are," I replied. "Mandy, were you able to get anything new out of Mrs. Curtain?"

"Not much. Phil was retired. Running his store," she said. "Fishing when he had the time off. She said that he felt awful about the Odell Watkins shooting. He lived with it every day. She said he almost quit the force the day after it happened."

"I'm not surprised. The common misconception is that these cops are dispassionate about the lives they upend when they make a mistake like that. It isn't true. They're human beings too. Janet Driscoll told me how haunted Mickey was about the Jamal shooting," I said. "I guess calling administrative leave a 'paid vacation' is really unfair. Killing a person, justified or not, messes with a cop's head. The last thing you want is for him—"

"Or her," Mandy interrupted.

"Or her," I corrected, "back on the street the next day."

"I talked to a lieutenant over at Bryant Street. She told me that before they're let back on active duty after a shooting incident, there's a psych eval and everything, part of the reason Mickey

Driscoll took some leave beyond the admin time off," she said. "He wasn't ready to go back to work."

"We've got some good stuff," I said. "But there's more to this story. We have three dead cops."

Mandy asked, "You and Lynn making any progress?"

"One step forward, two steps back," I told her.

"The serial murderer Cha Cha," Stu said.

"I want you to talk to Martha Isherwood. This time on camera," I decided.

"Why? She says she has no idea where her kids are."

"Fresh eyes," I said. "I think Carla Isherwood is the key to this whole thing. Talk to her mother on camera. See if there's anything Lynn and I missed. Anything at all that might be a lead on where to find Carla and Brother Freddy."

"I really don't see what I'm gonna pick up that you guys didn't, but okay," Mandy agreed.

Stu ran long fingers through graying hair. "I'm with Mandy. I don't see what you expect us to learn, but you're the boss," he agreed.

"For now," I said. The words hung in the air, creating an uncomfortable silence.

"I'll go load up the camera," Stu said, leaving the editing bay.

Once we were alone, I turned to Mandy. "What's with you talking to my sister about Kendra?" I snapped.

"I'm concerned. I thought she needed to know."

"Why? Why did my sister need to know?"

"Because we love you, dumb ass. We know you aren't in a good place right now. You haven't been since Sarah left. You've been drinking too much. Now, you've got to deal with the bullshit around here at work—"

"I'm fine," I said.

"You are a lot of things, my friend, but 'fine' isn't one of them," she stated.

"Just stay out of my business and help me finish this story before they throw my behind out on the street."

She shook her head, grabbed a clipboard and a stack of papers, and left me alone in the editing bay.

I looked at the frozen image of Janet Driscoll on the monitor. She looked less haggard than she did the day of the funeral. More put together and relaxed. The bun was gone, and her hair was down, cascading gently over her shoulders. Her makeup was flawless; the smudged mascara and red eyes from crying were nowhere present. They say that resolving grief is just a matter of time and distance.

I pressed PLAY.

"It's important to me that people know how Mickey lived. Not just how he died," Janet Driscoll said.

Funny, that's the same thing Sheila Williams said about Jamal. They're both keepers of their loved ones' legacies.

"What was he into?" Mandy asked off camera and picked up by Janet's lavalier mic clipped to her blouse. "I mean, when he wasn't working?"

"He loved classic cars," she was saying. "I don't think I was the love of his life. His old Thunderbird was. He restored it himself. Spent five years of Saturdays on that damn car. He had just finished driving it when . . ."

Her voice trailed off.

"It's okay," Mandy could be heard saying. "Take your time."

Janet Driscoll wiped her eyes. There goes the mascara.

"I'm sorry," she said. "What was the question?"

"Mickey's other interests," Mandy repeated.

"He was a terrible golfer," Janet said, composing herself. "But he liked it. He kept trying to get me to come out and play with him. Chasing a white ball around with a metal stick is not my idea of a fun afternoon."

"Mine either," Mandy laughed.

"I did go fishing with him occasionally. He liked Lake Chabot in Castro Valley. Sometimes, he'd fish at the Berkeley Marina or Alameda Beach."

I pressed the pause button.

Alameda Beach.

I pulled out my phone and dialed the number I had for Janet Driscoll. She picked up on the first ring.

"Hi, Mrs. Driscoll. It's Topher Davis."

"Hello, Mr. Davis. This is a nice surprise."

"I wanted to thank you for talking to my crew on camera."

"Mandy is a sweet girl. I was glad to do it," she said.

"How are you doing?" I asked.

"I guess about as well as can be expected under the circumstances. I've only had one good cry today."

"I'm glad to hear that you're hanging in there."

"Getting through this one tear at a time."

"I was watching the footage of the interview you were kind enough to give," I said. "You mentioned that Mickey liked to fish."

"Next to driving his T-bird and golfing, it was his favorite thing in the world to do," she said.

"Do you, by chance, know where he bought his fishing gear?"

She thought for a moment. "There is a fishing tackle store in Alameda. It's owned . . . it was owned . . . by that other officer who was killed."

"Do you know how long Mickey had been going out there?"

"Not very. He'd been buying a lot of his stuff from Amazon. About a month before he died, he started shopping at the store in Alameda," she stated. "Why do you ask?"

"Just background information for our piece," I told her. "That's all."

"Feel free to call me anytime. Anything I can do to help," she said. "Do you know if the police have any leads? They aren't telling me anything. Do they know who murdered my husband and those other officers?"

"I understand they're pursuing several different angles," I said.

I heard a slight sniffle on the phone.

"I'm sorry," she said. "It comes and goes."

"Of course. I'm sorry. I didn't mean to upset you."

"No. I want to help," she told me. "I need to do something. Feel useful."

"You're being very helpful. I appreciate you talking to us."

"Anything to find out who did this," she said.

"Tell me . . . When Mickey would go fishing in Alameda, would he go alone?"

She thought for a moment.

"I really don't know. I don't recall him mentioning anybody else," she said. "Fishing was like therapy for him. He said it gave him time to think."

"Did he ever mention the name Carla Isherwood?"

"Oh . . . her." Janet Driscoll said as though she was spitting something terrible out of her mouth.

"What's *she* got to do with this?" she asked.

"Just more background," I said. "What do you know about her?"

"Not much," Janet Driscoll reported. "Mickey was paired with her for a minute during her probationary period. He said she was a real loose cannon. Real gung ho. Too macho even for him." She laughed. "Can you imagine?"

"Did you ever meet her?"

"Once. I dropped off some lunch for Mickey at the station, and he introduced her."

"You don't sound like a fan," I said.

"I don't like passive-aggressive people. Especially when they're other women."

"She was aggressive?"

"Like I said, 'passive.'"

"How so?"

"Lots of ways. Like when Mickey introduced her, I put out my hand for her to shake, and she squeezed like she was trying to break every bone in it. It was like she was saying, 'I don't shake hands like a girl,'" Janet said. "It was just weird."

"Do you know what happened to her? Do you know if Mickey ever saw her again once she was dismissed?"

"It's funny you should ask that."

"Why?"

"We were at dinner a few months ago. Mickey had been keeping a low profile since the . . . incident, but I finally got him to take me out to dinner in the city. The Slanted Door. You know that fancy restaurant on the pier where all the movie stars go when they're in town?"

"I know it well," I said.

"We ordered, and I went to the ladies' room. When I got back to the table, a woman was leaving. Mickey was as white as a sheet. I thought another one of those nuts threatened him about the shooting."

"What did he say?"

"That it was nobody. Just some woman who recognized him from the news and said something nasty. He was very evasive, so I let it go."

"Did you get a look at her?"

"Just the back of her head. She had long, blond hair."

"What makes you think the woman was Carla Isherwood?"

"I don't know. Just a feeling, I guess. I do know that whoever this woman was in the restaurant, she creeped Mickey out. There was something about Carla that did the same thing to him. I could be completely off base," she said. "I never saw her face. Poor Mickey was so shaken up that he didn't even eat his dinner."

I heard her sniffle.

"It was the last time he took me out."

"I'm sorry."

"What does Carla have to do with this?"

"We'd just like to talk to her. That's all. Will you do me a favor and holler if you remember anything else about her? Anything that might help us locate her?"

"Of course," she replied.

"How are your girls doing?" I asked.

"About as well as can be expected. Like me, they're taking it all one day at a time. Grief ebbs and flows."

"That it does," I said. "That it does."

I called Lynn and told her about my conversation with Janet Driscoll.

"So, he was in touch with Phil Curtain. Not unusual. They knew each other when they were both with the department," she said. "They were both part of the Isaac Wilson incident."

"Try this on for size," I said. "Mickey takes his wife out to dinner, and he is approached by a woman she thinks may have been Carla Isherwood. The woman says something to Mickey that puts the fear of God into him. So much so that he looked up Phil Curtain so that they could put their heads together and decide what to do about it. Unfortunately, they both ended up dead before they got the chance."

"Okay," she said, "I'll play along. Let's say it was Carla in the restaurant. What does she have over Mickey that would spook him like that? And where the hell has she been all this time?"

"That's what we need to find out."

TWENTY-NINE

"**I**'VE GOT GOOD news," Kendra said as she handed me my second Johnnie Walker Blue of the night.

"You're going to spend another evening playing house with me?"

"Besides that," she said.

"Okay, I'll bite," I said, taking a pull from the scotch. "What's your good news?"

"The department is settling in the Jamal Williams shooting."

"When was this decided?"

"This afternoon. I got a call from their general counsel that they've agreed to a number my client can live with. I guess they just want this over. Especially with all of this police murder stuff in the news."

"That makes sense," I said, taking a second sip of my drink. It was nice that she was stocking my favorite liquor at her place.

"I just have to dot a few i's and cross a few t's, and my business is concluded," she informed me.

I pulled her onto my lap. "What about our business?" I asked.

"Oh, that's far from concluded," she said, kissing me.

"So, how much did they settle for?"

"Now, you know I can't tell you that," she said, kissing me with gin-and-tonic-coated lips. "Besides, what about our agreement about church and state?"

"Thought that only applied to my house," I said, draining my glass.

"Let's just say that you won't be picking up dinner checks for this girl for quite a while."

"Congratulations."

She gave me a deep kiss. It was one of those kisses that made you feel like you'd never truly been kissed before that very moment.

"Why don't you take me into the bedroom and congratulate me properly?" she asked.

"Well," I said, taking her by the hand, "can't be rude."

The next morning, Sergeant Dale Harris walked into The Egg as I was polishing off my second cup of coffee, and Lynn was finishing her tea. Even though he was tall and reed thin, Dale had a build that looked thick around the middle when he wore his bulletproof vest as he did that morning. He pulled up a chair and sat at the table between us.

"What do you hear? What do you say?" he said. "Sorry I'm late—three-car accident on I-680. Acura slammed on its brakes and got rear-ended by an Intrepid going 70, which was then rear-ended by a Mazda going 80. It's a miracle that nobody got killed."

Jared appeared with an empty cup and a pot of black coffee. He placed the cup in front of Dale and poured it before refilling a cup for me.

"Want some more tea, babe?" he asked Lynn.

"I'm fine for now, honey. Thanks," she said.

He turned his attention to Dale and me.

"And what will you gentlemen have this lovely morning? Pancakes?" he asked Dale.

"Nah," Dale said. "Your wife is buying. I'll have corned beef hash and eggs."

Jared took out his pen and began scribbling. "Poached or over easy?" he said, writing.

"Over easy, please," Dale said. "And let's make it three eggs instead of two. And some dry rye toast."

"Be right up," Jared said. He looked at me and Lynn.

"Just coffee for me," I said.

"I'll have your hash right up, Dale," Jared said, leaving the table.

Dale took three packets of sugar, tore them open simultaneously, and dumped them in his coffee. He then poured in some cream, stirred the concoction, and took a satisfied sip.

"Diabetes much?" I asked.

"Hey, the extra boost keeps up my energy."

"What'd you find out?" Lynn said.

He pulled a folded pink piece of paper from his shirt pocket, unfolded it, and gave it to Lynn.

"You didn't get this from me," he said.

Lynn nodded, looking over what he'd given her.

"Your Dr. Stevens wasn't as lucky as the three I just left," Dale said. "He was driving his Jaguar and rear-ended a semi. Hell, he practically drove under the thing. The top of his car was sheared off, along with his head."

I let out a "Good Lord."

"Any idea what happened? Was he texting or something?" Lynn asked.

"No idea. We haven't gone through his phone yet."

He took another sip of coffee, grimaced, and poured two more sugar packets into his mug. "One thing's for sure. The doc apparently wasn't up on his auto maintenance."

"What do you mean?" I asked.

"His brake lines. Not a drop of fluid in them."

Jared returned to the table with Dale's breakfast and refilled the officer's coffee cup.

Dale repeated his three-sugars routine.

"Any idea if his brake lines were tampered with?" I asked.

"Too early to tell," he said. "They'll go through what's left of the vehicle sometime today."

"But it *is* possible somebody drained them?"

"I supposed it's possible," he said, raising a fork to his lips.

He put the fork into his mouth and chewed. Then he reached for the saltshaker and sprinkled a generous amount on his food.

"How are you still alive the way that you eat?" I asked.

"Good genes," he said. "Grandpa Harris made it to 103."

"Tell me," Dale said, "what's this all about?"

"Maybe nothing," Lynn replied.

"And maybe . . .?" Dale said before refilling his mouth.

"I'm not sure," she said.

I filled him in on what we knew about Odell Watkins, his shooting by Phil Curtain, and the caginess of Dr. Stevens.

"Ya know," Dale said, his mouth full of hash, "Watkins was old. Maybe he really was too sick to talk to you."

Lynn's phone buzzed, and she answered it.

"You're kidding," she said. "We'll be right there."

She turned off her phone and dropped it into the pocket of her windbreaker.

"What's up?" I asked.

"They just picked up Freddy Isherwood."

THIRTY

LICENSE PLATE READERS have been the bane of privacy advocates ever since they were first introduced into the arsenals of some Bay Area police departments a few years back. They consist of a camera, processing unit, and software installed in a patrol car. As the cop car makes the rounds, the scanner photographs the license plates of every vehicle it passes. The photographs are then instantly processed through the software to see if the plates are linked to any crime or if the vehicle is stolen.

Privacy advocates say that this technology constitutes an illegal search. Proponents say there is no expectation of privacy when you're driving an exposed license plate down a public street. So far, the courts have agreed.

Freddy Isherwood was driving a white Prius down East 14th Street in San Leandro when he passed an SLPD patrol car. San Leandro was one of the first cities in the region to employ the new technology, which was unfortunate for Freddy, whose plates had been reported as stolen. He was pulled over, and while the plates, registration, and insurance information were all listed as belonging to Charles Woodbridge, Freddy's license had his own name on it.

He was arrested and placed in a holding cell in the downtown San Leandro PD. Luckily, Lynn knew the San Leandro police chief and was able to get us some time alone with him.

The chief, Chuck Burke, was relatively new to the position. A handsome six-footer in his early forties, he had grown up in San Leandro, been with the department since the Academy, and distinguished himself working through the ranks, eventually earning the top job when it became available. Lynn had known Burke since he was a patrolman and a regular at The Egg. She explained the situation as Burke walked us down a long hall past photos of all the chiefs since the city's incorporation in 1872.

"He said anything?" Lynn asked.

"Not a word. Not even to the officers who initially stopped him," Burke said. "He's an odd one."

"Was he carrying anything?" she asked.

"Yeah," I added, "like a .38-caliber revolver?"

As if it would be that simple.

"He's clean," Burke said. "Nothing but a wallet and his car keys."

"How'd you know who he was and know to call me?" Lynn asked.

"Your department put out a BOLO on him. He matched the description, and his license was in his wallet. When we ran his prints, he was in the system," Burke said.

"Here's his jacket," he told her, handing her a file folder.

I looked over her shoulder at the file.

"Mostly petty stuff," Burke stated. "Shoplifting, disturbing the peace."

Lynn flipped to a mugshot of a young Freddy. He looked to be about eighteen. It was pre-tattoo.

"Anything violent?" Lynn asked.

"One item of interest," Burke said, turning a page in the file.

Lynn read it.

"An arrest for ADW," she said.

"Yeah. He got into it with a woman at Costco over a Bugs Bunny DVD, of all things. The situation escalated, and he pulled out his fingernail clippers," Burke said, laughing. "He opened it to the nail file and attacked the woman."

"Was she hurt?" I asked.

"With a pair of nail clippers?" he laughed.

"9/11 started with a couple of box cutters," I reminded him.

"True," Burke said. "The court found him to be mentally incompetent. He was sent to the psychiatric hospital in Napa until he was deemed no longer a threat to himself or others."

"How long was he there?" I inquired.

"Three years," Burke said. "He just got out a few weeks ago."

"That," said Lynn, "is why the Driscoll killing didn't happen sooner."

We stopped in front of a wooden door with a gold plate that read INTERVIEW ROOM.

"Right now," Burke said, "as I see it, you have nothing to tie him to Driscoll. All we've got is a white Prius with stolen plates."

"He's close to his sister. Let me have a crack at him," Lynn said.

"Be my guest," Burke replied, opening the door.

We walked into a plain interview room with white walls and flat lighting. A dark wood conference table sat in the middle of the room with matching chairs on both sides. A sulking Freddy Isherwood sat with his left hand cuffed to a chair on the table's far side. He was a big, husky man. His large build reminded me of Hoss from the *Bonanza* reruns Lynn and I used to watch as kids.

He wore blue jeans and a Porky Pig tank top that showcased his muscular, tattooed arms. There must be one hell of a weight room at Napa.

Lynn sat in one of the chairs across from him. Burke and I stood leaning against the door.

"Hi, Freddy," Lynn said. "I'm Detective Sloan. You can call me Lynn."

"I want them," he said, pointing at Burke and me, "to go away."

His tone was that of a cranky little boy.

"They're okay, Freddy," she said in her best kindergarten teacher voice. "The policeman is Chief Burke. You've met him already. The other man is my brother, Chris."

"GO AWAY," he screamed at us.

Lynn gestured toward the door with her head for us to leave.

"It'll be all right," she told us.

Burke reluctantly opened the door and went through it. I followed. Once the door was closed, we stood in the hallway and watched the interrogation from a two-way mirror in the hall. Burke turned a knob on a speaker system that increased the volume enough for us to hear.

"It's okay, Freddy. They're gone," Lynn said.

Isherwood tried to fold his arms across his chest and failed, forgetting that his left wrist was cuffed to the chair.

"Freddy . . . May I call you Freddy?"

"That's my name, so I guess it's okay," he said. He spoke with the cadence and articulation of a child.

"And like I said, you can call me Lynn."

He said nothing, drawing imaginary pictures on the table with the index finger of his free hand.

"Freddy . . . I understand that you just got out of the hospital."

He said nothing—just more imaginary doodling.

"Did you like it at the hospital?" she asked.

He shrugged. "It was okay, I guess. On Fridays, we got green Jell-O."

"That sounds yummy!" she said so enthusiastically, even I believed her. "Where have you been since you left the hospital?"

He paused for a moment, thinking about the question. "Around."

"Are you staying with Carla?"

"Carla is dead!" he shouted.

"I'm sorry, Freddy," she said softly. "That must make you really sad."

He said nothing as he continued his imaginary drawing.

"What happened to Carla?"

"May I have some soda?" he asked.

"Sure. Any kind you want," she said. "What would you like?"

"Do you have 7UP? 7UP is my favorite. When I was in the hospital, they always let me have it."

I looked at Burke, who said, "The Coke machine is down the hall."

I walked down the hall. The floor was marble, and every footstep echoed.

I found the Coke machine, put my ATM card in, and paid two dollars to send a can of 7UP lumbering to the dispenser's opening. I grabbed the soda, took it to the interview room, and knocked. Lynn answered, took the soda, and mouthed, "Thank you."

I walked back over to Chief Burke and resumed my eavesdropping.

"Here you go," Lynn said, handing the can to Freddy Isherwood.

"My hand is stuck to the chair," he said. "Will you open it for me?"

"Of course," Lynn replied, popping the top.

Freddy Isherwood took the can in his free hand and downed the entire soda in seconds. He then let out a belch while singing the alphabet.

"A, B, C, D, E, F, G . . ." he sang.

He got as far as Q before running out of gas.

"That's pretty good," Lynn praised him.

"I made it all the way to Y once."

"Wow," Lynn said. "That's pretty far. I could never come close to that."

Freddy Isherwood went back to his imaginary drawing.

"You know who could make it all the way to Z?" she questioned.

"Who?" he asked, not looking up from his invisible masterpiece. There was a hint of admiration in his tone.

"My brother Chris, who you just met. He could get all the way to Z during a burp."

"Wow. That's cool."

"Could your sister do that? Could Carla get to Z?"

He chuckled. "Carla couldn't even get to E," he said. "She was no good at this game."

"Freddy, what happened to Carla?" Lynn asked softly.

Freddy Isherwood became agitated.

"She's dead. Carla is dead," he said.

"How did she die, Freddy?"

"The policemen killed her."

"What policemen killed her?"

Silence.

"How did the policemen kill her?" she persisted.

"Are you a policewoman?"

"Yes," Lynn said gently.

"Then I don't want to talk to you anymore! You killed Carla! The police killed Carla!"

"Well, there's your motive," Burke whispered to me.

"I didn't hurt Carla," Lynn said. "I would never hurt Carla."

Isherwood continued drawing on the table.

"Freddy, what are you drawing?"

Silence.

"Freddy?"

After a few more tries, Lynn got up and met us in the hall.

"Well, that was an experience," she said.

"Plus, you lied," I said. "I never made it past O during a belch."

Burke laughed.

Lynn gently punched my shoulder.

"The police killed Carla," Lynn said.

"So, he goes to Napa, and when he gets out, he kills the police he blames for her death," I said.

"Come on," Lynn pointed out. "You heard him. He's got the mind of a nine-year-old. Can you imagine him planning and getting away with three cop killings? Not to mention Odell Watkins and Dr. Stevens?"

"Let's not get ahead of ourselves. We don't know if Stevens and Watkins are even homicides," I replied.

"Okay, leave them out of it for now," she said. "You heard him, though. That's not a criminal mastermind in there. No way he planned all of this."

"Then who did? Because you're right. It sure as hell wasn't him," I said.

"He's being manipulated."

"Agreed. But by whom?" I asked.

Echoing footsteps quickly clicked their way down the hall as a young officer approached Burke. He was of medium height and build and had dark, wavy hair. What drew my attention was how youthful he appeared. He looked like he should be getting ready for the prom instead of carrying a badge and gun.

"This is Officer Fielding. He's the officer who apprehended your suspect," Burke said. "Fielding, Detective Lynn Sloan with SFPD and Topher Davis from Channel 6."

"Officer," Lynn nodded in his direction.

"Nice to meet you," I said.

"You might not think so after I tell you what we've got," Fielding nervously reported.

"What are you talking about?" Burke asked.

"We ran the VIN on the Prius. It's registered to the perp."

"Shit," Lynn said.

"So what?" I asked. "He's still driving a car with stolen plates and registration."

"It's a vehicle code violation, sir," Fielding told me.

"A misdemeanor. A fucking ticket," Lynn said with disgust.

"Are you saying . . . ?" I asked.

"We have to let him go," Burke stated.

"That's crazy. It makes no sense," I said. "Who steals plates and puts them on their own car?"

"You'd be surprised," Burke said. "People who want to avoid parking tickets. Bridge toll evaders."

"So, he just . . . walks?" I asked.

"One upside," Lynn interjected. "The Prius. You've impounded it, right?"

"We have," Fielding said. "Sitting in the impound yard right now."

"Mind if my evidence tech goes over the car? See if anything ties him to our murders?" she asked.

"We can hold onto it for three or four days," Burke said. "He'll have to petition the court and pay a fine to get it back. And you're going to need a warrant."

Lynn pulled out her cell phone and hit speed dial. Someone quickly answered on the other end. She made niceties for a few minutes and then explained the situation.

"I know, Your Honor," she said into the phone. "At the very least, he's a person of interest in multiple homicides. Police homicides."

She looked at me and rolled her eyes.

"Yes, it's his own car, but he's driving it with stolen plates. And it fits the description of the vehicle seen at two of our killings," she said with frustration.

A brief pause.

"Chief Burke figures three or four days," she continued.

She sighed, deflated.

"Okay," she said. "I've got it. Thank you for your time, Your Honor."

She clicked off.

"Judge Grimes is usually pretty friendly regarding these types of things. He says we don't have enough probable cause. He can't sign off on a warrant."

"So now what?" I asked.

"Grimes says we can search the car while it's in impound. His bogus plates, which incidentally constitute possession of stolen property, allow us to do that. For the forensics team to actually go through the vehicle, we need a warrant . . . and that we ain't got."

I shook my head.

"All this, and the guy just waltzes out of here," I said. "Can't you hold him on the possession of stolen property?"

"You know the 'bail reform' we've got now," Burke said. "Bail only on serious felonies. He'll be cited and released."

"At least we'll have eyes on him now that we know where he is," Lynn said.

"I'll make sure nobody goes near the vehicle until you guys do," Burke promised.

"Thanks," Lynn said.

"Okay," Burke said, "I'll cut him loose and put a couple of plainclothes officers on him."

"Thanks," she said. "Much appreciated."

"Anything to catch a cop killer," Burke told her, his tone grim. "Anything."

THIRTY-ONE

LYNN AND I hung around the SLPD headquarters for an hour and a half. At the same time, they cited Freddy Isherwood with California Vehicle Code section 10852 VC for driving with the stolen plates and California Penal Code section 496 PC for possession of stolen property. He was briefed on the procedure to get his car back, and then, as Burke told us he would be, Freddy was released.

Two plainclothes officers from SLPD surreptitiously followed him to an AC Transit stop on East 14th Street, where he eventually hopped on a bus headed for Alameda.

Burke arranged for us to do a cursory search of the Prius. We had taken separate cars, so I followed Lynn about two miles through town to Crown Towing. Crown was the local towing company the city had given the contract to tow stolen cars, those illegally parked, or driven by drunks.

We found spaces on the street in front and walked into the yard past a lot filled with vehicles, including everything from a new Porsche with the dealer's sticker still pasted to the driver's-side door window to a 1969 Oldsmobile Cutlass that had seen better days. A cyclone fence topped by large loops of razor wire surrounded the whole operation. A small building stood at the rear of the lot, and we walked in.

Inside, we found a dingy little office with fake wood paneling. A filthy mid-twentieth-century sofa was nestled against the wall. In front of it sat a scarred and scratched coffee table covered with old copies of *Better Homes and Gardens* magazines. Apparently, there was some connection between the beautification of one's domicile and the forced confiscation of one's vehicle.

A heavyset woman in her mid-fifties sat on a stool behind a badly scratched counter in the rear of the building, bellowing into a phone headset. Her hair had been bleached so often that it had the consistency of straw. Bright blue eye shadow covered lids with long, fake lashes. A fresh coat of red lipstick covered her mouth with traces apparent on her two front teeth.

"Sir, you'll need to bring a valid California Driver's License, current registration for the vehicle, and a $200 vehicle release fee," she bellowed into the headset.

She paused.

"That's right. There's also vehicle storage due at $105 a day. Your car has been here . . ."

She tapped on the keyboard of a computer in front of her.

"Five days," she said. "That's another $525 in storage. That brings your grand total to $725."

The man she was talking to was so furious that we could hear him yelling through her earpiece from the other side of the counter.

"I'm sorry, sir, but that's what's owed as of today. If you pick it up tomorrow, that's another $105 in storage fees."

The caller could be heard yelling louder. Who could blame him? $725 to get his own car back?

"Sir, please don't yell at me," she said. "I'm not the one who parked in a tow-away zone. Those are the fees."

She paused, listening.

"Fine. We'll hopefully see you today. Have a good afternoon." She pressed a button on the headset, shutting it off.

"Guy parks his Acura directly in front of a bright red sign that says, "TOW-AWAY ZONE, NO PARKING," and it's somehow *my* fault he got towed," she said, shaking her head.

"I guess some people will never get it," Lynn replied, using her sympathetic tone when she wanted to ingratiate herself with someone.

"What can I do for you folks?" the woman said.

Lynn flashed her badge.

The woman looked at it carefully.

"San Francisco," she said, impressed. She looked me over.

"Aren't you the guy from TV?" she asked.

"Topher Davis," I said, extending a hand.

Long, red-lacquered nails embraced it. Her skin was coarse. It was like grabbing a hunk of steel wool.

"I'm Michelle," she said. "I watch you all the time."

"Thank you, Michelle," I said, smiling.

People like to hear their own names repeated to them. Winning friends and influencing people. Thank you, Dale Carnegie.

Her tone suddenly shifted.

"You're not doing one of your, what do you call them? Exposés on us, are you?"

Come to think of it, that wasn't a bad idea. $105 in "storage" fees for a car they took involuntarily would draw a lot of viewers.

Focus, Davis.

"No, ma'am," I said.

"Police business," Lynn chimed in.

"What kind of police business?" Michelle demanded.

"You have a white Prius here. It was picked up this morning after an arrest. We need to have a look at it."

Michelle picked up a walkie-talkie next to the computer, pressed the transmit bar, and spoke into it.

"Kyle, can you please come to the office right away?" she ordered. She returned her attention to us. "It'll be just a minute. Have a seat."

Lynn and I looked at the filthy couch and declined.

About five minutes later, a lanky kid of about twenty entered the office. He had red hair, freckles, and milk-white skin that had begun to burn from exposure to the warm spring sun. I've never had a sunburn before. Score one for melanin.

"You called me?" Kyle said to the woman behind the counter.

"These folks are with the police," Michelle said. "They need to look at that white Prius that came in this morning."

"The police tow?" the kid said.

"Yes," Lynn replied.

"Follow me."

We thanked Michelle and followed Kyle to the far end of the lot. The Prius was parked next to a blue Chevy Corvair, the sight of which immediately brought me back to the age of sixteen. I'd been working after school at the local produce market and saving money to buy a car. One of the cashiers had a '64 Corvair she was willing to part with for six hundred bucks. When I told Auntie my plans, she was apoplectic.

"Don't you know those damned things flip over?" she lectured.

"Great," Lynn said. "He can be like Fred Flintstone when he gets that big order of ribs at the end of every show."

I ended up with a silver 1975 Chevy Vega. Nice car to drive . . . if you happen to own your own oil refinery. Putting oil in it was like pouring a bottle of 10W-40 into a sieve. The experience made me swear I'd always drive a nice ride. Hence, the Lexus.

"You can go on in," Kyle said. "The door is unlocked. I've got some other stuff to do, so I'll leave you to it."

He headed off in the direction of the building.

The Prius was a late model and looked like it had just rolled off the showroom floor. From the outside, it was easy to see that it was meticulously maintained. Lynn opened the door to find an immaculate black interior. The car was an automatic. I guess it makes it easier to shoot straight when you don't have to worry about downshifting.

She stuck her head in the passenger side, opened the glove box, and pulled out a few papers.

"Anything?" I asked. "Gun? Black ski mask? A pair of Warriors tickets?"

"Vehicle registration and proof of insurance in the name of Charles Woodbridge. The address lists the real owner of the plates as being in Emeryville."

She said nothing as she pushed the button that popped open the trunk. It was as clean as the rest of the car. She lifted the interior trunk compartment to find a donut and jack securely fastened in place. I hate donuts. Is it really that more costly to sell a car with a full-size spare?

"Nothing?" I asked.

Lynn reached inside, pulled out a glossy paper, and examined it.

"Check this out," she said.

I took the paper and looked at it. It was a brochure for the Black Sentinels for Justice.

Lynn slammed the trunk shut.

She climbed back into the driver's seat and checked the GPS.

"Damn," she said. "Not a goddamned thing. All of the previous trips have been deleted."

"I wonder if forensics would find anything?"

"Unless we can find probable cause for a warrant, I guess we'll never know, now, will we?" she said sarcastically.

"Hey, I'm on your side, remember?"

"Sorry," she said. "This is just so damn frustrating."

We returned to the building where a middle-aged man who looked like a cover model for the current edition of *Meth Addicts Weekly* counted out cash that he carefully placed on the counter. Once he finished, Michelle took a pair of keys from the collection of dozens that hung on the wall behind her and handed them to the guy.

Once the man left, she turned her attention to us.

"Find what you were looking for?"

"Not yet," Lynn said. "Can you do me a favor?"

Lynn pulled a business card from the holder in her pocket, wrote her cell number on the back, and handed it to the woman.

"Would you call me at that number if somebody comes to pick up the Prius?"

Michelle studied the card. "Homicide?" she asked. "Who got killed?"

"I can't really talk about an open investigation . . . but you might be a big help in catching a killer," Lynn told her.

"Will I get to be on TV?" Michelle said, looking at me.

"You never know," I told her. "You help us solve this case . . . You're a real hero."

Michelle thumbtacked the business card on the wall next to the rows of car keys.

"Call me anytime. Day or night," Lynn said.

"I'll call you the second somebody comes by for that car," she replied with an air of duty and resolve.

"Thanks," Lynn said.

Once we were outside the gate, Lynn spoke. "So, Freddy is mixed up with the Sentinels."

"Think Otumba is our Svengali?"

"By any means necessary," she said.

THIRTY-TWO

LYNN AND I parted ways at the tow yard. She headed back to 850 Bryant. I headed into the station. We had a solid lead now that we knew Freddy Isherwood was somehow connected to Malik Otumba and his radical group. Unfortunately, we only had one lead. We couldn't tie the Prius to the murders, meaning we couldn't connect them to Freddy. I still believed that Carla was the key to all of this.

"Carla is dead!" Freddy had shouted during his interrogation. "The police killed her."

What did that mean exactly, "The police killed her"?

What police? And when?

It appeared to me that, somehow, the catalyst for this whole thing was that beating that cost Carla her career in law enforcement twenty-five years ago. We needed to know more about it.

As I got on the upper deck of the Bay Bridge, I called Lynn on her cell.

"What now?" she answered.

"Aren't we the 'glass is half-empty girl' today?"

"Sorry."

"No worries."

"What's up?"

"What do we know about the man Carla beat? Isaac Wilson?" I asked.

There was silence on the other end of the line for a moment. "Not much," Lynn replied.

"Why don't we talk to him?"

"What for?"

"If Freddy is to be believed, Carla is no longer with us. There were six people at the scene of that incident: Carla, Driscoll, Curtain, Martin, Wilson, and Wilson's girlfriend, Sharica Jones. So, if Freddy is correct, and we count Carla, four of those six people are now dead. Isaac Wilson and presumably Sharica Jones are the only ones left," I said.

"Unless somebody's gotten to them too," Lynn said.

"Why don't we find out? Think you can track him down?"

"Let me see what I can do," she replied. "Ready for this?"

"What?"

"Burke just called me. You'll never guess where his guys trailed Freddy."

"The headquarters of the Black Sentinels for Justice on San Pablo," I asked.

"Nope. Phil Curtain's store," she replied.

"The Angler? Why?"

"He even had a key to the front door and let himself in."

"Burke's guys are gonna sit on him for a while and see if they can figure out what's what with his ties to the place."

"A big, blond muscle-bound white guy with fucking Tweety Bird tattoos on his arm shacking up with the sexagenarian widow of a dead cop?"

"I see what you mean," she said. "Talk about the odd couple."

"Let me see what I can find on Isaac Wilson," she responded. "And let me know if any more inspiration hits you."

"You'll be my first call."

She hung up. My phone lit up with an incoming call as soon as she did.

"Hello?"

"Boy, you don't call. You don't write," the high-pitched, nasally voice on the other end said.

"Carter!" I exclaimed. "How are you?"

Carter Stone was the owner of Smash Comics on Castro Valley Boulevard. I wasn't kidding earlier. I really am a grown-ass man who still reads comic books. I have specific titles that I keep on standing order so that I can get the new books when they come out. Mainly, I collect Golden Age books—rare superhero stuff put out before 1955. Carter keeps an eye out for those hard-to-find gems for me.

"You haven't been here in over a month," Carter said. "Ya got books piling up."

"Sorry," I apologized. "I've been busy working on a story."

"Anything good?"

"Nothing that I can talk about. Tell you what. I'm headed into the station now. I'll swing by on my way home."

"Sounds good, dude," he said. "Got in a nice Golden Age book too. A Superman Number Seventeen."

"The one with the World War Two cover?"

"1942," he said. "Supes has got Hitler in one hand and Hirohito in the other."

"Don't you *dare* show that book to a soul until I get there," I warned.

He laughed. "See you tonight."

I hung up just as I was pulling into the driveway at the station. When I went inside, I found Mandy again toiling away in an editing bay.

"Whatcha got?" I asked.

"Sound from Twain Harte on the Martin shooting. Just the sheriff pontificating," she said.

"Grab Stu, and let's have a quick production meeting," I told her.

Mandy, Stu, and I sat in my office fifteen minutes later.

"This story has sure morphed into something different than we originally envisioned," I stated.

"Well, that's for gosh-darned sure," Stu said in his Texas drawl.

"Three cop bodies and counting," Mandy added.

"Maybe four," I said.

I filled them in on Carla Isherwood and brother Freddy.

"Wow," said Mandy. "What are we gonna do with all that?" She took out her reporter's notebook and began scribbling notes.

"For now, stay on the path we're on," I said. "Let's make them all real people in this story. Mandy, you've done a good job with the stuff on Jamal. Really humanized him."

"Thanks," she said.

"Now, make sure we do the same thing with Driscoll and the other officers."

"Already on it," Mandy replied. "We got great sound on Driscoll from Janet. His favorite food. His love of classic cars. Mrs. Curtain talked about Phil and his fishing. Not too much on Martin. I'm working on him. Folks in Twain Harte didn't know him well. I'm gonna go knock on some doors in Petaluma. It was Martin's primary residence for years."

"That all sounds great, but there's something I need you to do first," I said.

"What?" she asked, not looking up from her notepad.

"San Leandro Police tailed Freddy to The Angler. He had a key and everything. I want to know why."

"You want me to go back there?"

"Yes. Tell Edna Curtain you've got a few follow-up questions and see if Freddy Isherwood is there. If not, see if you can find out why he has a key to that store. I'd go myself, but Freddy's seen me. If he's there, I don't want to spook him."

"What if he *is* there?"

"Don't make a big deal out of it. Just casually see if you can find out what the deal is and why he has a key to that shop."

"Gotcha," she said, flipping her notebook shut.

"Just remember . . . We're on the clock with this one," I said.

"As if we could forget," she responded. "What are you gonna do?"

"Track down Isaac Wilson. I want to hear his side of that ass whipping he took from Carla Isherwood."

"Well, I guess we've got our marching orders," Mandy stated. "Come on, Stu."

"Fishing for clues at the fishing store," he said. "I like it. Might even pick up a new reel while we're there."

Once I was alone, I opened my laptop to see if I could find out anything about Isaac Wilson. The name was too common. There were Isaac Wilsons everywhere. I had no way of knowing which one, if any, was the man I was looking for. I picked up the phone and dialed Lynn.

"What is it with you today? Can't a girl get a chance to catch her breath?"

"Sorry. You know I'm up against the clock on this one. Wondering if you had a chance to look up Isaac Wilson?"

"Jesus," she said, "you just asked me to try to find him."

"I did, didn't I? Sorry."

"Lucky for you, I did," she said gleefully.

"You did? How?"

"DMV records. I called him, and he'll speak to us. Ten o'clock tomorrow morning."

"That's great. I sure wish the station would give me more time to finish this."

"Don't worry, Chris. We'll finish this," she said.

The sympathy in her voice was evident.

"I'll see you in the morning. Meet you at The Egg. Quit calling me every five minutes. Goodbye."

I hung up.

The last thing I wanted or needed was anybody feeling sorry for me. I gathered my things and headed home. Traffic was a bear. I was not going to miss that commute once this gig ended.

It took me thirty-five minutes to get up Battery Street to the lower deck onramp, and ninety minutes later, I found a parking spot right in front of Smash Comics. I walked in to find Carter Stone sorting new books. Carter was a nice kid. Went to college, got his degree in mechanical engineering, then discovered he hated it. He had worked hard, saved his money, and used it to buy this place.

At first, I patronized him because he was a nice kid. Now, I do because I love the place. Next to the station and The Egg, it's been my home away from home.

He looked up from his work as I entered.

"Well, look at what the Catwoman dragged in."

"Ouch. That's bad."

"Oh, now you're a critic too?"

"Let's look at the Superman book," I suggested.

He went into the back room and brought out the book. He removed the cardboard backing, pulled the book from its plastic comic bag, and gently handed it to me.

It was an excellent copy with white pages and bright colors. It had minimal wear along the spine, but not bad for a seventy-five-year-old comic book.

"What are you grading this?"

Comics are graded on a 1–10 scale. The higher the grade, the more valuable and expensive the book is.

"I'm thinking 6.5," he said.

"That looks about right. How much?"

The main rule of negotiating: the first one to mention a number loses.

"Three thousand," he said. "For you, twenty-seven fifty."

Golden Age comic collecting is an expensive hobby. Fortunately, I can afford it.

"Make it an even twenty-five hundred, and you've got a deal," I said.

Carter stroked his chin. "You're robbing me blind here, ya know?" he said. "I've got a lot of overhead here with the rent going up and sales of new books down."

I said nothing.

After a few moments of silence, Carter extended his hand and reluctantly said, "Deal."

I gave him my American Express Black Card, and a few minutes later, I was seated in the Lexus, my Golden Age treasure on the passenger seat beside me in a plastic Smash Comics bag. I was just getting ready to pull out of the parking space when I remembered that I had forgotten to pick up the current issues Carter had been holding for me.

I put the car back in park, turned off the motor, locked the doors, and returned to the comic book store.

"Hey, Carter, I forgot—" is the last thing I remember saying.

The blast from behind picked me up off my feet and threw me headfirst into a wooden display rack of graphic novels. There were comics, posters, plaster, and wooden debris everywhere. The front window with its bright neon SMASH COMICS logo was completely blown out, leaving shards of glass everywhere. The blast was so strong that some shards were glass projectiles lodged into the wall at the far end of the building.

From my vantage point on the floor, I looked through the space that had been the store's front window and saw the wreckage of my Lexus.

The body was gone, blown to pieces that were strewn all over Castro Valley Boulevard. The frame, though twisted and contorted, was intact. It was also in flames, sending plumes of black smoke into the air. I could feel the back of my shirt getting wet and sticky. Apparently, not all of the glass projectiles were lodged in the store walls.

Everything else is a blur. The sirens. The sheriff's deputies. The paramedic asking me if I knew who and where I was and how many fingers she held up. The ambulance. Eden Hospital's ER. It was all like a surreal dream.

I awoke, heavily sedated, in a hospital bed, Lynn at my side.

"What did that note with the bullet say again?" I asked.

"How you feeling?" she asked.

"Woozy. Did they give me good drugs?" I croaked.

"Only the best for my big brother," she said. "You have a concussion and a few cracked ribs. Some of the glass lodged into your back, so you also needed a few stitches. Other than that, you're gonna be fine."

"What the hell happened?"

My sister took a deep breath. "Witnesses saw a helicopter-shaped drone fly into your car. The bomb squad boys think it was loaded with C4," she said. "Thank God you weren't in it at the time or . . ."

It had been a long time since I saw Lynn choke up. It took a lot to get her emotional after she returned from the war. Not to mention the things she saw on the street working for the SFPD.

"What happened? That kid Carter said you had already left the store."

"I forgot some books. Went back inside to get them."

"Your shitty memory saved your life," she said.

"Is Carter okay?"

"Just a little shaken up. He had gone into the back room to get some comic books or something when the bomb went off. He's fine, but his store is toast."

"Tell him not to worry about that," I said. "I'll pay for the damage and repairs. I'm the reason the whole thing happened."

"NO! YOU'RE NOT!" Lynn yelled. "That fucking cop killer is."

"We backing off?" I asked.

"The day after they convict his ass," she replied gravely.

The door to my hospital room opened, and Kendra walked in, holding a cup of coffee.

"Oh, thank God," she said. "You're awake."

"I had Mandy call Kendra," Lynn said. "I thought she'd want to know. Mandy and Stu are out in the waiting area."

"You made the six o'clock news," Kendra said.

"Lovely. That's all I need. To be a part of the story," I replied.

At least, that's what I think I said. The drugs must have put me out because the next thing I remember is Mandy and Stu sitting in my room and a nurse asking me if I'd like dinner. The clock on the wall said it was eight forty-five in the evening. My head was killing me, and there was a ringing in my ears. They had me sleeping on my side because of the stitches in my back. I had a terrible crick in my neck.

"You are one lucky feller," Stu drawled.

"Yeah, look at me. I'm a goddamn four-leaf clover," I said. "Where's Lynn?"

"She's meeting with the bomb squad to see what she can find out," Mandy said.

"And Kendra?"

"She went to your place to get it together for you."

I felt a sudden panic come over me.

"My house! Is my house all right?"

"Your house is fine," Mandy declared, reassuring me.

"So, it was just my Superman Seventeen they were after?" I joked.

"What?"

"Nothing. The car was the target."

"YOU were the target," she stated.

I told the nurse I wasn't hungry, and she left us alone.

Once she'd gone, Mandy gently put her hand on my arm. I was connected to an IV drip.

"Topher," she said. "Maybe it's time we let this one go. Let Lynn and the police handle it. No story is worth getting killed over."

"Quit?" I exclaimed. "All because of a little car bomb? Woman, have you taken leave of your senses?"

"I'm serious," she replied.

I looked into her eyes. They were beet red. It looked like the poor kid had been crying all day.

"This is what they want," I said, putting my free hand on Mandy's. "They want us to quit. The fact that they're trying to kill me means we're getting close. Close to something they don't want us to find out."

"But—" Mandy started to say.

"It's our last story, and we've got a week. We can't stop now," I said. "We just can't. Our team—you, me, and Stu—we don't quit."

Her eyes filled with tears as she drew in half a breath and reluctantly nodded.

"We may get fired, but we don't quit."

She brushed her moist eyes with the back of her hand, continuing to nod.

"Now," I said, "when can I get the hell out of here? I've got work to do."

THIRTY-THREE

OVER THE DOCTORS' objections, I made the hospital release me at about eight the following day. Mandy gave me a ride home. On the way, I called Carter on his cell.

"Dude! Are you all right?" he asked.

"Just a few bumps and bruises. I'll be fine."

"Great. You gave me a good scare."

"I'm sorry about the store."

"Yeah, it's totaled. But hey, that's what insurance is for, right?"

"If you need anything or have to pay some kind of deductible or something, you let me know. I'll pay for any damages your insurance doesn't cover."

"Dude, you don't have to do that."

"Yeah," I said. "I do. I'm the reason for this mess."

"Knock that shit off," he said. "The bomber is the reason for this mess. You just rest up."

"Thanks, pal," I said. "One favor, though . . ."

"Anything."

"Find me another Superman Seventeen."

He laughed and hung up. Good-natured kid to be able to laugh when his livelihood has just been blown to shit.

Mandy drove past two Alameda County sheriff's vehicles and Lynn's unmarked as she pulled into my driveway.

I walked in the front door, and Sophie bounded up to me, standing on her hind legs, her front paws on my shins, demanding to be picked up. I tried to bend over to grab her, but the stitches in my back made it difficult.

"Let me do that," Kendra said, picking up the dog and putting her in my arms.

Sophie immediately started licking my face.

"Somebody missed you," Kendra said, kissing me. "Let me help you to the couch."

She guided me to the couch, where I sat down just as Lynn walked into the room from the kitchen with two Alameda County Sheriff's deputies. I recognized them from The Egg.

Rusty Jones was an athletic guy in his early twenties. He was forever training for marathons and Iron Man competitions. Martin Gates had ten years and twenty pounds on Rusty, but he was not a guy to be messed with. Both were seasoned officers.

"How do you feel?" Lynn asked.

"Head hurts some. A little ringing in my ears. Doc said it would be like this for a day or so."

Kendra fluffed a pillow and put it behind my head.

I looked back and forth between Lynn and Kendra.

"So . . . You've met," I said.

"Yes," Kendra responded. "At the hospital yesterday. Remember?"

"Not really. I was pretty doped up. Lots of holes in my memory."

"Not exactly the dinner I had hoped for, but . . ." Lynn said.

"Well, I'm glad you connected," I replied.

"So, what are the Katzenjammer Kids doing here," I said, gesturing to Marty and Rusty.

"Well, it's good to see you too," Rusty said with a smirk.

"We're here to keep an eye on you," Marty said. "Somebody just tried to kill you."

"I asked them to make sure he doesn't get a second chance," Lynn told me.

"Lynn, they're using drones with C4. They can fly one into the house, the backyard, or while I walk down the street. There's no protecting me. We've got to find a way to nail Freddy Isherwood and whoever is behind him."

She thought momentarily before letting out a reluctant, "Agreed."

"Didn't we have a meeting set for today?" I asked.

"After what happened, I rescheduled it for tomorrow."

"Okay," I said. "I'm going."

"All right," she conceded.

"Okay?" I said. "No argument? No pushback?"

"Not today," she replied. "I'm just glad you're alive."

"Wanna pick me up? I seem to be in need transportation."

"I'll get you at nine," she said. "Provided you get some rest tonight."

"Yes, Mother."

Rusty said, "Marty and I will spend the night in your living room. Just in case."

"We're arranging for sharpshooters on the property to take out any drones that happen your way."

"All right," I said. "Just don't shoot up some twelve-year-old kid's birthday present."

We chatted a few minutes longer. Then Kendra put me to bed. I needed to rest and be at least somewhat coherent for our meeting with Isaac Wilson.

THIRTY-FOUR

KENDRA FIGURED I needed the bed to myself and took up residence in the guest room. Smart girl. It was a restless sleep. I couldn't lie on my back because of the stitches, and lying on my side was excruciating because of the cracked ribs. The doctor sent me home with some pain pills, but I didn't take them. I'm not a big fan of opioids. I don't like the way that they make me feel. At about three a.m., I got up and poured myself a double Johnnie Walker Blue. That did the trick; I was out like a light in no time.

At eight o'clock, I was awakened by Kendra carefully placing a breakfast tray across my legs.

"My turn to spoil you," she said, lifting plate covers to reveal Eggs Benedict, home fries, and freshly squeezed orange juice.

"No rose?" I asked.

"I'd hit you in the face with a pillow right now, but I'm afraid you'd pop a stitch."

"Thank God for small favors."

"Eat. Your sister is coming by to get you in a bit."

She kissed my forehead and left me alone, where I could hear her cleaning the kitchen.

I was surprisingly hungry. I hadn't really had a decent meal in a few days. I ate everything on the plate and contemplated licking it to get the remaining hollandaise sauce when Lynn stuck her head in the doorway.

"How's the patient this morning?"

"Well fed," I said, rubbing my full belly. "Otherwise, a little stiff and sore. Whatcha got?"

"Bomb squad says it was definitely C4. The drone was a common one you could pick up for seventy-five bucks at any toy store, mini-mart, or online. They figured the range would have been about a quarter mile, so whoever was operating it remotely was nearby. We're checking street cam footage now," she said, "but we don't expect to find much. Whoever operated it could've been sitting in a car, an apartment, or pushing a cart at Safeway while they were piloting that thing."

She walked into the room.

"I'm going to see Isaac Wilson. Still want to come with?"

"You bet I do."

I tried to climb out of bed but was too stiff and sore.

"This is embarrassing, but will you please help me get dressed?"

"Men," she said. "Such babies."

I stuck my tongue out at her.

Lynn walked to my closet and pulled out a pair of black slacks and a Tommy Bahama shirt.

"How's this?" she said, holding up the ensemble.

I nodded. "That's fine."

She hung the clothes on the closet door and then eased me out of bed.

"I hope you're wearing clean underwear because, either way, I'm not touching it."

She gently got me out of my black silk pajamas and into the clothes she'd chosen.

"I think I can brush my teeth." I went into the bathroom and, with Herculean effort, brushed my teeth, washed my face, and dragged a comb through my hair.

Soon, we were on the freeway in Lynn's unmarked, headed toward downtown Oakland. We took Interstate 880 to Broadway and pulled into the underground garage of a gleaming gold office building a few blocks from the Paramount Theater. Lynn parked the car in front of a glass booth and handed her keys to a young Asian valet.

"Valet parking?" I asked. "You must be expensing this."

"His suite of offices is upstairs," she said, her index finger pointing skyward.

"Suite of offices??"

"Yep. Mr. Wilson has done very well for himself over the past twenty-five years," she declared.

We took the elevator in the garage to the twelfth floor and got out. When we stepped out of the elevator, the first thing we saw were glass double doors adorned with the letters IWP etched in a stylized font. We entered just as a pretty, young receptionist answered the phone, "Isaac Wilson Properties."

I looked at Lynn and silently mouthed, "Isaac Wilson Properties?"

She nodded her head.

"Not the same knucklehead who used to beat up his girlfriend," she whispered.

"That remains to be seen," I countered.

The receptionist finished her call and then turned her attention toward us.

"How may I help you," she said.

I let Lynn do the talking.

"We have an appointment with Mr. Wilson. Detective Lynn Sloan."

The receptionist tapped a few keys on her computer before saying, "I have you right here. We're running a little behind this morning. Please have a seat. Mr. Wilson will be with you shortly. May I offer you some water or coffee?"

"No, thank you," Lynn said.

"I'd love some black coffee," I replied.

"Right away, sir," the receptionist said as she quickly walked out of the room, clicking high heels with every step.

A white couch that reminded me of some kind of modern art piece was across from the receptionist's desk. We sat just as the woman returned with a white saucer, balancing a white square-shaped cup of coffee she handed me. I thanked her and sipped the best coffee I'd ever tasted.

"Better than ours at 850 Bryant, huh?" Lynn asked.

"I'd rather eat gas station sushi than drink the coffee in your office again," I replied.

"Noted," she said.

A glass coffee table stood before us with the latest *Forbes, Inc., Entrepreneur*, and *Oakland Magazine* editions. All the covers showcased a smiling, middle-aged African American man over various iterations of the caption, "*Isaac Wilson, Oakland's Real Estate Czar.*"

I opened *Oakland Magazine* and thumbed through it until I got to the cover story. It began with a two-page color photo of Wilson standing in front of an ostentatiously large mansion in the tony neighboring city of Piedmont, where Lynn and I were raised. It was an enormous all-white home, fronted by a circular driveway accessorized with a Mercedes, a Bentley, and a red Lamborghini. I showed the photo to Lynn, who nodded her head, impressed.

According to the story, Wilson's IWP had become one of the East Bay's most prominent developers, landholders, and landlords after a little over fifteen years in business. The company owned apartments, single-family homes, and office buildings, including the one we sat in. The article talked about how Wilson had been a down-on-his-luck, unemployed warehouse laborer when he was given the opportunity to go to business school through the largess of a benefactor. After he graduated, he got his real estate license, and his benefactor provided the seed money for his first acquisition, a dilapidated six-unit building in a rough part of East Oakland. Wilson renovated it, rented it out, and was off to the races. He owned or managed twenty such properties within five years and formed the current company.

I handed the magazine to Lynn, who was skimming through the story when the receptionist returned.

"Mr. Wilson will see you now," she said.

We followed her down a narrow hallway lined with offices filled with realtors we could overhear wheeling and dealing. At the end of the hall were wooden double doors with the name ISAAC WILSON stenciled on them in large gold leaf.

The receptionist opened the door on the right, made a sweeping "and here they are" gesture with her hand, and left, closing the door behind her.

Isaac Wilson was a man of medium build with distinguished gray tufts of experience at his temples. The magazine had done him justice. He was lean and muscular. You could tell he cared for himself, from his buff body to his manicured nails. He looked just like his photograph as he rose from his enormous desk to greet us at the door. He wore a gray suit tailored perfectly to fit his frame. His shoes were Italian and expensive. I like nice things, but I don't think I'd spend what they must have cost.

"Isaac Wilson," he said, extending a hand. Lynn took it.

"I'm Detective Sloan, and this is—"

"Topher Davis," he said, cutting her off and grasping my hand with both of his as though we were old friends. "Nice to meet you in person. It's a pleasure to meet you both. Please, have a seat."

He gestured toward two leather chairs in front of his desk, and we sat in them.

"Like the desk?" he asked. "It's a replica of the Resolute Desk in the White House."

"It's lovely," Lynn said.

The room was all done in brown wood with an occasional hint of brass strategically placed on the doorknobs and other places around the office. Framed photos of Wilson on the covers of various periodicals, including the one we'd just read, adorned the walls. A gigantic tank filled with brilliantly colored tropical fish was built into the wall at the far end of the office.

I really like fish and had been thinking about getting a koi pond like the one a psychologist friend of mine in L.A. has. I've got too many critters on my property, though. I'd just end up feeding the raccoons.

"So," he said, "what can I do for San Francisco's finest?"

"We're conducting a murder investigation and have a few questions."

"Murder investigation? I don't know anybody who's been murdered."

"Actually, you know at least three people," she said. "Three of the four cops who arrested you the night you were beaten have turned up dead."

"I did read something about that," he said. "Wait a minute . . . You don't think *I* had something to do with it, do you?"

"Did you?" I asked.

"No way. The day that woman beat some sense into me was the luckiest day of my life."

"How so?" Lynn inquired.

"I sued the department. I got a two-million-dollar settlement. After legal fees and such, I ended up with a cool million all to myself."

A million dollars. His benefactor with the "largess" had been the City of San Francisco taxpayers.

"I used the money to get my act together. Got my BA at San Francisco State. Went to business school. Got my real estate license. Bought my first properties. Now, look at me."

"What about your girlfriend?" I asked.

He laughed a hoarse, hearty laugh.

"Sharica? I haven't thought about her in ages. She was what we liked to call 'pretty poison.' Beautiful girl but always creating problems that ended up with me in handcuffs. Some people should just not be together. We were two of them."

"Do you have any idea where we might find her? I want to talk to her as well," Lynn said.

"Try one of the cemeteries over in Colma. I heard she overdosed about ten years ago. See what I mean? Poison. If we'd stayed together, I'd probably be buried next to her."

"Don't you find it odd that everyone involved in the incident that night—the police, your girlfriend—are all dead?" Lynn asked. "Everyone except you."

"I hadn't thought about it, to be honest. I'm too busy. IWP owns or manages almost 200 properties in the East Bay. I don't have the time for much else. My attention was elsewhere," he said. "I don't read or watch a lot of news these days. No offense to Mr. Davis."

"None taken. What happened that night?" I asked. "The night of the incident."

"Mr. Davis, I'm sure there's a police report with all the details."

"We'd like to hear *your* version of events," Lynn said.

"Let me think. It's been a lot of years. As I said, I was cuffed by the police on a number of occasions. They all kind of blur."

"I'm sure you didn't get a two-million-dollar settlement as a result of the other encounters," Lynn said. "Think. I'm sure your memory will refresh."

"And you'll keep this between us?" he asked. He made a sweeping gesture of the room, indicating his magazine covers.

"As you can see," he said, "I'm quite publicity conscious. You promise to keep my name out of it?"

"The press won't hear about it from us," I said. "We're off the record."

"I give you my word," Lynn added.

He tented his fingers and put them gently across his lips, thinking.

"Well," Wilson said, stroking his chin, "we were fighting about something. We were always fighting. Usually because we were drunk, high, or both. Thank God I don't do that shit anymore. Clean and sober eighteen years next September."

"Congratulations," I said.

"Thank you. One day at a time. Anyway, we were fighting about something, and it got physical. She came at me with a cast-iron skillet. She was always throwing things or coming at me with a knife, pan, or whatever she could grab. Eventually, somebody would call the police, and since I was the man in these domestic disputes, I was always the one with my hands cuffed behind my back."

"Not uncommon," Lynn said. "It's unfair, but the man is usually assumed to be the aggressor in these kinds of calls, even though many times, it's the woman. So, somebody called the cops?"

"Yeah, one of the neighbors, I guess. Two cops show up. Curtain and this rookie woman, Carla something. I forget. This was a lifetime ago."

"Carla Isherwood," I said.

"Yes. Her. Curtain I'd known for a while. I used to deal for him."

"Excuse me?" Lynn said.

"I used to deal for him. Coke, pot, meth, heroin. Whatever he happened to have that week. I think he was getting the stuff from your evidence locker. He'd bring me the drugs. I'd sell them, and he'd collect 75 percent of the take."

"How long did this go on?" Lynn asked.

"Six, maybe eight months. He'd meet me on Tuesday afternoons near the projects where I lived. I'd give him an envelope with his money. He'd give me a brown paper lunch bag filled with the junk he wanted sold."

"What ended this lucrative little side hustle?" I asked.

"One Tuesday, he comes by to collect, and I tell him I'm not dealing anymore unless I get 50 percent. I wanted half. I was taking all the risks. I was the one who'd end up in San Quentin if I got caught."

"And what did he say?" Lynn asked.

"He called me an ungrateful bastard. Said I should be happy just for the opportunity to work with him," Wilson replied. "He also said, I'd be sorry."

"So, a week later, me and my lady fight. Somebody calls the cops, and Curtain shows up with the lady cop, Isherwood. They drag me out into the hallway and cuff my hands behind my back like usual, then Curtain says to Isherwood, 'He needs to learn some manners. Jack his ass up.'"

"Curtain said that?" I asked.

"Yeah. The lady cop is reluctant. She wants to know why. I'm already in custody. I'm no threat to anybody. Curtain says, 'This is why I don't like women on the force. They're too weak to do what needs to be done.' *That* set her off, and she started whaling on me with the baton."

"I heard you called her a nasty name," I said.

Wilson laughed. "Yeah, that was their excuse. I never said anything to that woman before she went off on me. The whole time, Curtain is egging her on. 'Hit him like a man,' he's yelling. So, she starts hitting me harder, more aggressively, holding the baton with both hands while hitting me in the face, my head, and my ribs."

As he spoke, I put my hand on my own broken ribs.

"Sharica jumped in and tried to help me, and Curtain laid his baton across the side of her head. She went out cold.

"One of the neighbors had just bought a new VHS camcorder, and he started filming. Now remember, this is not that long after Rodney King. Relations were already tense between the Black community and the police."

"The more things change, the more they stay the same," I said.

"Ain't that the truth?" Wilson replied. "So anyway, this neighbor gets her on video beating my ass. Eventually, two other officers show up—"

"Driscoll and Martin," I said.

"Yep, that's them," he confirmed.

"They're dead now too," Lynn clarified.

"Wow," he said, shaking his head in disbelief. "They pulled her off me."

"Where'd this story about you calling her the 'c' word initiate?" Lynn asked.

"Once it was on tape, there needed to be a justification. Curtain couldn't just say, 'I'm teaching him a lesson because he wants a larger share of my drug money,' so he came up with this cock-and-bull story that I called her a nasty name and resisted arrest. The neighbor gave the tape to the DA's office."

"I'm surprised the tape wasn't given to the press," I remarked.

"Like I said, the Rodney King riots were still fresh in everybody's mind. I guess the guy didn't want to see San Francisco get torn up like L.A. did. As far as I know, the press never saw it.

"I did call a civil rights lawyer, though, and we sued. We settled out of court. As you know, I got some money."

"And you never reported Curtain about the drug money?" Lynn asked.

"I wasn't suicidal then, and I'm not suicidal now. He told me to keep my mouth shut, and I did. I went along with his story. I never said a word to anyone until now. I figure any statute of limitations on dealing is up by now, so I can't get busted. Plus, you tell me Curtain's dead, so he can't do anything to me.

"There was a settlement conference. All four cops were there. We settled. Then I heard they fired the lady cop. A lot of people who saw that video wanted her in jail."

"And the other officers?" I asked.

"'Administrative leave,' as they call it. Then, back to work."

"And you?" Lynn probed.

"I just wanted the whole damn thing over with," he said. "You think my case has something to do with these deaths?"

"We don't know," I answered.

"We just needed to know what happened, and you're apparently the sole survivor from that night," Lynn said.

"That lady cop dead too?"

"That's what we're told."

"Wow," he said, again shaking his head. He thought for a moment.

"Do you think I'm in danger?" he asked. "Is somebody coming after me? Do I need protection? A bodyguard or something?"

"I doubt it," Lynn said. "Whoever it is appears to be targeting cops."

"You said that the remaining three officers went on administrative leave and then back to work," I said. "How do you know?"

"Well, like I said," he began, "I used the settlement to go back to school. Got my GED and then SF State. One day, maybe a month later, I leave my home to go to class, and Curtain's across the street leaning against his patrol car smoking a cigarette."

"What did he say to you?" Lynn asked.

"Nothing. Not a word. He just puffed on his smoke and glared at me. The message was clear. 'Tell anybody about our business, and you're dead.' Message received. I never saw him again after that. I moved to my grandmama's house here in Oakland to get away from all of that. Been here ever since. I've got nicer digs than my granny's these days, though."

"I saw the magazine pictures," I said. "You have a lovely home. Congratulations on all of your success."

"Aw, I didn't do anything that anybody couldn't do with hard work, determination, and a million-dollar head start. Like I said, getting my ass whupped like that turned out to be the best thing that ever happened to me. You know, it's funny," Wilson said. "I haven't thought or talked about this shit for years. Now, within the space of a month, two cops show up asking me to swing down memory lane."

"Who else talked to you?" Lynn asked.

"That cop who shot the kid at the party. The one who pulled the lady cop off me."

"Driscoll?" I said.

"Yeah, Driscoll. I don't know why I keep forgetting names," Wilson said. "He was here about three weeks ago asking the same questions. Did Curtain deal? Did I help him? What was my role in it? How long did it go on? How big was his operation?"

"What'd you tell him?" Lynn asked.

"Nothing. Curtain was still alive, and I planned to stay that way myself," he said. "I gave Driscoll a lot of, 'I don't remembers' and 'I can't recalls.'"

He lifted his left arm and glanced at the platinum Rolex on his wrist. "Now, if you'll excuse me, I have another appointment in a few minutes. Some muckety-muck from Chevron looking for something . . . palatial. And he's got deep pockets."

We talked to Wilson for a few more minutes, and then Lynn gave him her card and told him to call if he remembered anything else. We then went down to the garage, got Lynn's unmarked from valet parking, and headed back to Castro Valley.

"I really should go into the station," I said.

"No, you shouldn't even be here. You're going home to rest."

There are times to fight with Lynn and times to shut up and give in. This was the latter.

"Do you buy it?" I asked. "That Curtain was a dirty cop? And that Driscoll was looking into him?"

"Anything's possible," she said. "I've got a friend in the Internal Affairs Bureau. Let me see if IAB has anything on him."

"He was with the department for years after that incident. If he were, in fact, selling drugs that he stole from the department, somebody would have known," I said. "He'd have been fired and then sent to jail."

"Do you have any idea how hard it is to get rid of a bad cop?" she asked.

"Come to think of it, not really. But I do have an inkling."

"First, if another cop finds out, you can pretty much throw out any hope of his cooperation. As a general rule, cops don't rat out other cops."

"The thin blue line again," I said.

"Then you've got to have a DA willing to prosecute if the cop is dirty or bring the case in front of the grand jury. District attorneys are reluctant to do that since they see us as all as being on the 'same team.' They know that they'll need cop testimony in future cases. They are reluctant to do anything that might jeopardize that relationship.

"Then you've got the biggest impediment of all—the police union whose job it is to fight for cops' rights, no matter what Right or wrong, the POA is behind the officer."

"Isn't there a citizens' review board?" I asked.

She laughed. "They're a joke. Their job is to make recommendations regarding the department and officers accused of misconduct. A 'recommendation' that is neither binding nor adhered to by the powers that be."

"They're toothless, in other words," I said.

"Exactly. Then, in the rare and unlikely event that you're able to actually charge a cop and put him on trial, the jury is generally comprised of older white people, the only ones with the time to sit on a jury. They tend to believe that the police can do no wrong and that the officer needs to be given the benefit of the doubt. Nine times out of ten, no matter how guilty or dirty the cop is, he walks."

"But IAB—" I started.

"Does the best job it can, but they're despised. Nobody likes cops who make their living by investigating other cops. That's why they're called 'The Rat Squad.' To see that a dirty cop is fired and prosecuted, you have to climb a fucking mountain," she said.

"They fired Carla Isherwood," I stated. "Where was all of this machinery to help *her* keep her job?"

"Carla was still in her probationary period. That's a whole other ball game. A bad rookie is much easier to get rid of. Remember, Curtain, Martin, and Mickey Driscoll threw her under the bus."

We rode in silence for a few minutes, and then I said, "What about Wilson? As you pointed out, he's the sole survivor from that incident."

"I just can't see him involved. He's living a charmed life now—big house. Fancy cars. Lots of money. Magazine articles. I don't see him risking all of that. Remember, he didn't tell anybody the real story behind the beating. If his story is true, Curtain still scared the shit out of him," she said.

"I believe Wilson," I said. "He sounded credible to me too. You know, if Curtain weren't one of the vics, he would be at the top of my suspect list right now."

"But he *is* one of the vics. There's no better alibi than being dead," she said.

"So, what was Mickey Driscoll doing?" I wondered.

"Perhaps we should have another chat with Mrs. Driscoll and find out."

"Perhaps we should," I agreed.

We got to my house, and Lynn helped me walk in. Kendra was in the kitchen cooking something that smelled scrumptious. Sophie was asleep, curled up in the little bed I keep for her in the corner of the kitchen.

"What are you still doing here?" I asked.

"Well, hello to you too," Kendra said with a smile.

"Sorry. I didn't mean that the way it came out. Just surprised to see you. *Pleasantly* surprised, that is."

"I took the day off to look after you."

"I'm fine. Really."

"No, you're not," Lynn said. "Stop arguing. You're outnumbered here."

"Why don't you put him to bed, and I'll bring in some lunch," Kendra suggested.

"Whatcha making?" I asked.

"Grilled cheese sandwiches and Campbell's tomato soup. When I was a kid, my mother would always make this for me if I was sick. It made me feel better."

"I'm not sick," I protested.

"You're injured," Lynn said. "Close enough."

Lynn helped me to the master bedroom, and I changed back into my pajamas.

"The Katzenjammer Kids still watching the house?" I asked.

"Until I tell them otherwise. They're watching the house 24/7," she affirmed.

I gingerly climbed into bed. The girls were right. I did need rest. My whole body ached. Soon, Kendra came in and placed my lunch tray across my legs. The grilled cheese sandwich and tomato soup were revitalizing. As with breakfast, I cleaned my plate and bowl.

"Sorry you hated it," Kendra said with a smile.

"Eggs Benedict for breakfast. Tomato soup for lunch. I am *definitely* going to keep you around for a while."

"I'm counting on it," she said, kissing me softly on my forehead. "I'm counting on it."

THIRTY-FIVE

AFTER LUNCH, I fell asleep and napped until 4:30. I guess my body needed more rest than I realized. My ribs were still sore, but my back felt fine . . . until I tried to lie on it. The pain was excruciating in the places where I was stitched up. I guess I let out a yelp or something because Kendra came rushing into the room.

"What is it, baby? You okay?"

"I'm fine. Just forgot about the stitches and tried to lie on my back."

"Lemme see. Lie on your stomach," she said.

I did as instructed, and Kendra lifted my pajama top to examine my back.

"Everything is still in place," she said. "You haven't broken any of the sutures."

"Thanks," I said. "I'll try to be more careful."

"The doctor prescribed some ointment to rub on it. It'll help you heal and will deal with the itching when it starts."

"Itching?"

"Yes, he says that as the wounds heal, they'll itch. Let me get it. I'll be right back."

She left for a few minutes and then returned, opening the cap on a silver metallic tube. "Stay on your stomach," she said.

I did as commanded while she gently massaged a cream of some sort onto my back. The sensation was cool and soothing.

"Can I talk to you about something?" she asked.

"Anything," I said.

"You're hurt. You really shouldn't be here by yourself."

"I'm not by myself," I said. "I have Sophie."

"Sophie can't rush you to the hospital if you get an infection."

"I don't know. She's a pretty smart dog."

"True, but can she drive or dial 911?"

"With the proper training, I bet she could."

"Be that as it may, how would you feel about my moving in with you for a few weeks until you're all healed?"

I stroked my chin in contemplation. "Let me think about it," I said. "Okay, I've thought about it. Yes!"

"Good, I already have a packed suitcase in your guest room."

"You were *that* sure I was going to say yes?"

She said nothing. She just smiled.

"Come here," I said, carefully sitting up.

She leaned in close. I gently brushed one of the black ringlets out of her right eye and passionately kissed her.

"Wow," she said, smiling. "You should get blown up more often."

Kendra went into the kitchen to make dinner. I picked up my cell and called Mandy to fill her in on what we learned from Isaac Wilson.

"Do you think it's true? That Curtain was dirty?"

"I don't know. What reason would Wilson have to lie now? It's been twenty-five years, and he's parlayed the money he got from that civil suit into a gazillion dollars."

"I got no vibe like that when I talked to Mrs. Curtain," Mandy said. "If her husband was up to no good, I don't think that she was aware of it."

"The wife's always the last to know," I said with a smile in my voice. "Anything new in Petaluma?"

"Not much," Mandy said. "Martin's neighbors didn't know him very well. They described him as standoffish. He lived there for over twenty years, and some of his neighbors didn't even know he was a cop until his murder was on the news."

"Sounds like he really kept to himself,"

"One thing," Mandy said. "In the two weeks before he permanently moved to Twain Harte, he had a visitor two or three times."

"Any idea who it was?"

"I showed pictures of Mickey Driscoll and Phil Curtain to the neighbor who told me this, and she positively identified Phil Curtain."

"I don't see anything sinister in that. They were old cop buddies."

"That may be true, but Curtain comes to visit, and Martin abruptly leaves town. That's not odd to you? Put it together with some woman spooking Mickey Driscoll in a restaurant, and it's all weird."

"So," I said, "Some woman spooks Mickey Driscoll, and Phil Curtain abruptly starts visiting Martin."

"That's about it," she said. "What does it all mean?"

"That is the $64,000 question. And there's more," I said. I repeated what Wilson told us about Mickey Driscoll questioning him.

"I want to talk to Mrs. Driscoll again. See if she knows anything about Mickey's activities while he was on administrative leave."

"You're in no shape to play Columbo," she told me.

"Columbo?" I said. "You're dating yourself."

"When my mother was recuperating from her back surgery, I watched the reruns with her," she said. "I'll talk to Mrs. Driscoll. How are *you* feeling?"

"Sore. Can't lie on my back. I'm pretty uncomfortable," I said. "Kendra will be my nursemaid for a few days until I'm fully up and around."

Silence.

"What is your problem—with her?"

"Let's call it woman's intuition," she finally said.

"Talk to Janet Driscoll and keep canvasing Martin's neighborhood in Petaluma. You don't live in a place that long and leave no trace behind."

"Will do. Take care of yourself."

"I will. I promise."

She hung up.

I lay in bed on my good side and thought. Driscoll is approached by a mystery woman who spooks him. He immediately reaches out to Phil Curtain, who, in turn, alerts Martin, who hightails it to Twain Harte. Within ten days, all three cops have been murdered with the same gun.

Our primary suspect, Freddy Isherwood, drives a car he owns with stolen plates and has a key to the business of one of the vics. Malik Otumba has an uncle who just died from injuries received during a shooting from Curtain twenty-odd years ago. The uncle's doctor won't let us see him. The doctor ends up dead. Carla Isherwood is the key somehow, but her brother says she's dead at the hands of the police.

Could she have found out about Curtain's dealings and threatened to tell IAB? They could examine his police record and his finances. Could he have been killed by someone over a drug deal gone bad? If so, why would Freddy Isherwood be the assassin? And what's any of this got to do with the killings of Driscoll and Martin . . . unless they were part of it?

Could *that* be it? The three of them were in it together, and they were afraid rookie Carla would turn them in. So, they set her up to beat a handcuffed Wilson, knowing that she'd be fired for it.

Two of the three were retired, and one was getting ready to. If they were stealing drugs from the evidence locker, and the department found out, they couldn't be prosecuted because the statute of limitations had long passed, but they could lose their pensions. Why not leave their fates up to IAB?

And who was this mystery woman who gave Mickey Driscoll the willies?

I went through what we had learned over and over until I again drifted off to sleep.

THIRTY-SIX

I **WAS TOO BORED** and impatient to wait for Mandy to call Janet Driscoll, so I called her about the mystery woman myself.

"I didn't get a good look at her," Janet Driscoll said. "She was halfway out the door when I returned to the table."

"So, you got a glimpse of her from behind?"

"A quick one as she was leaving. Blond. About five foot five. Nice figure."

"Would you please do me a favor and let me know if you remember anything else?" I asked.

"Do you think that woman had something to do with my husband's murder?"

"I don't know," I said. "I'm no cop, but if I were, I'd definitely consider her a person of interest. We need to find out who she is and what exactly she said."

"If I think of anything else, I'll call you," she said. "The girls and I want this solved."

"Trust me, so do we," I said. "You ladies take care of yourselves."

"We will. It's just difficult dealing with the fact that there is a 'new normal.'"

"I can imagine."

"Some days, it's hard just to put one foot in front of the other," she said.

"But you do."

"I do . . . most days. Grief ebbs and flows. One minute, I'm fine; ten minutes later, I'm a mess."

"Hang in there," I said. "You can't believe it right now, but it *will* get better."

My thoughts drifted back to the days after Mama was killed. There is a surrealism that accompanies an unexpected death. It takes a while for the brain to realize that the unthinkable has happened. That the person is gone, and you'll never see them again in this life. It's a hard thing to wrap your head around.

We said our goodbyes, and I hung up the phone just as Kendra walked in carrying a breakfast tray.

"Ya know, I can come to the table. I'm not a total invalid."

"I know. I just figured that breakfast in bed would be nice."

"It is, and I appreciate it," I said, lifting the silver cover on my plate to reveal a lovely crab and cheese omelet. If this was going to be my new normal, I could certainly get used to it.

"Who was on the phone?" Kendra asked.

"Janet Driscoll. I had a few more questions about Mickey's last days for my story. Speaking of which, I need to go into the station today."

"No, you don't," she said in the tone of a mother chastising a child.

"I'm in the middle of my final story. I've got to get this right, and I'm running out of time."

"What you've got to do is heal," she said. "You aren't going anywhere, mister."

She put a forkful of omelet into my mouth to silence my protests. It was good. Not as good as the omelets at The Egg, but good.

"Can I at least work from home, Doctor?"

"You may do light tasks. Like phone calls. I talked to Mandy, and she's coming over with some of your files."

"You talked to Mandy?" I would have loved being a fly on the wall during *that* conversation.

"Can I at least work in my den?"

"You're on bed rest. Anything you need, I'll get for you," she said.

"When did you get to be so bossy?"

"Like the saying goes, 'You ain't seen nothing yet.' Your insurance agent called. She's arranged a rental car for you to drive until you can replace your Lexus. They'll drop it off this afternoon. I'll handle that for you if you'd like."

"I would. Thanks."

"I've got a brief I need to work on. Is it okay with you if I use your den?"

"Well, since my bossy girlfriend won't let me use it, go ahead. Knock yourself out," I said.

She kissed my forehead.

"I'll knock you out if you get out of this bed today," she warned. She looked at me and smiled.

"What?"

"That's the first time you've referred to me as your girlfriend."

"I guess it is," I said after a thoughtful bit of silence. "The times they are a-changin'."

"I'll check in on you in a bit. Enjoy your breakfast," she said, leaving the room.

After I ate, I pulled out my reporter's notebook, tore out several pages of notes, spread them out on the bed, and returned to putting together the pieces of the jigsaw puzzle that was these murders.

I thought for a while, then dialed Lynn on her cell.

"I'm on my way into the office," she said. "Just got off the phone with Burke. His Ds sat on The Angler for three days. They got zip. Edna Curtain comes and goes. Freddy never left the building."

"Is the Prius still in the impound yard?"

"Freddy will have to pick the car up himself since he's the owner of record."

"And if he doesn't?"

"If he doesn't pick it up in ninety days, it's sold at auction with the proceeds going to the San Leandro Police Department."

"We need to get a warrant somehow so that your forensic team can go over every inch of that car," I said. "Either that or wait until it's sold at auction and buy it."

"The Prius is no good to us now. It's been out of his possession so long that some crafty lawyer can squawk about the chain of custody of the evidence."

"Any other thoughts?"

"None without new evidence popping up."

"I know a few friendly judges in Alameda County—" I said.

"You do? How?"

"I've emceed a few events for the Bay Area legal community. Maybe I can get one to do us a solid."

"And you're just telling me this *now*??"

"Sorry. I didn't think of it when you were calling San Francisco judges. Let me call you back."

I hung up and dialed Joe Wyatt. Wyatt is an Alameda County Municipal Court judge I once did a favor for. I came and spoke to his kid's fifth-grade class about television and how we put together the news.

I dialed his cell, and he picked up on the third ring.

"Good morning, Your Honor," I said. "Topher Davis."

"Topher! How are you?" he said in his deep baritone. I've always liked his voice. It's rich and authoritative. What you'd expect from a Central Casting judge.

"How's the family," I asked. "How's Garrett?"

"We're all fine. It's been what? Three years now? Garrett is still talking about the visit you made to his school. You made quite an impression. He says he wants to go into television."

"Tell him to be a judge instead. Better job security," I stated.

He let out a hearty laugh. "What can I do for you?" he asked.

I explained the situation.

"So," he said, "all you've got are stolen plates?"

"Technically, yes. But the car fits the description of the vehicle used in two of our homicides."

"I don't think that's enough, Topher."

"How about this?" I said. "I can put the driver at one of the murder scenes. Saw him there with my own eyes."

I told him about Freddy being part of the crowd at the Curtain shooting in Alameda. I also explained that Freddy evidently lives there.

"And you've got video of a car just like it at two of the murder scenes?"

"That is correct, sir."

Judge Wyatt paused for a minute, thinking.

"Okay, I'm going to give your sister her warrant, but the grounds are shaky. Tell her not to hang her whole case on anything she might find. An appellate judge may invalidate the warrant as being without sufficient probable cause, meaning anything you find is inadmissible. It'll be 'fruit of the poisonous tree.'"

"I'll make sure she knows. We're just looking for anything that ties Freddy Isherwood to these killings. Thank you, Your Honor," I said.

"Glad I can help."

"If Garrett ever wants another Career Day presentation, let me know."

"I'll be sure to do that," he said before ending the call. "Don't think I won't."

I immediately called Lynn and let her know she got her warrant.

"Great! My forensics team will be there this afternoon."

After Lynn hung up the phone, I felt a burst of adrenaline surge through my veins. It's a charge I get when a story is starting to heat up. It's like the runner's high that marathoners get. I love that feeling. I'm addicted to it. It's things like this that make the impending end of my job so difficult. With time quickly slipping away, I won't have too many more opportunities to experience this. God, how I hate that this is all ending. I guess what Janet Driscoll said really is true. Grief ebbs and flows.

THIRTY-SEVEN

By EARLY AFTERNOON, I was in agony. My body felt like I'd been hit by a Muni bus. My back itched like crazy in all the places where it was stitched together. That was a good sign. As Kendra said, it meant that the wounds were healing. I finally broke down and asked Kendra to bring me one of the pain pills. I swallowed it with a glass of water, and it knocked me on my ass. I slept like the dead for the remainder of the afternoon.

Around six o'clock, I was awakened by a gentle kiss from Kendra. Something was cooking in the oven. The house was filled with its aroma.

"How you feeling, Sleeping Beauty?"

"Like a scotch. Johnnie Walker Blue," I said.

"Sorry, but no. Not when you're taking pain pills."

I glanced at the clock on my nightstand.

"That was hours ago," I protested.

"You've still got the drug in your system, so no booze," she said firmly.

I wondered if she was this stern in court. My guess was, absolutely.

Statistics say that married men live longer than single men do. It's always been my contention that it's because women make you go to the doctor, and then they make you follow the doctor's orders once you get home. Most single guys I know, including yours truly, would walk around for a week with a bullet in the arm before they'd sit in a doctor's office. And even then, it would be under duress.

"I'll fix you a nice sparkling water with a squeeze of lime," she said.

"Lucky me. Can you at least make it a ginger ale with a squeeze of lemon?"

"Sure," she said. "You can sip on it while we're waiting for our guests."

"What guests? And what smells so good?"

"We're having a dinner party. Everyone wanted to come and check on you anyway, so I just invited them all to dinner. Mandy, Stu, Lynn, and Jared are coming. What you smell is homemade chicken pot pie."

"I LOVE chicken pot pie. Auntie would make it from scratch when we were kids."

"I know," she said. "You told me. That's why I'm making it. I thought it would be nice for you and Lynn."

It was a nice gesture, but I was more concerned with the guest list. Inviting Lynn and Mandy, who both wanted to put her under the microscope, was either brave or reckless. Probably a combination of both. And I was in no shape to referee.

"Everyone should be here in about an hour. Do you need help getting cleaned up?"

"No," I said. "I think I can manage."

I felt much better after getting some good sleep.

"Okay then. Go ahead and get cleaned up and dressed."

"And what is the attire for this shindig?"

"Relax. You don't need to break out your tux. It's casual," she said. "I need to check on my pot pie. Holler if you need any help."

She left the bedroom and headed for the kitchen.

I made my way to the closet and pulled out a pair of black slacks and a black dress shirt. I figured that if I were to break a suture and start bleeding, the black fabric would hide it. I showered, shaved, and got dressed. I was a little slow, but I managed to pull it off.

I walked into the living room to find Jared and Lynn on the sofa. Mandy and Stu were in the matching chairs on the far side of the coffee table. I liked this room. I should use it more often. I hadn't entertained since Sarah left.

"There he is," Jared said, walking over to give me a bear hug.

"Careful," I said. "My stitches . . ."

"Sorry," he said. "I'm a little excited. Just glad you're still with us."

"You and me both," I said.

"How you feeling?" Mandy asked.

"Stiff and sore. About what you'd expect from a guy who almost got blown up by a drone. Anything new in Petaluma?"

"I have one rule this evening, ladies and gentlemen," Kendra chimed in. "No shoptalk. Just a nice, quiet dinner."

We all agreed. Lynn's acquiescence surprised me a little. She's not someone who likes to be told what to do . . . funny after a career in the military and law enforcement, where you're constantly being given orders.

I noticed that the glass of red wine Lynn was sipping was almost empty.

She handed me the glass, and I took it over to the bar cart, where I found that Kendra had decanted a bottle of Pinot Noir. I refilled Lynn's glass and then pulled out a glass for myself that I poured a little scotch into. I was just about to take a sip when Kendra said, "That had better be ginger ale."

Jared stood and walked over to me.

"I'll take that off your hands," he said, relieving me of my beloved Johnnie Walker.

I took Lynn her glass of Pinot. She took the glass and whispered in my ear, "I like her."

One down, one to go. I wasn't as concerned about what Stu and Jared thought. Guys are generally more easygoing about issues like this. Whether they like Kendra or not is irrelevant. In other words, they mind their own business.

"Stu, can I get you a beer? And, Mandy, you still a Chardonnay girl?"

They both confirmed, and I fixed them fresh cocktails.

Kendra returned to the room and poured me a glass of ginger ale before heading back into the kitchen.

I distributed the drinks and then stood nursing my ginger ale. We were all quiet.

"Come on, guys. Are you telling me we have nothing to discuss besides these murders?" I asked.

"You know how it is when we're working on a story," Mandy said.

"Same as when I'm working on a case," Lynn said. "Tunnel vision."

"Well, let's get it out of the way before Kendra returns. Lynn, anything from forensics on the Prius?"

"Not yet. I asked the evidence techs to put a rush on it. We'll know if we've got anything in the next day or two."

"A little something of interest in Petaluma. Martin's neighbor across the street has one of those RING video doorbells. She has Curtain recorded visiting Martin a couple of weeks ago, and ... get this ... Martin packing his things into his car. He moved to Twain Harte that night."

"So," I said, "a blond mystery woman says something to Driscoll that freaks him out. Driscoll tells Curtain, who, in turn, tells Martin, who is so freaked out that he moves a hundred miles away in the dead of night."

"That about sums it up," Lynn said.

"I want to know who our mystery blonde is and what she said."

"Don't we all?" Lynn replied.

"I think it was Carla Isherwood. Janet Driscoll said Mickey looked like he'd seen a ghost," I said.

"But," Mandy interjected, "Brother Freddy said she was dead. That the police killed her."

"Just because Freddy said it doesn't make it the truth," Lynn said. "Remember, that guy's elevator doesn't go all the way up to the top floor."

"It could be drug related. Remember what Isaac Wilson told us. Curtain was stealing drugs from the evidence room and putting the stuff back on the street through him back in the day. Maybe Driscoll and Martin were involved somehow, and this woman, whoever she is, let Mickey know that she knows," I speculated.

"To what end?" Lynn asked. "The statutes of limitations on these crimes ran out ages ago. The law can't touch them. Martin and Curtain are, or rather were, retired so that they couldn't be fired. Worst-case scenario, they'd lose their pensions."

"You're assuming that Isaac Wilson is telling the truth," Mandy said. "There's zero proof."

"Why would he lie?" I asked. "As you said, it's too late to charge him with anything. Plus, thanks to his settlement and real estate acumen, he's got more money than God."

"Speaking of money, I ran the financials on our dearly departed. With Driscoll, nothing out of the ordinary. Savings account with maybe thirty thousand in it. Checking account appropriate for running his household. A healthy 401(k)."

I sipped my ginger ale, wishing it was scotch.

"Martin had over a hundred grand in his account," she continued. "A lot of money, but not really when you remember he was a single guy with no kids. Makes it easy to save." She took a healthy swig from her cocktail.

"It's with Phil Curtain that things get interesting. One point five million dollars spread out among several banks. I discovered he had a safety deposit box and got a warrant to open it. I found another fifty thousand in cash."

"There's no way that isn't drug money," I said.

"You think he was still dealing out of his fishing store?" Mandy asked.

"Where would he get the drugs? He has no access to confiscated drugs since he retired. Pot's now legal, so there's no money in it if you aren't a dispensary."

Mandy laughed. "Maybe he was able to get a prescription."

"Maybe he was," I said. "For opioids. Oxycontin. Major business the last few years."

"And what if he was getting it from Dr. Stevens," Lynn said.

"That's one hell of a theory," I answered.

"But it makes sense," Lynn said, pulling out her cell phone. "Rodney, it's Lynn. I need to see Dr. Stevens' prescriptions for the last year."

Silence as she listened.

"I know about HIPPA laws and patient privacy. I don't need patients' names. I just want to know if he was prescribing an excessive amount of controlled substances, like Vicodin, Valium, Xanax, and Oxycontin," she said. "Stuff like that. I don't care who he prescribed them to. The names are probably phony anyway. I want to know if he prescribed the drugs on an excessive basis. Okay. Thanks."

She clicked off.

"Let's see how Curtain was making his money. He sure as hell didn't make a million dollars selling trout flies," Lynn stated.

"Anything on Sheila Williams' missing .38, Mandy?" I asked.

"Nada. She says it just plain vanished along with her valuables." Mandy replied. "Lynn, you still looking at her as a suspect?"

"There are better ones," Lynn said. "But until we locate that gun and ballistics show that it isn't the murder weapon, she's not in the clear as far as I'm concerned. I did have the local pawn shops check for her stolen valuables. We came up empty."

"So, where's that leave us?" Mandy asked.

"With a whole lot of speculation and conjecture," Lynn said.

"I'd prefer the word 'theories,'" I said. "I think all roads lead back to Carla Isherwood. And . . . I don't buy that she's dead. Not based on her brother's word alone. We find her, we find some answers."

Kendra came back into the room.

"Dinner is served," she announced.

We walked into the dining room where Kendra had set a beautiful table with white linen, my good china and silverware (family heirlooms that had belonged to Auntie), and some crystal wine goblets I reluctantly purchased a few years back when Mandy was selling Princess House Crystal on the side.

Next to each setting was a small plate of herb salad tossed with raspberries. The table was centered by a crystal vase (also from Princess House) filled with wildflowers from my property. Next to the flowers was the golden crust of the pot pie.

"Everyone, please, dig in," Kendra said.

She took everyone's plate and served them a portion of pot pie from its glass baking dish. This one I bought when Sarah went through a Pampered Chef phase.

The pot pie was delicious. One bite, and I was a ten-year-old kid again having dinner with Lynn and Auntie on the rickety old card table we used for dining before she started making some real money.

"This is delicious!" I exclaimed.

"I aim to please," Kendra said, smiling.

"It tastes just like Auntie's."

"It should," Kendra said. "It's her recipe. I got it from Lynn."

"Where'd you find her recipe?" I asked Lynn.

"I have a book with all of her recipes in it. If she cooked it, she wrote down how she did it. I made a copy and gave it to Kendra."

"Now I can make all of your favorites from when you were a kid."

"Wow. The women in my life are conspiring against me," I said.

"Don't include me in that," Mandy said. "I just brought the ginger ale."

We finished dinner, and Kendra served strawberry shortcake. She had baked the little cakes herself from scratch.

After dessert, we sat in the living room drinking Rémy Martin from heated snifters. Kendra had decided that enough time had passed since I took the pain pill and allowed me to partake.

"Mandy, I'll be at the station tomorrow," I said.

"That's way too soon for you to be up and around," she said.

"I'm running out of time. We have to finish this story before I'm let go, or it will never be finished."

"And when will you consider the story finished?" Mandy asked.

"When we've solved these murders," I replied, taking a healthy sip of the Cognac. It went down easy and warmed my chest as I drank it.

We sat around for a while longer and made small talk before everyone rose to leave. Mandy hugged me and said, "I'm glad you're okay. You gave me quite a scare."

"Don't worry. You'd need kryptonite to take me out."

She laughed.

"By the way," she whispered, "The jury is still out on Martha Stewart over there."

"Lynn likes her," I said.

"Well, I'm not Lynn. I'm not saying I don't like her. I'm saying that I haven't decided yet."

My turn to chuckle. "Any idea when you'll make this final determination?"

"You'll be the first to know. Feel better," she said, kissing me on the cheek on her way out the door.

Once we were alone, Kendra looked at me and smiled.

"Thanks," I said. "That was really nice."

She gave me a peck on the lips. "You have nice friends."

She helped me undress and put on my pajamas.

Kendra kissed me good night and headed to the guest room.

I could definitely get used to this.

THIRTY-EIGHT

WHEN I AWOKE the following day, I wasn't as sore as I had been when I went to bed. I was rubbing the fog from my eyes when Kendra came in with a breakfast tray.

"You don't have to keep doing this. I can make my way to the kitchen," I said.

"I like doing this," she said, gently placing the tray of plates with silver covers across my lap. "I like taking care of you."

I lifted the silver cover on the plates to reveal two eggs, over medium, turkey sausage patties, and freshly made hash browns. I lifted the cover on a smaller plate to find two pieces of dark rye bread lightly toasted. No butter.

"How'd you know I like dry rye toast?"

"Jared told me some of the things you like to order at his restaurant."

"Girlfriend does her homework."

"Girlfriend?" she said, a slight hopefulness in her voice. "There's that word again."

"Okay, honey, you've got the job," I said.

She giggled like a sixteen-year-old girl who had just been given the varsity quarterback's class ring to wear around her neck on a chain.

She gave me a deep kiss.

"You weren't serious when you said that you were going to work this morning, were you?" she asked.

"About as serious as a heart attack. I have things to do and little time to get them done."

She looked at me in a way that said she didn't like it, but she understood.

"They were supposed to drop off a rental car for me to use until all of this was over, right?"

"There's a silver Mercedes sedan parked in front of the house," she said. The keys are on the coffee table in the living room.

"Awesome. I'd been thinking about trading the Lexus in any way. This way, I can see if I like the Benz better."

"If you're going to be stubborn, can I at least drive you in?" she said, "I have some work at my own office I can do."

"Sure. That would be nice."

I ate my breakfast, and Kendra took the tray out. I was undressing to jump in the shower when my phone rang. Lynn.

"What have you got?" I asked.

"Well, good morning to you too," she said.

"Good morning," I said. "What have you got?"

"Evidence techs found traces of gunpowder residue on the steering wheel."

"A good defense attorney can give us a million reasons for that," I said.

"I wasn't finished," she said like a little girl with a secret.

"Are you gonna tell me, or must I guess?"

"In the trunk, they found minute traces of C4."

"What?"

"At some point, the son of a bitch transported his explosives in that car."

"Tell your techs they've done a hell of a job," I said. "Now, you can pick up Brother Freddy and hold on to him this time."

"No, I can't."

"I don't understand."

"Remember what your judge friend said? The warrant is . . . shaky. I can't count on it to make my case because anything found in the search could potentially get tossed."

"Fruit of the poisonous tree," I whispered.

"Exactly," she said. "One upside, though . . . Whoever is pulling Freddy Isherwood's strings is nervous. He wants you out of the way. He thinks that's gonna stop the investigation."

"What now?"

"We can't use anything we find as a result of that forensics examination, but we *can* use things that we can reasonably argue we'd find anyway, like the brochure for the Sentinels. Let's visit Otumba again. Shake *that* poisonous tree and see what falls out," she said. "Then we'll take a little fishing trip to The Angler."

"Are your guys still watching the building?" I asked.

"Yep. Our friend Michelle called from the tow yard. Edna Curtain drove Freddy in to pick up the Prius. She paid the fee in cash. They left with Freddy driving the Prius. Give me half an hour, and I'll meet you at your place," she said.

"Kendra will drop me off at your office. How's that?"

"I told you I liked that woman. See you in an hour."

I managed to shower, shave, and dress myself, just like a big boy. Kendra had to tie my shoes because I couldn't bend over to reach my laces.

We fed Sophie, locked up the house, and headed outside.

A gorgeous silver, two-door Mercedes C 300 convertible sat in my circular drive.

"You drive the Mercedes," I told Kendra. "I'd like to see how she handles."

We hopped into the Benz with Kendra behind the wheel. Per my instructions, she didn't drive straight to the freeway. She took an alternate route that allowed us to try the twists and turns of some of the narrow roads in Palomares Canyon.

"This car is fun to drive!" she exclaimed.

"It sure does handle the curves well."

"Speaking of handling curves well . . ." She leaned over and kissed me.

"Eyes and lips on the road, please," I said.

Eventually, we hopped on I-580 and headed into the city. Traffic was moderate as Kendra dropped me off at 850 Bryant Street.

"When do you want me to pick you up?" Kendra asked.

"I'm not sure. Can I text you when I'm ready?"

"Only if you kiss me goodbye."

I did.

"Topher's got a girlfriend," she sang.

Kendra sped off, her hair blowing in the breeze of the Mercedes with its top down. I went inside and made my way to Lynn's office.

"You look like your old self. The rest has done you good," she said.

"Yeah. Other than having limited movement in my back because of the sutures, I feel fine."

"Good. Let's go visit some Black radicals."

"What are you going to tell them?"

"Everything."

THIRTY-NINE

"**T**HIS IS POLICE harassment. You can't just come barging into our place whenever you feel like it," Malik Otumba said.

He was flanked by the two bodyguards from before.

"Call a cop," Lynn said. "Oh, wait . . . There's one here."

"How's your head?" she asked the guy whose skull she had bounced off the desk on our last visit.

"Fuck you," he said, rubbing the Band-Aid on his forehead.

"Get out," Otumba demanded.

"Sure. We can talk down at 850 Bryant if you'd prefer. Grab a jacket. It's a little chilly in San Francisco today."

He paused for a moment . . . thinking.

"What do you want?" he barked.

"Some answers."

"Answers to what?"

"To start with, what's your connection to Freddy Isherwood?"

"He's got your leaflet in his car," I said.

"Lots of people have my literature. People who are tired of the destruction of Black and brown bodies by the pigs."

"Enough with the Huey Newton routine. Has Freddy Isherwood been here?" Lynn asked.

"Before you claim you don't know him, I should warn you that we know you went to school with his sister, Carla," I added.

Otumba motioned for the bodyguards to leave the room. They exited, shutting the door behind them.

"How'd you find out about that?" he demanded.

"You knew the Isherwood sibs at San Francisco State," I said.

"We knew each other. I was studying Computer Science. Carla was majoring in Criminal Justice."

"And Freddy?" Lynn asked.

"Freddy was a squatter. He was just there staying in her dorm room. Went to some of Carla's classes. Partied with us some."

"Carla was a partier?" I asked.

"Nah. Not really. A beer or two when we were kicking it. We got Freddy to hit a joint once. He coughed up a lung. It was hilarious."

"So, you were close," Lynn said.

"We weren't partners or anything, but we hung out some," Otumba said. "When he got out of the nuthouse, he showed up on my doorstep and asked if he could stay here for a couple of days."

"Why here?" Lynn asked.

"He saw my picture in the paper or something. I was surprised he came here. Like I said, it wasn't like we were partners. I knew him some in college. I let him sleep on the couch in the basement. He was here for three or four days before telling me he found a job in Alameda and would be moving to a place he found to stay out there," Otumba said. "He packed up his shit and left. That's all I know."

"When was he here last?" I asked.

"About three weeks ago," Otumba said, scratching his head to remember.

"Did you have him do errands for you?" Lynn demanded.

"What kind of errands?"

"Oh, I don't know," Lynn said. "Cop killing, maybe."

"I told you I got nothing to do with those pigs getting smoked. I'm not sorry it happened," he said, "but me and my boys had nothing to do with it."

"Tell me about your uncle Odell. We know that Phil Curtain was pressuring people to deal drugs for him in the past. Was Odell one of them?" Lynn questioned.

There was a long silence.

"The man is dead, Malik. So is Curtain. There's nobody left for you to protect."

"And nobody for you to be afraid of," I added.

"Except me," Lynn said.

Long silence.

"Yes," Otumba finally said. "Uncle Odell had been pushing meth for him. He'd supply Odell and tell him what he wanted sold."

"So, why did Curtain shoot him?" I asked.

"Curtain was taking 80, 90 percent of the money. My uncle is putting his ass on the line selling this junk, and if he gets caught, *he's* going to jail."

"If he got busted, he could have implicated Curtain," I said.

"It's his word against a cop's. Who do you think they're gonna believe?" Malik retorted.

"Same situation as Isaac Wilson," I said.

"Who?"

"Another guy Curtain forced to deal for him," Lynn stated.

"Unc thought that the reward should be equal to the risk."

"So, Odell starts skimming," Lynn said. "How much?"

"Total? Around ten thousand dollars," Malik replied.

I whistled.

"It wasn't all at once. A little here. A little there. It adds up," Malik continued.

"And Curtain found out," I said.

"And decided to make an example of him," Malik said.

"Curtain's shooting into that car was deliberate. Retribution. Hell, an execution," I said.

"That's why Dr. Stevens didn't want us talking to him," Lynn speculated.

"Stevens? That son of a bitch was in on it. After my uncle got shot, he prescribed all kinds of shit in his name and gave it to Curtain to sell. Why do you think he was in that hospital? He could have lived on his own. Hell, he could've lived here. Curtain wanted him close to make sure he wouldn't talk," Otumba said. "It also made the number of prescriptions Stevens wrote look less suspicious if he's under twenty-four-hour care. They used my uncle til the day he died."

"Did you have anything to do with Stevens's death?"

"That cracker is dead too?" He laughed. "Damn."

"I'll take that as a no," Lynn said. "I'd better not find out that you've lied to me, or . . . I'll be back."

We turned and headed for the exit.

"You know," I said. "You sounded just like Arnold Schwarzenegger when you said that."

"Practice, Big Bro," she said, "practice. Why didn't you tell me you found out Malik went to State with the Isherwoods?"

"Because I didn't."

"You ran a bluff??"

I looked at her and smiled.

"Remind me never to play poker with you," she responded as she got in on the driver's side of the unmarked.

"Where to?" I asked. "The Angler?"

"No more calls. We have a winner," she said.

"Do you still have the file on the Wilson beating with you?"

"It's in my briefcase in the backseat."

I grabbed the briefcase and thumbed through the file while Lynn drove to Alameda.

"Bingo!" I shouted.

"What?"

"It's been bothering me that all of the cops in this case were murdered with a .38 while Stevens's killing was clearly a staged car accident. Somebody drained his brake fluid. Now I know why."

"And that's because . . .?"

"Stevens was the EMT who arrived at the scene to give Wilson and his girlfriend medical aid the day of the beating. He and Curtain go *way* back," I said.

"And I'm sure he must have testified at the hearing," Lynn surmised.

"That's right. Whoever's pulling Freddy's strings wants everybody to think they're racially based revenge killings. Shooting Stevens throws that theory out the window. With a random car crash, the deaths don't look connected."

"You know," Lynn said, "you really are quite bright despite what people say."

We found a parking spot about three blocks from The Angler. Inside, Edna Curtain was showing a customer the various trout flies she had available. The man picked them up one at a time, examined them, and then put them back on the counter. Lynn and I waited until he chose three multicolored specimens and handed them to Edna to ring up and bag. This is why I don't fly fish. I don't have the patience to pick the damn flies, let alone wait for some trout to bite on one.

We didn't see Freddy Isherwood anywhere on the sales floor.

"Good afternoon, Mrs. Curtain," Lynn said, flashing her badge. "I'm Lynn Sloan with SFPD Homicide. This is my associate, Mr. Davis."

"I've already talked to the Alameda police, and I've already talked to Mr. Davis's associates from the television station. I told them everything I know about my Philly."

"We're aware of that," Lynn said.

"Well . . . Have you caught the son of a bitch who killed him?"

"We have some very strong leads we're looking at."

"What do you want?"

"Just a few more questions, ma'am," Lynn said.

"All right, I guess," she replied, returning the unpurchased flies to the display case.

She was a small, stout woman in her sixties who was built like a fireplug: short, stocky, with meaty hands and sausage-like fingers. I was surprised by the dexterity of those large digits when dealing with the delicate trout flies.

"Mrs. Curtain," I said.

"Call me Eddie. Everybody calls me Eddie. My mother named me Edna after her grandmother. Always hated that name."

"Eddie," I continued, "did you and Phil run the store together? Just the two of you?"

"Why the hell do you think I'm standing here showing grown men fake bugs?" she asked. "Yes, the two of us ran it together. Why? You want to buy it? Make me an offer. This was Philly's dream anyway, not mine."

She put the last of the trout flies in the case and locked it.

Lynn said, "He means, do you have any help? Any employees?"

"Oh, you mean Freddy?" she said.

"Who's Freddy?" I asked, feigning ignorance.

"Guy who helps out around here," Eddie said. "I wouldn't really call him an employee."

"Why not?" Lynn asked.

"Because I don't pay him. He sweeps. Stocks the shelves. Watches the register if I have a doctor's appointment."

"And for all that, you don't pay him?" I asked.

"Who are you, the Labor Board?" she said indignantly. "In exchange, he gets room and board. He sleeps on a cot in the back room."

"Where was he when Phil was killed?" I asked. Like a good lawyer, sometimes it's best to ask questions you already know the answers to.

"He was out running some errands. He has his own car, so we send him out for stock, supplies, lunch. Only reason I was out getting lunch that day was because Freddy was at the wholesaler's picking up fishing line. If not, he'd have gone to pick up lunch, and I'd have been here. I'd be as dead as Philly. God rest his soul," she said. "The kid probably saved my life."

Her eyes began to water, and she wiped them on the sleeve of the Pendleton shirt she wore.

"How'd he end up here?" I asked.

"Just showed up on our doorstep one day," Eddie said. "Said his sister used to work with Phil when he was on the job. He asked for work in exchange for a place to sleep. Philly gave it to him."

"Is he here now?" I questioned.

"No, he's making a run to the wholesaler. Then he's headed to the cleaners to pick up my dress for . . . Philly's funeral," she said, her eyes watering again.

"I'm sorry for your loss," Lynn said.

"Thank you," she replied, wiping her eyes.

"Eddie," I said, "if it isn't too much trouble, can we have a look at Freddy's room?"

"I don't see why not," she said. "This way."

She led us down a short flight of wooden stairs to a musty little space, not much bigger than a walk-in closet. The walls were unfinished plywood. It was as if someone had begun a project to refurbish it but stopped before it was completed.

There was wooden shelving where brushes sat on top of previously opened paint cans. Other tools, a hammer, a handsaw, and a mayonnaise jar filled with nails, were strewn about the shelves.

A coatrack stood in the corner of the room, supporting several Pendleton shirts and a few pairs of blue jeans. At the base of the rack were two pairs of shoes. A spit-shined pair of black shoes you could buy at any mall discount store and an expensive pair of Nike running shoes.

An old army cot was in the center of the room with a neatly folded blanket and pillow at its head. A wooden crate was beside the cot as a makeshift nightstand that supported a Coleman propane lantern.

"Lift the crate," Lynn said.

I put the lantern on the floor and lifted the wooden box to find a framed eight-by-ten color photograph. I picked it up. Blond hair. High cheekbones. An aquiline nose. Carla Isherwood in her police uniform.

"Take a look at this," I told Lynn, handing her the photo.

"Academy graduation picture," she said. "Same one that's in her file. A reminder for him of why he does what he does."

She handed the photo back to me.

We then examined the other items under the crate: a .38-caliber Smith & Wesson revolver and a brick of a gray, clay-looking substance.

I let out an "Oh shit."

Lynn coolly and calmly told me to put the crate back over the explosives carefully. I did as she instructed. She then grabbed the portable police radio on her hip and hit the transmit button.

"This is Detective Lynn Sloan," she said into the walkie-talkie. "I'm in Alameda at The Angler fishing shop on Park Street. We've just discovered enough C-4 to take out a city block. We need the area evacuated and the bomb squad here at the store ASAP."

"Copy that," said a crackly voice on the radio. "Alerting the Alameda PD now."

"Copy," Lynn said, putting the radio back on her belt.

She turned her attention to Eddie. "Did you know about this?"

"Hell no! Do you think I'd work ten hours a day standing on top of a bomb?" she said incredulously. "This is all Freddy's shit. Ask him."

"I plan to. When did he leave?" Lynn asked.

"An hour ago," Eddie said.

"Where was he going first?" I asked.

"Wholesaler," Eddie said.

"What dry cleaner do you use?" Lynn asked.

"What?"

"You said Freddy was out picking up your dry cleaning. Which one is it?" I asked.

"Evans Dry Cleaning on High Street."

Lynn again removed the radio from her belt and gave dispatch the location of the dry cleaner and Freddy's description. Afterward, she removed the crate, took out her phone, and took pictures of everything: the gun, the C-4, their positions, the cot, and the photo of Carla. She then used a ballpoint pen from her vest pocket to pick up the .38 by the barrel to preserve fingerprints.

She dropped it in one of the plastic evidence bags she carried in her pocket.

Lynn said, "What did he have with him when he came here?"

"All I saw was a duffel bag with him. I didn't know what was in it. I assumed it was clothes, a toothbrush, stuff like that. I swear I knew nothing about this. If you think we'd have let him stay here carrying a brick of plastic explosives, you're crazy," she said with exasperation.

Lynn looked around the small room. "There's no duffel bag here," she said.

"He came carrying a duffel bag. I swear. It was a green canvas. Like something you'd find at an army surplus store," Eddie said.

"When was the last time you saw it?"

"I don't know. Maybe that first day he showed up here."

"So, a loaded .38 and a brick of plastic explosives," I said to Lynn. "Is *this* enough to hold him on?"

"Ask me again while I'm putting cuffs on the bastard."

FORTY

THE BOMB SQUAD arrived about ten minutes after Lynn had summoned them. They evacuated the area and went to work.

The SLPD surveillance of Freddy had ended the day before, so Lynn put out a BOLO on him. She described the Prius sans license plates because there was no telling what plates he'd use. She told dispatch to have officers watching the dry cleaners and the fishing equipment wholesaler Eddie told us about. The suspect was to be considered armed and dangerous.

We stepped outside, where the whole street had been cordoned off for six blocks. Uniformed Alameda PD cops were diverting traffic and keeping the press (including Mandy and Stu) and onlookers at bay.

We approached a beefy African American officer who appeared to be in charge of the operation, and Lynn flashed her badge.

"Detective Lynn Sloan SFPD," she said, extending a hand. "I'm the one who called it in."

"Sergeant Luther Denton," he responded, shaking Lynn's hand.

"You've got a brick of C4 under a wooden crate in the basement."

"Anything else we need to know?" he asked.

"I'd sweep the building to see if the suspect found any other hiding places for explosives," Lynn suggested.

"We're on it," Denton said as he entered the fishing store.

As he left, a call came through for Lynn on her radio. Freddy was at Evans' Dry Cleaners. The cops had surrounded the place, and Freddy had an AR-15 and hostages.

Well, at least we knew what was in his duffel bag.

We jumped in Lynn's unmarked and raced to the scene.

The cleaners was a two-story stand-alone building with the business on the ground floor and a personal residence, presumably the owners', on top. A plate glass window in front of the business area of the store had been shot out.

We made our way through the throng of police, their guns drawn, surrounding the building. Across the street was a Bank of America. Sharpshooters had positioned themselves on the roof, peering through the scopes of their rifles that were trained on the cleaners below.

Lynn and I made it to the cop in charge, a blond-haired, blue-eyed sergeant named James Somers. Lynn flashed her badge.

"Detective Lynn Sloan, SFPD." She gestured toward the cleaners. "The gentleman responsible for all of this commotion is a suspect in multiple homicides I'm working. Police homicides. He's a cop killer. What have we got?"

"The suspect was in the cleaners with a green duffel bag over his shoulder. Two of our officers watched him enter and saw that he matched the description on the BOLO. They parked their squad car directly in front of the cleaners, and the suspect pulled a long gun out of his bag and started shooting. We haven't returned fire because we have a hostage situation."

"How many hostages?"

"We figure about half a dozen—mostly the Korean family who own the business and live upstairs. A few customers who were in the wrong place at the wrong time are also present. The hostage negotiator is on his way," Somers said.

"Would you mind if I talked to him?" Lynn asked. "We have history."

"I'd prefer to wait for the hostage negotiator, Detective," Somers said sternly.

He was tall, lean, and muscular—the kind of man whose every utterance came across as a command.

"I've talked to him before. He knows me. Let me see if I can get those people out of there."

Somers stroked his chin and thought for a minute. "All right, I'll give you five minutes," he said.

"We need him alive," she told him.

I stood next to Somers just as I saw Mandy and Stu setting up across the street. Lynn reached inside Somers's squad car, grabbed the mic, and put it in loudspeaker mode.

"Freddy," she said into the mic, "It's Lynn Sloan. Remember me? We talked in San Leandro."

Silence came from the dry cleaner. Freddy was standing inside the cleaners behind the counter. He had a terrified young Korean girl next to him. She looked to be about fourteen or fifteen. Tears were streaming down her face. The barrel of Freddy's assault weapon was pressed against the back of her head.

"Freddy, we talked about Carla, remember?" Lynn said into the mic.

"The police killed Carla," he screamed. "Now they want to kill me!"

"Nobody wants to hurt you, Freddy," she said softly. It was like an adult talking to a wayward child.

"Yes, they do," he screamed. "They want to shoot me. They all have their guns pointed at me."

"They're just scared, Freddy. Like you are. Nobody wants to see anyone get hurt."

Freddy began to cry.

"Freddy, I'm coming in. Just me, nobody else. Is that okay?"

Freddy thought about it for a moment. "Just you?" he finally said.

"Just me."

"How do I know you won't shoot me?"

Lynn walked to the front of the army of police and squad cars. She pulled her Glock from its holster, knelt, and put the gun on the ground. Then she stood up with her hands in the air.

"I'm not armed, Freddy. See? I put my gun down. I just want to talk, just you and me."

"Just you and me?" he repeated.

"Just us. I promise."

"I don't want to talk to the police. The police killed Carla."

"Do you think that this is what Carla would want? You hurting innocent people?"

"They're not innocent."

She took a few steps toward the shattered window.

"Let the girl go, Freddy. Let her go, and you and I can talk."

Lynn took a few more steps forward.

"Stay there," he demanded.

Lynn stopped dead in her tracks.

"You don't want to hurt anybody, Freddy. Let's you and I talk, and we'll get the cops who killed Carla."

"And you won't shoot me?" he asked.

"You saw me lay my gun down on the ground."

Freddy looked at the people in the cleaners . . . an older Korean couple, presumably the girl's parents, and a young African American man in a pullover sweater with his dress shirt collar exposed. I pegged him as a college student. A woman in her fifties who was so scared she was chewing her fingernails to the quick was also there.

"You'll help me?" he asked Lynn.

"I'll help you," she said, walking closer, "but you'll have to let the people go, Freddy."

He looked at the hostages again. "Tell the police to stop pointing their guns at me," he demanded.

"Let them go, Freddy," she repeated. "They haven't done anything."

"If I let them go, they'll shoot me."

Lynn turned toward Somers. "Have your people stand down," she said.

Somers looked at her momentarily, shook his head, and picked up the mic in his squad car.

"Officers, stand down," he said over the loudspeaker. "I repeat, stand down."

The officers complied and stopped pointing their weapons at Freddy . . . all except the sharpshooters on the bank roof across the street. They didn't move a muscle as they continued to look through their scopes.

"No one is going to shoot you, Freddy. See? They aren't pointing their guns at you anymore. Let the people go so we can talk."

Freddy looked at the hostages. "Get out of here," he said, shoving the girl away from the muzzle of his gun. "All of you, get out."

The hostages ran out of the building and took cover with the officers behind their squad cars and out of harm's way.

Lynn walked up to Freddy, who then trained his rifle on her.

"You don't need that," she said gently. "Let me have it so we can get the people who hurt Carla."

"You'll help me?" he said with the innocence of a four-year-old.

Lynn had her hand on the gun and slowly pushed the barrel down to point it at the floor.

"Freddy, can I tell them we're coming out?"

Silence.

"Freddy?"

He nodded his head.

"We're coming out!" she yelled.

"Why don't you give me the gun?"

He began to point the gun in Lynn's direction just as a sniper's bullet tore through his chest from the bank across the street.

Somers grabbed his mic.

"Goddamn it, I said stand down!" he shouted.

Lynn took the rifle from Freddy's hands and cradled him in her arms.

"We need a bus!" she screamed.

A crimson stain in the middle of Freddy Isherwood's chest began to expand.

"It's gonna be okay," she said gently.

"I told you," he rasped. "I told you they'd shoot me."

EMTs were already on the scene and rushed to the cleaners to see what they could do.

Ten minutes later, Freddy Isherwood was dead.

FORTY-ONE

A FURIOUS LYNN watched as the coroner's van came and took Freddy's body away.

"What the hell happened?" she said to Somers.

"One of our snipers got a little trigger-happy. He says he thought the suspect was about to shoot you," Somers said.

"What he was about to do was give me the gun and surrender himself peacefully," she said angrily.

Rarely had I seen her so mad ... unless, of course, it was at me.

We went to the Alameda PD Headquarters, where Lynn and I were interviewed about what we found at The Angler as well as the hostage standoff. After about three hours, we were released. Lynn was still furious.

"I don't see why you're so mad. The guy was a serial cop killer, for Christ's sake. Good riddance," I said.

"But he died before we could figure out why ... and who was behind him," she said.

"Does the reason really matter? We took a killer off the streets. We should feel good about that."

"And Geppetto?" she asked.

"Maybe there was no Geppetto," I said.

"A lone nut acting alone?"

"It wouldn't be the first time," I said.

"It's not that simple. There's more. My gut tells me there's more."

Lynn's instincts are what make her such a great detective . . . but she's not infallible.

Lynn dropped me at my house in Castro Valley and then headed to the city in her unmarked. She wanted ballistics tests on that .38 Smith & Wesson just as soon as she could get them. I entered the house and was greeted by yet another wonderful smell from my kitchen.

Kendra met me at the door with a kiss and then put a double Johnnie Walker Blue in my hands.

"You haven't been taking any pain pills today, correct?"

"No, Mother, I haven't."

"Then sit on the couch and enjoy your scotch. Dinner in about half an hour."

I took a healthy whiff of the aroma.

"Prime rib?"

"Not the Hopper, but I think you'll like it."

I eased my way onto the couch. Sophie sprang onto the cushion beside me and rested her head on my thigh.

"I missed you, too, honey," I said, scratching behind her ears.

Soon, Kendra called me into the dining room, where she had already cut two generous, blood-rare pieces of prime rib and plated them with baked potatoes and some freshly ground horseradish. A Caesar salad sat in wooden bowls next to our plates.

We had a pleasant evening. After dinner, she worked from my den and finished her tasks. I told her what I could about my afternoon without jeopardizing sensitive information. Church and state.

We ended the evening with lovemaking for a nightcap. Kendra had to be gentle because of the stitches, but she pulled it off. Afterward, we lay in bed sweaty and exhausted.

"Think I'll go home tonight," she said. "I've got a few more things to work on."

"I really wish you wouldn't," I said.

"Excuse me?"

"I've kind of gotten used to you. I wish you'd stay."

"What exactly are you asking me, Mr. Davis?"

"You've got some of your stuff here . . . Why not bring the rest of it?"

"You mean . . . You want me to move in?"

"I know it's only been a couple of weeks, but you just . . . fit."

She leaned in and kissed me. "I'll think about it," she said with a coyness in her voice. "I'll think about it."

"Take all the time you need."

FORTY-TWO

"**I**T'S OUR MURDER weapon, all right," Lynn said.

"Are they sure?"

I was driving across the Bay Bridge in the rental Mercedes when Lynn called to give me the news.

"They're positive. It's a match for all three homicides."

"Who's it registered to?" I asked.

"No idea. The serial number has been filed off."

"I wonder if it's Sheila Williams's missing .38."

"It's possible."

"What now?" I asked.

"I have the unenviable task of telling Martha Isherwood that she needs to make arrangements for her son's body. Freddy's name hasn't been released to the media, pending notification of his next of kin."

"I've been thinking about what you said about there being a mastermind," I said. "You're right. We can't call this case closed. Anybody with a brain in their head can see that Freddy Isherwood didn't have the mental capability to pull off something like this by himself."

"Well, somebody's certainly changed their tune from last night."

"I thought about it, and the more I pondered it, the clearer it became. He didn't act alone."

"Conspiracy's a tough thing to prove. They still don't know who killed Kennedy," Lynn pointed out.

"Want me to go with you to Martha Isherwood's to make the notification?" I asked.

"Sure. If you'd like."

"I'll meet you there."

I got off the bridge at Treasure Island, turned around, and headed for Fairfield.

Traffic was light, and I made the trip in half an hour. It gets hot in Fairfield this time of year. As soon as I crossed the Carquinez Bridge, the temperature immediately jumped into the triple digits.

This wasn't my first death notification. I'd gone with Lynn several times concerning stories I was working on. I don't know how she's able to do it as often as a homicide detective has to. It's hard for me. You never know how the family member is going to take it. Some cry. Others scream and become hysterical. One woman fainted.

We found Martha Isherwood gardening in the front yard. She wore a dark green sundress, gardening gloves, and an oversized floppy straw hat as she dug in the dirt with a small spade, planting geraniums. I thought about how, on a beautiful sunny day, we were about to change this poor woman's life irrevocably.

"Detective. Mr. Davis," she said as we got out of our cars. "What a lovely surprise. Can I offer you anything? Iced tea? Lemonade?"

"No, thank you, ma'am. I'm afraid that this isn't a social call," Lynn said.

"Oh?" Martha replied.

"I'm afraid that I have some unfortunate news to give you ..."

"Did you see the news last night or this morning?" I asked. Coverage of the standoff was exhaustive.

"No," she said. "I read some and then went to bed early. Why?"

I looked at the ground. Lynn was silent as she tried to find the right words.

Martha Isherwood's tone changed. "Which one?" she asked.

"I'm sorry?" Lynn said.

"Which one is dead? Freddy or Carla?"

Lynn drew in a big breath before exhaling the word "Freddy."

"We're sorry for your loss," she said.

"I've expected this news for years. It was only a question of which one would be first," Martha Isherwood said.

"I think I can use a glass of iced tea," she said, standing up. "Let's get inside out of this hot sun."

Lynn and I looked at her. Not the reaction we were expecting. But as I said, you never truly know what to expect.

We followed her into the house and then into her kitchen, where she opened the avocado-colored refrigerator and pulled out a clear glass pitcher of iced tea with thinly cut lemon slices floating at the top.

"Mr. Davis, would you please be a dear and hand me one of the glasses in the cupboard behind you?"

I turned around and opened the wooden cupboard door to find a neatly sorted array of drinking glasses and coffee mugs. The glasses had a yellow flower pattern all over them. I took out one and handed it to her.

"Are you sure I can't offer you anything?"

"Yes, ma'am. We're fine," Lynn said.

Martha Isherwood poured herself a glass of iced tea and took a large swig, draining half the glass. Then she refilled and took a smaller sip.

"What happened?" she asked.

Lynn explained about the homicides, Freddy's declaration that Carla was dead, and his shooting.

Martha shook her head.

"Both of them gone. Twenty minutes ago, I had two kids. Now, I have none."

"Is there someone we can call? Someone to come and be with you?" Lynn asked.

"No, thank you," she said, taking another sip of iced tea.

"Want to hear something funny?" she asked. "I can't cry for them. They were my children, and I loved them, but I can't cry for them. Isn't that strange?"

"People react to grief in different ways," I said. "There's no right way or wrong way to do it."

"For me, Freddy and Carla have been dead for years. I can't cry for them. I guess I'm all cried out."

"We don't have confirmation of Carla's death. That came from Freddy. He didn't give us any details. He just said that Carla was dead and that the police had killed her. After she left the SFPD, she fell completely off the radar. We can't find a trace of her," Lynn said. "Do you know what Freddy meant when he said that 'the police killed Carla'?"

"Not a clue," Martha Isherwood said again, filling her glass. "I know that she loved being a police officer. I can only imagine what she must have felt when she lost that job."

"Do you think their father might have any useful information?"

"I doubt it. Even though the kids blamed me for Fred Senior leaving us, once he took up with his office bimbo, I know he didn't have much contact with the kids on his own. He was too consumed with . . . *her*."

I could feel the venom dripping from the word "her." Some hurts and resentments last a lifetime.

"Do you have any idea where we might reach Mr. Isherwood?" Lynn said. "I'd like to talk to him."

"Why in the world would you want to do that? He has nothing of any value to say to you or anyone else," Martha declared.

"I think we should notify him as well," Lynn said.

Martha let out a big sigh, took a sip from her iced tea, and then said, "Last I heard, he was still working at the Jelly Belly factory with his whore."

I've often wondered why spurned wives always start throwing the word "whore" around when it comes to the other woman. It's the husband who's breaking his vows. Although, in these situations, there's usually enough vitriol and blame to go around.

"Are you sure there's no one we can call for you? Someone to come and sit with you for a little bit?" Lynn said.

"I'll be fine. I'm just going to go back to my geraniums," she said. "I'm a whiz at raising plants. Too bad I wasn't as good with raising kids."

We said our goodbyes and went to our respective cars. Lynn called the Jelly Belly factory. Fred Senior no longer worked there, but his former assistant (this time a male) was able to get a current cell phone number for him. Lynn reached out, and he agreed to meet us for lunch at the local Denny's.

FORTY-THREE

IT WAS AROUND 12:15 when Lynn and I slid into an orange booth at the Fairfield Denny's. I like Denny's. There's something comforting about knowing that you can walk into any Denny's in the country and get the exact same menu with the exact same food that tastes the exact same way. I love consistency as much as I hate change.

The waitress, a thin, towering brunette about six feet tall and twenty-two years old, poured us steaming mugs of coffee.

"May I take your order?" she asked.

"Not quite yet," I said. "We're waiting on a friend."

"You wouldn't happen to know Fred Isherwood by chance?" Lynn asked.

"Big Freddy? Everybody knows Big Freddy. He comes here for lunch every day. Sometimes dinner too."

"Would you please do me a favor and have the hostess point him to our table when he gets here?" I said, slipping her a ten-dollar bill.

"I'll personally escort him here myself," she said, slipping the bill into her apron pocket.

Once she'd gone, Lynn and I sat drinking our coffee.

"Why do I feel like I'm cheating on Jared by eating here?" I asked.

"It's okay," Lynn said. "It's lunch, not breakfast. And you're not ordering an omelet, are you?"

"No."

"Then I have the power to grant you special dispensation," she said.

"Thank you, Father. Want to hear my confession now too?"

I glanced up to see our skinny waitress friend leading a silver-haired gentleman in our direction. He too was tall, six foot two or three. He wore a pair of brown slacks, a white dress shirt, and a tweed blazer, even though it was a billion degrees outside. Based on what we knew about him, he had to be pushing eighty, but he didn't look it. He was lean and muscular. He obviously took good care of himself. He could easily have passed for a man twenty years his junior.

"Which one of you is Detective Sloan?" he said upon reaching our table.

"That would be me," Lynn said, extending her hand.

Fred Senior shook it.

"And you would be Topher Davis from the TV."

"I thought you looked familiar," the waitress said.

"Thanks for watching," I replied.

"Yep, we got us a genuine celebrity in the house," he said, with "genuine" coming out of his mouth as "genuwine."

Fred Sr. and I shook hands. He had a firm, tight grip. The same bone-crushing handshake people said Carla offered.

Lynn scooted over toward the window.

"Please, sit," she said.

Fred Sr. slid into the booth next to her.

"Want your usual, Freddy?" the waitress asked.

"That sounds good."

"Okay," she said, writing in her notepad. "Grand Slam. Eggs over medium, pancakes, bacon, and hash browns."

Then she directed her attention to Lynn and me.

"What can I get you?"

"Cobb salad, no bacon. Low-calorie dressing on the side," Lynn said.

"That sounds good. I'll have the same," I said.

The waitress wrote down our orders, then said, "Back in a jiff."

"So, how did you get my number?" Fred Sr. asked.

"We called the jellybean factory," I told him. "They told us how to reach you."

"Retired from there three years ago," he said. "I'm still too damned young for a rocking chair, so I've been buying and rehabbing houses."

If he was too young for a rocking chair, I *definitely* was. Maybe I can rehab and flip houses once my TV life is over. Who am I kidding? I call in an electrician to change my lightbulbs.

"On my way to look at a duplex in Vallejo once we're done here," he said. "So, what can I do you for?"

The waitress returned to the table and poured Fred Sr. a mug of coffee. She then headed back toward the kitchen.

"I'm afraid I have some bad news," Lynn said.

"Oh?"

"I'm sorry," Lynn replied. "There's no easy way to say this. Your son, Fred Junior, was killed last night."

Isherwood sat stone faced. It was as though Lynn had told him that cantaloupes were on sale at the local market. No reaction at all. Just like Martha.

Lynn told him about the standoff, the murders, and Carla.

"We're very sorry for your loss," I said.

"I'm sorry for your loss" is the standard cop line for all survivors of deceased loved ones. It's a formulaic show of empathy. I've adopted it myself on many occasions, like this one.

As I said before, people grieve in different ways. Like Martha, Fred Sr. was almost blasé about the news.

"I lost them both long ago when I left their mother for Gina," he said.

"Your current wife?" I asked.

"Current *ex*-wife," Fred Sr. corrected. "We were married about six years. Then I caught her in bed with one of the guys from the shipping department. Fired him. Divorced her."

"I'm sorry," I said.

"If she did it *with* you, she'll do it *to* you," he offered.

"Why the estrangement from your kids?" I asked. "Martha said that Carla blamed her for the breakup."

"You've been talking to Martha?" He chuckled. "How is the old gal? Still in the Fairfield house I gave her?"

"Planting geraniums," I said.

"Those were always her favorite flowers," Fred Sr. smiled. "As for the estrangement, Carla and Gina hated each other's guts. After Martha and I split, Carla and Freddy tried living with us for a few months. It just didn't work. It came down to my having to choose between my wife and my kids. My kids were practically adults at that point, so I chose my wife. Then I find out she's screwing around on me," he said, shaking his head.

The waitress returned and set our meals in front of us. Fred Isherwood Sr. smeared a healthy amount of butter on the pancakes in his Grand Slam breakfast and drenched them in syrup. He then poured syrup over his eggs, bacon, and hash browns.

The waitress had called this his "usual." How in the world did he look so fit on that kind of diet?

"We're trying to figure this whole thing out. We don't believe Freddy acted alone," Lynn said. "When was the last time you saw him?"

"A few weeks back. He'd just been released from a mental hospital." He took a bite of a pancake.

"In Napa," I said.

"There was always something 'off' about that kid," he stated.

"You act as though these killings don't surprise you," I remarked.

"When you get to be my age, nothing surprises you, son. You learn that anybody is capable of anything under the right or the wrong set of circumstances."

"What did he say? Where did he tell you he was going?"

"He showed up on my doorstep one Saturday and said he'd just gotten out of the mental hospital. He told me that the police had killed Carla."

"Did he go into any more detail than that?" Lynn asked.

"No. I asked him too. He just said Carla was dead and that the police had killed her."

"Then what happened?" I asked.

"I told him that he could stay with me if he wanted. He said he already had a place to stay in Oakland and was looking for a job."

"That must have been when he stayed with the Sentinels," Lynn conjectured.

"The who?" Fred Sr. asked.

"The Black Sentinels for Justice," Lynn said. "They're an antipolice group in Oakland. Your son stayed with them for a few days after he was released from the hospital."

Fred Sr. took another bite of his syrupy concoction.

"Anything else?" Lynn asked.

"He asked me if he could borrow some money until he found work somewhere. He said he needed a car, so I wrote him a check for fifteen grand. Guilt money. It was the least I could do. He said he'd pay me back when he could. I told him not to worry about it, and that was that."

That explains how he got hold of the Prius.

We finished lunch and gleaned what information we could from Fred Sr., but Martha was right. He didn't have much new information to share.

He ate some more, and then it was like something hit him out of the blue. "Man," he said, "both kids gone."

Lynn gave Fred Sr. her card and wrote the number of the Alameda County Coroner's Office on the back.

"Someone will need to claim the remains," she said. "Just call the coroner's office. They'll guide you through the process. I also wrote down Martha's number in case you'd like to talk and do this together."

With that, his veneer cracked as tears began to well up in his eyes.

"Again, sir, we're very sorry for your loss," Lynn said.

The check came, and before I could get it, Fred Sr. snatched it off the table. "This is on me," he said.

We thanked him, and we all walked out into the parking lot together. We said our goodbyes, and Fred Sr. got into his car, a late-model maroon Cadillac. He fired up the engine and zoomed out of the parking lot.

"What do you think?" I asked.

"I think that is one fucked-up family. Dysfunctional doesn't even begin to describe it."

"Yeah," I said. "Too bad everybody can't be The Brady Bunch like us."

"Shit," she said with a laugh.

Lynn's phone rang, and she answered it.

"Sloan."

She listened for a minute, then said, "Stay with him and keep me apprised." After that, she clicked off.

"I've got OPD watching Otumba."

"Why?"

"I want to know if he was the one pulling the strings," she said. "Now that Freddy's dead, I want to see what he does."

"If it's true, how in the world will we prove it?" I asked.

"We'll drive off that bridge when we come to it."

FORTY-FOUR

"**W**HAT THE HELL do you mean you lost him?" Lynn yelled into her hands-free cell.

We had dropped the loaner Mercedes off at my place, and I was now in Lynn's unmarked. She was driving me into the city to do my final broadcast. She remained on her hands-free cell.

"We lost the tail. He knew we were behind him, ran a red at a busy intersection on Grand in Oakland, and vanished," came the voice from the other end.

"Well, what about the tracker?" Lynn said. "You *did* put a GPS tracker on the vehicle, right?"

"We did, ma'am. He apparently found it. It led us to a garbage can on University Avenue in Berkeley."

"Damn."

"What should we do now, ma'am?"

"What the hell do you think you should do?" she yelled. "Find him!"

She hung up the phone.

"Of all the incompetent . . ." she ranted.

"We don't have anything on the guy. It's all conjecture and speculation," I said.

"Malik Otumba is involved in this. I know he is. We'll find him, and he'll make a mistake, and when he does, I'll be ready for him."

"Looks like all of the other agencies believe you closed this case. Freddy Isherwood Jr. did all three cops to avenge his late sister," I said. "Maybe we should just take the win, Sis."

"It's too pat, Chris. All tied up in a nice little bow," she said. "Freddy Isherwood didn't plot those killings by himself. He was directed. I won't call this thing closed until I find out exactly who that director was."

We sat in silence as she dropped me off at the station for what would be the last time. Stu and Mandy had shot and put together a great package on the Jamal Williams killing and the slayings of Driscoll, Curtain, and Martin. There was background on how Sheila coped and how Driscoll struggled with the incident. There was info on the Curtain shooting and Odell Watkins. There were brief interviews with Edna Curtain and Janet Driscoll. Mandy put in what we had on Freddy, including footage of his own shooting. We left out the part where I was almost blown to bits.

I had thought about doing a final sign-off and thanking the audience for watching all those years, but I didn't really see the point. It seemed too self-serving. I signed off as I always did. We went to commercial, and everyone gave me a round of applause. That was nice. Mandy had packed up my dressing room for me and arranged for the contents to be dropped at my house. I came home to Kendra with a huge bouquet Curt had sent over with a heartfelt thank-you from the station for all my years of service.

And with that, my television career was officially over.

FORTY-FIVE

THE WARMTH OF the Saturday morning sun woke me as it beamed through my bedroom skylight and bathed my face. Lying there in Kendra's arms, I felt . . . rejuvenated. She slept with her head on my shoulder, her breathing in tandem with mine. I carefully extricated myself so as not to wake her up. I put on my black silk bathrobe and slippers, headed toward the redwood deck that abuts my bedroom, quietly opened the sliding glass door, and went outside.

It was a beautiful morning. It sounds corny, but I couldn't think of any description other than "picture perfect." The sky was that shade of blue you see in old MGM Technicolor musicals. So blue that you know it's just got to be a soundstage in Hollywood someplace. God doesn't make mornings with skies like this. Only this particular morning, He did. I took it as a sign. If God can make a morning like this, nothing is impossible. It was the beginning of a new day, a new venture, and a new life.

I walked off the deck and over to my lemon tree, where I plucked two fat, ripe citrus specimens.

Then I went back inside and brought the lemons into the kitchen. Next, I took two English muffins from the bread box and placed them on the counter. I opened the refrigerator and pulled out a stick of butter, eggs, asparagus, and some crab meat wrapped in butcher paper. I spread the ingredients all over the kitchen island. Then I returned to the fridge and took out an ice-cold bottle of Taittinger I'd been saving for a special occasion. I popped the cork, filled two champagne flutes, and set them on the counter. I sipped from one of the flutes. Yummy. I love Taittinger almost as much as I love Johnnie Walker Blue. Not quite, but almost.

I was filling the coffeemaker with French Roast when I heard a voice behind me.

"Is this for me?" Kendra said, indicating the full flute of champagne on the counter. She was barefoot, wearing nothing but the pink silk robe I'd given her as a "just because" gift.

"It sure is," I said, refilling my own glass.

"What's the occasion?"

"The beginning of a new life."

"Oh, are you pregnant?" she asked, sipping from her flute.

"Damn," I said. "I was hoping I wouldn't show for another few weeks."

Kendra laughed.

"A new venture," I said. "Mandy, Stu, and I are starting a new media company. We'll continue doing the same work we've been doing, except we'll do it for podcasts, YouTube, and the web. The best part is that we'll own the whole thing, and we'll decide what to cover and when."

"That's wonderful," she said.

"Isn't it? I'm too damn young to retire. I've got more money than I know what to do with. I figured, why not tell the stories I want to tell in the way I want to tell them."

She walked over and kissed me.

"Here's to your new life," she said, clinking our flutes together. "Congratulations."

I pulled a small brass saucepan from the cupboard, put the stick of butter in, placed it on the stove, and lit the burner.

"Whatcha makin'?" she asked, refilling her glass.

"Crab Benedict. Have a seat."

Kendra sat on one of the stools in front of the island and watched as I separated the eggs and squeezed the lemons. I then whisked the juice in the saucepan with the melted butter and egg yolks.

"Hollandaise from scratch," she said. "Your culinary skills continue to astound."

"Oh, I'm full of surprises. Wait and see," I replied.

"Do you know what your first story is about yet? The first thing you'll take on for the new company?" she asked, taking a small sip of champagne.

I grabbed my large butcher knife from its block and turned away to the cutting board to slice the asparagus.

"We're gonna pick up the Driscoll story right where we left off," I said.

"Haven't you been through enough with all that? It's time to move on. Let it go."

"I can't," I said. "It isn't finished yet. There's too much we still don't know."

"I'm pleading with you to drop this. Please," she said.

"Are you worried about my safety?"

"More than that," she said.

The bullet's force in my left shoulder was enough to spin me one hundred and eighty degrees. I slumped to the floor facing Kendra. She stood on the other side of the kitchen island. She had a small silver pistol in her right hand. Auntie's snub-nosed .38. Damn it, Lynn must have left it here even after I told her I didn't want a gun in my house. If I don't die today, I'm going to kill her.

"You just couldn't leave well enough alone," Kendra said, her eyes welling up with tears.

As she stood there holding the revolver, it was as though she'd taken off a mask, and I was seeing her, *really* seeing her, for the first time. The high cheekbones. The aquiline nose. Her hair, eye color, and skin tone were different, but it was the same woman.

"Carla Isherwood," I whispered.

The pain in my shoulder was agonizing. A pool of blood began to spread across my robe around the bullet hole.

I tried to speak, but I could only get out: "Why?"

"I tried to warn you off. I've grown to . . . care about you," she said. "Most sane people would have quit once the bullet came in the mail, but not you."

"What about the Lexus? The drone? Was that you trying to kill me?"

"If I'd wanted you dead that day, you'd be dead," she said. "I sat in my car about half a mile from that comic book store and watched you on the drone's video feed. I tried to give you one more warning to back off. I waited until you were mostly clear of the blast area before I detonated the C4."

My voice was weak . . . my breathing labored. Tears were beginning to stream down Kendra's cheeks.

"Now look what you're making me do," she said, using the back of her free hand to wipe her eyes. "Why are you making me do this? Why couldn't you just leave it alone?"

I needed to stall for time. If she was talking, she wasn't shooting.

"That night at the House of Prime Rib, were you tailing me, or was that a coincidence?"

"Your sister told you. There are no coincidences," she said. "I'm really going to miss her."

"What do you mean?" I asked. My voice was getting weaker by the second.

"I can't let her live now. After we finish here, I have to . . . I didn't want to hurt you. I swear I didn't. I only wanted the bastards who destroyed my life. Driscoll, Curtain, and Martin. They got me fired and labeled a racist for doing what Curtain, my superior officer, ordered me to do," she said. "As you well know, they kill unarmed Black people, they get administrative leave with pay, and then, they get to keep their jobs."

"Why didn't you just tell IAB about Curtain?" I asked. "Surely, they wouldn't have fired you if they knew what was really going on."

Her tears were flowing harder and faster now. So was the blood from my shoulder.

"That blue wall is made up of 'good ole boys.' IAB wouldn't have given me the time of day."

"Why all of . . . this?" I said, indicating her appearance.

"I wanted to disappear, and I got tired of being called a racist after that beating incident, so I decided to see what it would be like to live my life as a Black woman. Darkening my skin and hair wasn't hard. The toughest part was getting Freddy to stop calling me 'Carla.' I finally drilled into his head that Carla was dead. Curtain, Driscoll, and Martin had killed her."

The police killed Carla.

I needed to keep her talking until I could figure a way out of this . . . if I didn't bleed out first . . .

"Let me get this straight. You're fed up with white male cops getting a walk for killing unarmed Black people, and you want revenge for your firing, so you have Freddy kill them, figuring the cops would look at it as retribution from a radical anticop group like the Sentinels," I said. "Then you try to implicate Malik, who's advocating the killing of cops, by putting his leaflet in Freddy's car."

"Malik is a pussy. He hasn't got the balls to kill anybody. He talks all this shit, but he won't do anything. He was just a useful idiot. He started getting press for the Sentinels shortly before Freddy was released from that hospital in Napa."

"So, you sent Freddy to stay with him once he got out."

"Malik knew us when we were at San Francisco State. I was sure he'd take Freddy in. I needed a convenient place for cops and the press to point fingers."

She wiped her teary eyes again.

"Damn you! Goddamn you!!" she said, sobbing, her crying growing fierce.

When she shot me, the butcher knife I had been cutting with had fallen on the floor. It was about eight inches from my right hand. The searing pain in my left shoulder was almost unbearable.

"Freddy. You got your own brother killed."

I watched as a combination of sadness and anger crossed her face.

"No," she said, her eyes again filling with tears. "*You* did. You and your sister both."

"What about your name and law license?" I said, inching slowly toward the butcher knife with my right hand. Thank God the stitches were gone. That gave me a little more flexibility and range of motion. Not much, but I hoped it would be enough.

"I went to the cemetery and found the grave of a baby girl born the same year I was. Her name was Kendra Robbins. Getting a birth certificate and Social Security information in her name was a piece of cake. I forged college grades good enough to get me into law school. I got in because they were trying to increase diversity," she said, shaking her head. "First, I'm a racist, then I'm 'diversity.' I discovered that I liked being a Black woman, and I liked practicing law, so I became a civil rights lawyer."

"You figured you'd get your revenge through the courts . . ." As I talked, I slowly moved my right hand closer to the butcher knife.

"What did you say to Driscoll at the restaurant that night?"

"I put on a blond wig and told him I knew about Curtain's drug-dealing business and that I was going to the press to implicate him along with Curtain and Martin. I'd destroy all three."

"But Driscoll wasn't a part of any of that," I said. "He was a clean cop."

"Driscoll killed an innocent Black kid holding a phone. Fuck him. He didn't even recognize me at first."

"So . . . What was the point of confronting him?"

"Driscoll was all over the news. I knew he wouldn't let it go. He began conducting his own investigation off the books. I knew Curtain would freak out when he discovered Driscoll was looking into his extracurricular activities. I didn't know he would take Freddy's car and kill the man."

"Curtain killed Driscoll?"

"Driscoll must have been getting close to the truth."

I inched closer to the knife. *Just keep her talking*, I thought.

"He put on a ski mask, used Freddy's car, and took out Driscoll," she said. "It was Curtain who stole the plates of other white Priuses, and it was Curtain who fired the same number of bullets in Driscoll as Driscoll had fired into Jamal. Clever touches, I thought. So, I borrowed them."

I said, "You plotted and planned the other murders."

"Freddy followed my directions to the letter."

"Geppetto," I whispered.

"What about me?" I asked. "Why come after me?"

"You were the loose end. I knew that, eventually, the police would let this case go cold. We left no clues, and we worked over multiple jurisdictions. We knew local law enforcement agencies couldn't get their dicks out of the way long enough to get coordinated and solve this. But you have no jurisdiction. You'd never let it go until you solved it. Once you kept going even after the bombing, I was afraid that we'd end up here."

I lunged for the knife and grabbed it. Kendra fired another round, narrowly missing my right arm.

"I love you, damn it," she sobbed. "You made me fall in love with you. Now, you're making me—"

I sat on the kitchen floor with my back pressed against the dishwasher. The pool of blood on my robe was bigger now. The whole thing was sopping wet. I felt like I was going to throw up. I clutched the brown handle of the knife firmly in my right hand and crawled to the far side of the rectangular island, keeping us on opposite ends. Blood continued to seep from my left shoulder. I thought I might pass out.

"Come on out, Topher," she said sweetly. "I want to make this as painless as possible."

"So, it was all a lie," I said. "Our entire relationship was a lie."

"We could have been so good together," she said. I could hear the regret in her voice. "So good."

I tried to stand but couldn't. I was too woozy and weak. I crawled around the back side of the island . . . just in time to meet Kendra there.

She pointed the gun at my head and prepared to pull the trigger. "I'm sorry," she said. "I have no choice."

Then Sophie lunged at her, biting her on the calf. She kicked the dog and momentarily turned the revolver away from me.

I reversed my grip on the butcher knife, swapping the wooden handle for the pointed edge of the blade. Using every bit of strength I could muster, I threw the knife as hard as I possibly could.

The butcher knife made one revolution before plunging right below Kendra's chin and into her throat.

FORTY-SIX

ONE MONTH LATER...

"**Y**OU KNOW, MAYBE you should go back to covering jugglers and knife throwers," Lynn suggested, fluffing a pillow behind me on my couch. "Turns out you have a knack for it."

"Imagine the trouble she'd have been in if I'd used the fire-eating tricks I picked up," I said.

It had been a month, and I was starting to get restless. My shoulder was stiff and sore. I had to keep my arm in a sling, but I felt better by the day.

I had been lucky. The last thing I remember is throwing the butcher knife at Kendra. I must have passed out afterward because my next memory is the ambulance ride to Eden Hospital, Lynn by my side.

She was in the neighborhood and dropped by to see if Kendra and I wanted to join her for brunch at The Egg. Instead, she found a trail of Sophie's bloody paw prints leading to the kitchen. She found us and called 911.

Kendra was pronounced dead at the scene. My lucky throw had severed her jugular vein, killing her instantly. I was alive,

294

unconscious, and bleeding like the proverbial stuck pig. The doctor said that I'd have bled out if Lynn hadn't found me when she did.

The bullet in my shoulder had gone clean through without hitting anything vital. But since I'd lost so much blood, the hospital kept me for a week before sending me home with orders to take it easy and rest. Little sis was there to make sure that, for once, I did as I was told.

There was a light rap on the front door, and Jared came in, followed by Mandy and Stu. They had brought a care package consisting of platters of bagels, lox, cream cheese, cheese blintzes, assorted sandwiches, and fixings.

"How's the patient?" Jared asked.

"Fine," I said, "if Nurse Ratched over here will give me a little room to breathe."

"Get used to it," Lynn said. "I'm not going anywhere until you're up and around."

That would be in a few days, at the Coroner's Inquest. As expected, Kendra/Carla's death was ruled self-defense shortly after Freddy's shooting was ruled justifiable homicide.

Martha Isherwood claimed the bodies of both her children. In death, as in life, she got no help from their father. I hear she had them cremated and keeps their ashes in an urn on her coffee table next to their childhood photo. Her kids had finally come home.

As for Malik Otumba, he wanted no part of any of the goings-on. He was caught using forged documents to cross the Tijuana border in San Diego. He was returned to the Bay Area, where he cut a deal to spill his guts to avoid a conspiracy charge for harboring Freddy. He would serve six months for the forged documents. Upon his release, he dropped the Malik Otumba moniker, disbanded the Sentinels, and returned to being just plain old Taronte Rogers, computer programmer.

Ballistics would later prove that Sheila Williams's .38 was
not the weapon used in the murders. Sheila's gun turned up six
months later in a liquor store holdup in Hayward. Kendra had
Freddy burglarize the woman's home. He stole her gun and put it
out on the street to cast suspicion on Sheila—one more attempt at
misdirection for the authorities.

As police would later verify, Kendra was telling the truth
when she told me that Freddy didn't kill Mickey Driscoll. Phil
Curtain did. After Kendra confronted Driscoll in the restaurant
and accused him of being a part of Curtain's drug-dealing
operation, just as she said, Driscoll began his own investigation
and discovered that Curtain was still dealing with the aid of Dr.
Stevens and his prescription pads. When Curtain found out what
Driscoll was up to, he took Freddy's white Prius, swapped out the
plates, put on a ski mask, and killed him with a .38 revolver he'd
carried as a "throw down" when he was on the job. Curtain had
access to the car when Freddy was hired to work at The Angler.
That was another piece of Kendra's plan. She wanted Freddy close
to her original target, Curtain. She remembered that Curtain
was always looking for ways to save a buck and figured if Freddy
offered to work for room and board, he'd let him.

Kendra had played them all like a chess master. Driscoll
hoped to regain some of his reputation by uncovering a drug ring
run by an ex-cop. Curtain was removing a threat to his income
and possibly his freedom. Kendra was getting revenge.

It's unclear whether Curtain knew that Kendra and Carla
were the same person, but once he killed Driscoll, he met his
demise through Freddy, who shot him with his own .38. He then
used Curtain's gun to kill Martin.

It was brilliant, really. The whole time, investigators were
looking for someone seeking revenge on police officers who killed

unarmed Black people when, in actuality, the murders were the brainchild of one sick, disgruntled ex-cop.

It turned out that there was nothing nefarious about Odell Watkins's death. He did indeed die of natural causes. Dr. Stevens, on the other hand, was another victim of Curtain's. With Driscoll sniffing around, Curtain wanted to eliminate anybody who could tie him to his drug business. Dr. Stevens owned several cars. All Curtain had to do was drain the brake fluid from one, sit back, and wait for the fireworks the next time Stevens decided to drive it.

Mandy took a bagel, sliced it, and smeared it with cream cheese. She placed a healthy amount of lox, a slice of tomato, and a teaspoon of capers on top and handed it to me.

"You remembered," I said.

"How you take your bagel? Of course, we've been together for seven years," she said with a smile.

"Thanks for not saying it," I said.

"What?"

"'I told you so' about Kendra."

She said nothing, just giving me a little smile that seemed to say, "But I *did* tell you."

"One thing bothers me," Mandy said. "How did Kendra darken her skin enough to appear African American?"

"She took a page from the book *Black Like Me*," I told her.

"Isn't that the book where a white man posed as Black to see how bad Jim Crow was in the South?" Lynn asked.

"Yes," I said. "Kendra did what he did. She took massive doses of the vitiligo drug Oxsoralen."

"Isn't that the medicine Auntie used to take for her psoriasis?" Lynn asked.

"Yes," I said. "I noticed that Kendra kept some in her medicine cabinet and assumed she was taking it for the same reason. She wasn't. The skin darkens when an Oxsoralen user is exposed to excessive amounts of ultraviolet light. She changed her eye color with brown-tinted contacts and dyed her hair. Her own mother wouldn't have recognized her."

The publicity surrounding my shooting and solving the cop murders convinced corporate to reverse their decision about shuttering our bureau. Weil was authorized to offer me a contract for five more years. I politely declined.

Mandy, Stu, and I had other plans. During my convalescence, we wrote and recorded the story of the case, including interviews with Martha Isherwood, Edna Curtain, and Janet Driscoll. We turned it into a twelve-part podcast. The first episode would garner a million downloads, topping the iTunes podcast rankings for the next month. Soon, we had more advertisers than we knew what to do with. We were off and running.

The podcast's success made us even more attractive to corporate, and they backed a Brink's truck full of cash up to my front door. Funny how they can always find the money when they *really* want to. I talked to Mandy and Stu, and we decided to sell corporate exclusive rights to our content as well as our production and on-air services for the station. We'd own everything and maintain full creative control. They'd pay us for the rights to air my investigative reports and post our digital content and podcasts on their platforms. The truth is, it wasn't about the money. I needed the credibility of a press pass for future stories.

I bit into my bagel. Mandy had prepared it perfectly. Sophie hopped up on the couch next to me, and I gave her a small piece of lox. It was the least I could do. I owed her my life.

"Nice wheels!" Jared said, pointing a thumb toward my driveway.

"Thanks. I've only had her a week and I'm madly in love already."

Janet Driscoll wanted to thank me for being fair to Mickey in my reporting and for finding his killer, so she gave me a present . . .

the Black Beauty, Mickey's prized 1957 T-bird. It had been repaired and given to me sans bullet holes.

That was another reason for leaving the station as an actual employee. Payola laws would have prohibited me from accepting the gift. Now, as head of a private media production company, I can do whatever I want.

"So, what's next?" Mandy asked, plopping down on the couch next to me.

I looked into her eyes and said, "The possibilities are endless."

Jared turned on the TV just as Phil Wagner reported the story topping the noon newscast. A traffic stop in nearby Danville had resulted in the shooting death of an unarmed Black father of five by a white police officer.

And the wheels on the bus go round and round . . .

ACKNOWLEDGMENTS

The author wishes to thank…

My literary agent, Kimberley Cameron, for taking a chance on a first-time crime fiction writer.

Amy Rennert, who was the first one to recognize the novel's potential.

Shawanda Williams and Kreceda Tyler at Black Odyssey Media for believing in a novel from an "unknown."

Elaine Petrocelli, who told me that I had a great story when she became the first person I ran the idea past.

Pam Jones for being my biggest cheerleader.

Jesse Kellerman for his encouragement and friendship.

Jonathan Kellerman for being the world's greatest crime fiction mentor and pal.

Rick and Cindy Simons for their unwavering support in all of my creative endeavors. Special thanks to Rick for driving me around Palomares Canyon in Castro Valley, California until I found Topher's house.

Wendy Miller for pushing me to do the things she believes I'm capable of doing.

My children Adam Copeland, Casey Copeland and Carolyn Copeland McKinney for their love and support and always telling me that "I can."

And last but not least, my manager, Jamie Grutemeyer for sticking with me during all the challenging times.

READING GROUP GUIDE

1. **Otumba's Perspective:** Do you agree with Otumba's assertion that individuals of color must be prepared to "defend themselves" from the police? Why or why not?

2. **Topher's Counterargument:** Does Topher make a valid point when he counters Lynn's concerns about the risks she faces as an officer by emphasizing her voluntary choice in joining the force?

3. **Lynn's Assessment:** In Lynn's view, how challenging is it to remove a problematic police officer? Do you believe her assessment is accurate?

4. **Analysis:** Can police shootings of unarmed individuals of color ever be justified as "an honest mistake?"

5. **Fair Adjudication:** Do you believe that police shootings of unarmed individuals are fairly adjudicated by the criminal justice system and those responsible for police oversight?

6. **Media Coverage:** Does the media cover the effects of police-related shootings of unarmed people of color fairly and accurately, taking into account all involved parties (police and victims)?

7. **Role of Broadcast Media:** Do you think the broadcast media serves the community well in cases involving police shootings of unarmed individuals?

8. **Nostalgia for the 1950s:** What do you think drives some people to have a nostalgic fondness for the 1950s?

9. **Prediction for Book 2:** What lies ahead for Topher Davis regarding his role in reporting and advocacy?

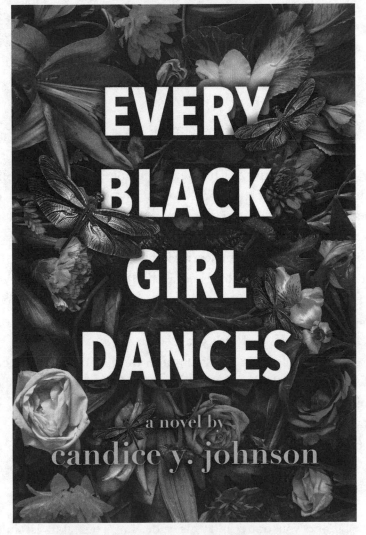

ONE

"GIRL, YOU ARE black as hell."

That's not exactly what the woman perched in the aisle seat says to me, but it's what I hear as our plane hits a second round of turbulence in half an hour. Even heaven seems annoyed by her incessant yapping about all things relevant to only her. Thank God, this flight only has a little more than two hours to go.

My row-mate is too cheery for six in the morning. I should be taking my first pee, not listening to a complete stranger with zero sense of boundaries or discretion, chattering about social media and current events while casually tossing in how pretty I am for a dark-skinned girl. Make that *extra dark*, as if I'm not already aware. Her thin lips latch onto the rim of her Styrofoam coffee cup as she flips her bright red curls, utterly oblivious of how insulting her backhanded compliment really is. Somehow, my blatant snub and wide-eyed silence isn't the effective deterrent I'd hoped it would be. Now, she's circling from waxing about visiting her elderly grandfather for a spell in Frisco, Texas, back to her fascination with my skin.

God, I don't have the strength to speak laymen's right now.

"I hope you don't find this rude, but your skin is simply luminous to be so . . ."

"Dark?" There. I finish for her. She knows it's rude before she alludes to it. My submissive face takes over as I lean against the window, observing her green eyes grow into saucers and soak up all this darkness in awe. "Makes you want a Snickers, huh?"

Her paltry giggle in response to my direct jab is a staunch reminder of the harsh scrutiny my particular shade of black forces me to deal with every day: she just doesn't get it. She chirps her name as if I care enough to register the pointless syllables in my memory bank. Sandy. Penny. Chrysanthemum. Hell, who knows what she just rattled off? For the rest of this flight from Los Angeles to Dallas, all I want to hear is my playlist while I catch a few zzz's.

What's-her-name blinks, taking a brief respite from her irrelevant musings to breathe. Facing me, she rests an elbow on the armrest and perches her head on top of her hand, curiosity etched across her heart-shaped face. Seriously, if she doesn't stop staring, I will invoice her for a counseling session. Sis acts like my skin's giving her third-world healing.

"Your braids are so . . . unique," she sings loud enough to provoke the passengers occupying the rows in front of and behind us to indiscreetly investigate for themselves as if I can't see them squirming in their seats just enough to judge whether her assessment's on point.

"So different," she mutters, intent on eliciting the response she didn't squeeze out of me the first time. One of her wiry hands gestures as if to reach across the empty middle seat between us to fondle my tailbone-length braids, regarding them with the wonder of a mythical creature she's discovered is actually real. A scowl replacing the excruciating smile I've managed to maintain this long prompts her to draw it back quickly. She darts an index finger toward them instead. "The colors weaved across the middle—I've never seen that before."

"Jamaica," I eek out as pleasantly as I can on the strength of the sigh which carries it.

"Your name's Jamaica?"

I giggle. Not because there's humor in the situation, but because I'm tired. These types of cultural interrogations are seemingly barren but never easy to birth. I'm a realist: no response I give this woman will make her see anything other than my skin. Her creepy gaze almost makes it impossible for me to restrain my snarky attitude, which is two seconds from reaching: *I wish you would.*

"No, ma'am, my name's not Jamaica. The color in my hair represents the Jamaican flag. Where my dead father's from."

"Oh."

She's uncomfortable now. One, because the bitter taste of ignorance isn't so tasty on her tongue. And two, I have yet to give up any useful intel on myself. Not even my name, which sis has been patiently waiting for since we strapped in for takeoff. But as long as I've mastered the resting "B" face—which I'm about to switch on effective immediately—silence shall ever be her portion.

"What did you say your name is? What is it that you do?" *See how intrusive she is?* When I saw our flight wasn't crowded, I expected to snooze all the way home to Texas. But instead, I got stuck with . . . her.

Maybe if I respond, she'll back down and stop leering at me like a puppy begging for a treat. Keeping my cool, I flash the smile the dental hygienist I hired to fix my teeth with my first Hollywood check and blurt, "I write and direct films."

"Oh yeah?" She perks up under the false impression that a bond is forming between us. "What kind of movies do you make? Anything I've seen?"

"Probably not," I hark a laugh as insipid as our wordy transaction. Obviously, there's no way this suburban duchess, who's probably never tasted a swear word, has been exposed to my gritty dramas. If she had, this conversation would've already detoured to mute.

"I make films exploiting Black trauma," I go on to explain. "You know, pimps, domestic violence, drug trafficking, crack babies. Real entertainment." I pull my denim jacket closed and lean closer to her, mimicking her pose on the other side of the armrest. "I write the real rough stuff. Families killing each other, men who can't keep their junk in their pants, silly, trifling baby mamas, and female doormats. Hood stuff like that. But I'm flying to escape the set of my latest film, *Crack Dreams*, because I'm sick of profiting off my brothers' and sisters' pain for the appeasement of people like you."

And just like that, sis turns away with a 'tude, reclines her seat, and pushes out a fake yawn. When she squeezes her eyes shut, I jam my earbuds in and press play on the first song in my playlist. Guess our meet and greet is over.

You've only got one reason not to love me,
But I can give you a thousand more
It's amazing how you hate me
Because my future's far from yours . . .

The jazzy tune by my best friend, Tati Ko, blares through the earpieces, and I recline my seat. Tati's being positioned to be the next queen of R&B music, but I'm flying back home to Parable to help celebrate her million-dollar win on *Battle Exes*, a wilderness-style reality competition show pairing ex-lovers and pitting them against their rivals from past seasons. Even though her ex helped secure Tati the win, she kept the entire bounty for herself. The Twitter crowd and I couldn't be happier that she got her revenge against the narcissist who's still threatening her and her family with violence over her selfish decision.

I peer out the window. The skies seem friendlier than the universe has been to me lately. Not that I'm anything close to a singer, but I can hum a mean tune, so I do it along with "Redeemed by Me," the song Tati wrote for my debut film, *Flogged*. *Flogged* chronicles the life of 16-year-old Nas, who was sold by her mother into the sex trade for drugs, and later convicted of murdering both her kidnapper and her mama. Like I told sis earlier, warm fuzzies.

Hard to believe, but a week ago, the same tune I'm jamming to now almost got me killed. Okay, maybe I'm being dramatic. But the incident was enough to make me come close to soiling the yellow sundress I planned on returning after sporting it at my girl Olivia's bachelorette party. Just because I have a few dollars tucked away in savings doesn't mean I'm not cheap.

Olivia's party was so lit, I stayed way longer than I originally intended. In my defense, *pole dance karaoke* far exceeded my expectations, killing my self-imposed curfew. But when the bride's mother slides from the top of the pole to the bottom in slow motion while killing the best of Whitney Houston in mezzo-soprano, you don't move. If nothing else, it helped me forget the crap day I had in preproduction for my next movie.

Anyway, I was zooming down the side streets on the way back to my loft, belching the remnants of the mini-mountain of mimosas I drank, feeling too good to notice I was pushing my red convertible Lexus well over the speed limit by 20 miles an hour. Didn't even see the police car waiting to catch an unsuspecting lawbreaker like me slipping until I flew by him, and the lights started chasing me.

"Great, just great. Hudson, I'll have to call you back," I told my boyfriend, who'd been on speaker the entire hour-long ride, to help keep me awake.

"What's wrong? Everything okay?" The slight panic in his voice did nothing to ease the fear swirling in the pit of my stomach as I eyed the wailing lights behind me. The way the flashes of blue and red intermingled with each other felt like a threat and made my stomach sink. Immediately, I wished I hadn't guzzled so many drinks.

"I'm not okay. I just got pulled over," I explained as I pulled to the side of the road and put the car in park. My trembling hands outshook my quaking voice. Minutes ago, the air was so cool; now, a trail of sweat immediately formed around my edges.

"Is that all?" Hudson chuckled. "Just comply with whatever they say, and you'll be fine." The amusement in my man's voice shook off any buzz threatening to keep me from walking a straight line if I was issued a sobriety test. Not to mention the one word that would ban my ovaries to him for the rest of our tenure together: *comply.*

What the entire hell?

"I have to go. I'll call you back." Ignoring Hudson's unsolicited advice, I reached to the dash where the phone was mounted and hung up. Then I started my video recorder and rested my hands on the steering wheel like my father taught me.

Breathe, girl, breathe. You're going to be fine.

Spying the officer creeping toward my car in the rearview, I was suddenly aware that my braids were secured in a bun at the nape of my neck. What if he mistook me for a man? Would it make a difference? Was there just a matter of minutes before I became a hashtag swimming in a pool of my own blood? Would there be protests in my name, or would I be quickly forgotten by the next day's news?

Would I be awarded a posthumous Oscar?

I won't lie. The officer's brown skin was a relief when he appeared at my window. After chronicling some pretty damning scenarios involving the boys in blue in my films, at least I was being stopped by a cop who looked like me . . . right?

"Good evening, ma'am. Do you know why I pulled you over?" His baritone thundered through my spirit. His broad chest heaved, and his badge issued a silent dare. *Try me.*

"I guess I was speeding," I said, not that my misdemeanor needed confirming.

"You were." His head tilted to the side, then quickly upright. "Hey, aren't you Hudson Pyke's girlfriend?"

No, I'm JC Burke, the dummy who let my blue-eyed lover get famous off my scripts while I literally became his shadow. But yeah, I'm her.

Eyes ahead, hands on the wheel. "Yes, Officer. That's me: JC Burke."

"Uh-huh."

I hesitantly allowed my head to inch left, scanning for the officer's name in case I needed receipts later. In the meantime, Officer Riggins's eyes darted past my face to the phone mounted on the dash.

Smile . . . You're this close to becoming viral.

"That last movie of yours - the cop was acquitted of attempted murder for shooting the kid in the back, right?"

I knew it. "Yes, he was, sir. I mean, the girl was running away after being suspected of shoplifting a T-shirt. And there was no excuse for swinging at the boutique owner when he tackled her, even though no stolen goods or weapons were found on her. At least she was only paralyzed, right?" I pressed my lips closed, bottling the rest of my opinion inside.

"Right. What was the name of it again? The movie?"

"*First-Degree Melanin.*"

His brows pinched together, broad shoulders hunched. "Yeah. The wife didn't care for that one too much." His low voice dodged my cell's audio as his fingers tapped against his ticket pad, which I preferred instead of on his holster. "She said the plot was unrealistic."

. . . in spite of the real Wisconsin news story I based it on?

"Look, it's hard to see out here. We don't want you having an accident, do we?"

You mean by car or bullet?

Without relaxing my tightened jaws, I peeled my stoic glare away from the badge, staring ahead. "No, sir, we don't."

"Good. Slow down," he warned. Taking a quick second to assess my threat level, he must've determined my 135-pound frame wasn't too menacing because he jammed the pad back into his pocket and exhaled the tension from his body. "Be safe out here."

The lump obstructing my throat didn't dislodge until Officer Riggins hopped back into his patrol car and left me reeling on the side of the road. How long had I held my breath? I slumped over the steering wheel in tears, trying to coerce my spirit to climb back into my mortified flesh, all while Hudson's instructions burned my chest.

Comply.

I slammed my hands against the dash until I swore I'd drawn blood. Without a shred of empathy, the rearview mirror gave me a glimpse of my runny mascara and snotty nose. *Comply* rang in my ears, breaking me down worse than the actual traffic stop.

After a few minutes, I turned the key in the ignition and pulled back onto the main road at a much-slower pace. Without bothering to call Hudson to give him an update, I powered off the phone. Let him worry whether I had *complied* for the rest of the night while I tried getting some sleep.

Once I got home and climbed in bed, I slept better than during the six weeks we'd been working on *Crack Dreams.* The next day, I powered through Olivia's wedding, then hit the reception with Hudson at my side. It was a grand affair of excesses and sparkle, so I didn't need to bring up his prior night's infraction until after the bride and groom's first dance. I think I did a pretty good job presenting the thousand other ways Hudson could've handled things better when I told him I got stopped; however, he made a conscious effort to misunderstand while *white-splaining* me instead.

"What's the big deal, JC? The drinks are flowing, and everybody's happy. There's no reason to walk around here with your face all twisted up." Hudson spun me as the other couples slow danced around us. His eyes were hidden behind his signature red frames. Tousled brown hair mussed from yanking it every two seconds while I patiently walked him through the source of our latest fight.

Hudson dipped me, but I locked my back to protect my breasts from spilling out of the strapless eggplant bridesmaid dress barely containing them. When he pulled me up, I pushed into his chest, hoping to feel the same security in his arms that I felt on our first date.

Nothing.

"At least you didn't get a ticket." Hudson's nonchalant assertion harbored dangerously close to amusement.

I backed away, dishing a death glare. "Have you heard *anything* I've said? I could've had my head blown off last night."

"Sure, in an imaginary scenario, which has absolutely no bearing on here and now." He smoothed a hand over my braids. "All I'm saying is don't waste your energy on something that didn't even happen. You've had 26 years to understand how traffic stops work. All you have to do is—"

"Don't you *dare* say, 'comply'!"

That word transported me back to the playground in elementary school when my bullies forced me to eat dirt pies.

Know what my teachers said when they gave me a spit cup to rinse the dirt out of my mouth in the bathroom? *"No one likes a tattler. Next time, walk away."*

What kind of a gutless waste of skin says that to a child who soiled her panties because she got jumped? *Code: comply.* Same disrespect, different recipe. And every time the man who rarely says he loves me outside of the bed brushes off my concerns with the standard refrain that I'm "just being emotional," it tastes like one of those disgusting dirt pies.

Hudson gently tugged me by the rhinestone belt cinched around my waist, pulling me closer. "Can we have one day without you swiping your black card?" As soon as the question dropped, his pale skin turned crimson when he noticed my lips pulled in a tight line. "I'm sorry."

"I am too."

Two minutes later, it wasn't hard convincing Olivia I wasn't feeling well and had to exit the celebration early. Hudson didn't call my name when I walked away from him. Didn't reach for my arm to hold me back or match my steps so I couldn't lose him on the way out of the gargantuan hall. By my estimation, he had at least 20 steps from where we were dancing to the parking lot to right his wrong.

But he didn't.

"Oh my, I didn't realize I'd fallen asleep." Sis is awake now, blowing stale air up my nostrils, which I quickly cover with a hand. Judging by her restored cheery demeanor despite our earlier exchange, she's still not woke, though.

"Just in time for landing." I grant her a smile, my fleeting apology for getting fly when she's only trying to make this trip pleasant for us. That's one thing I've hated about myself since I was a little girl. Being bold enough to buck, then too quick to nurse the wound when 'ish gets uncomfortable. I'm brazen on film, but I'm scared of being muted if I hit the wrong note.

Once we've landed and been given the go-ahead to exit the plane, sis stretches, then peels herself from the seat to retrieve her bag from the overhead. She grins and maneuvers into the aisle, pushing her way through the other passengers, all trying to get off the plane at once. "Enjoy your trip."

"You too." I don't follow behind her.

My backpack seems heavier when I hoist it over my shoulder, waiting for row after row of passengers to empty the plane. When there is finally nothing but empty seats in front of me, a kind gentleman allows me to squeeze into the aisle ahead of him. I'm praying the nice gesture will be indicative of my week at home.

Maybe.

People scurry past me as I slowly make my way to the baggage claim. By the time I get there, sis has already grabbed her stuff and is heading off. We lock eyes for a moment, and she waves like we'll see each other again in this lifetime. I wave back, thinking how at some point in our lives, every Black girl dances to someone else's expectations. It's about time I choreograph for myself.